Also by Jan Caston

The Year When Even The Dog Got Cancer
the little charity book which helps those who
support loved ones living with cancer
available via Amazon.

Who Needs Friends, Nelson Nutmeg?
the prequel book for 6-12 years olds which
introduces the characters starring in
Who Killed Nelson Nutmeg?
a live action film for all the family

Take a look at www.nelsonnutmeg.com
for details of both.

The screenwriting work of Jan Caston is
documented on
Imdb.com/jancaston

Or you can find out what Jan is currently doing
from her website
Jancaston.com

Jan Caston

Normal Dating

Brackenbrae
and
Ashby

First published 2017
by BRACKENBRAE AND ASHBY

1

ISBN 978-1-9998639-0-6

BRACKENBRAE AND ASHBY
Publishers

www.brackenbraeandashby.com

For Quincey and Bonnie,
our fun-loving, furry, loyal black girls who were the
inspiration for Benji, the dog,
and for George, who loved them both so much.

Chapter One
Dinner At Olivia's

The clock struck eleven times before the many bottles of pink Pinot Grigio Olivia served truly started working their numbing magic on Vera's jangling nerves. She hadn't drunk them all herself. They had been shared with her fellow guests, but as they'd followed a couple of rounds of pre-dinner Angosecs, no one sitting around the table was even remotely sober. 'Come to my eat-and-meet,' Olivia invited, and wouldn't take no for an answer. 'You'll love the other people who'll be there,' then changed the subject double quick before Vera could protest.

Love was hardly the emotion Vera was feeling, but obviously a form of love was exactly the reason Olivia was throwing this party. Ten people sat around the extended dining table. Candles replaced electric light. The food, prepared and served by a private chef, was delicious. Vera had even managed to eat everything from her plates without dropping a thing onto either of her two wobbly shelves at booby and belly height. That's a first, she thought, checking surreptitiously, but her lacy cream top showed not a mark despite her hand still shaking uncontrollably, just like it had from the moment she arrived.

Must be the booze, crossed her mind as she contemplated whether she could actually get off her chair and bounce her way to the bathroom without falling off her heels; not that she quite knew where her heels were at this precise moment. She'd slipped them off after the first course and since then they must have got kicked further under the table. It never crossed her mind either that she might be safer walking shoeless anyway, or that it was strange how an alcoholic stupor could abort all reasoning thought. She was simply just too drunk.

So, instead, she sat musing that as it was nigh on impossible to even get off her chair she'd have to cork it until she'd quaffed enough water to sober up a smidge. She said a little prayer that no one made her laugh too hard or she might have an embarrassing accident. What she needed was coffee, strong and black, the sort that usually kept her awake all night, but none seemed forthcoming. The chef had already gone home, leaving Olivia to clear up, a job Olivia obviously planned for the next day because she was now very drunk and chaotically pushing her way in between her seated guests with a freshly opened bottle of pink PG in one hand and a square bottle of brandy in the other, forcing even more drink onto them. There was no way she was capable of clearing anything away tonight.

'Use that one,' Vera zoned in to hear Olivia order Jez, the extremely young, bouncer-sized personal trainer who sat at the other head of the table. He laughingly protested he could take no more booze and leant back dangerously on the legs of his chair trying to avoid the brandy bottle Olivia waggled under his nose, hanging onto the table to stop himself falling over. Everyone else grabbed for their glasses to lift them to safety as the table rose, and then crashed back down with a loud bang.

Vera watched mesmerised as Olivia, undeterred, grabbed Jez's tumbler, capriciously slung the water out of it towards a drooping plant of indeterminate variety, poured a far too generous helping of brandy into it to replace the water and slid it towards him. 'Have one night off, you gorgeous man,' she ordered and stroked Jez's bristles seductively. Jez purred appreciatively. Taking her wrist, he kissed inside its curve. She let out a scream of pleasure, abandoned her bottles and pushed in to sit on his lap. It was a serious miscalculation. With thighs so musclebound, Jez could not sit with his legs together. Olivia landed between the gap, slid towards the floor and nearly cracked her chin on the edge of the table.

Her shrieks of laughter stopped all other

conversation. Their fellow diners turned to watch as Jez lifted and checked Olivia over intimately, something to which Olivia certainly did not object, while the rest of the table roared their advice where to check next. Olivia flapped her hand and ordered that they 'get on with their own stuff' as she pulled Jez into the noisiest thank you kiss. The poor guy came up for air with a puppy-dog grin and red lipstick smeared from the tip of one ear to his chin.

'Attagirl!' shouted Ian beside her. This was the same Ian who had told Vera when they were still sober that he was a starting-out solicitor specialising in conveyancing and that, sorry, but he never offered special deals as the rates were fixed so tightly he hardly made a profit. He said it so sheepishly, and with such a depth of remorse, that Vera, who was a property developer and who was in the process of selling the latest of her house renovations, popped in a mouthful of mozzarella and tomato and declared it delicious as she hid her mirth. She'd probably forgotten more over the years about property contracts than he'd yet learned, but she wasn't willing to discuss that as it would only reveal that she could easily be a contemporary of his mother. Instead, she wondered how astonished his own mother would be to witness the change from meek to predatory that had happened during the course of the evening with the help of alcohol. Ian practically had his nose in Etta's cleavage now, and it was pretty obvious one of his hands was heading towards the fastening of her bra.

Even Olivia was unaware of Vera's exact age. That was a most closely guarded secret, one she was never likely to divulge to these youngsters at this dinner party. What age would they be anyway? Suzette, the very pretty French girl who really ought to shave under her arms, had said she'd been teaching mathematics for ten years, so she was probably mid-thirties.

The Amazon of a girl Vera had spoken to before they sat down at the table, and who had introduced herself with 'Call me Hen! What a bloody stupid name my parents gave me because they really wanted a boy. Henrietta! I ask you,' was probably about the same age, though easily a foot taller than Suzette, with whom she now chatted intently across the table. Vera tried to remember what Hen said she did for a living, but it was gone. Was that a sign of tiredness, alcohol, old age or nothing worse than needing a wee? She plumped for the last and slid down her chair trying to find her shoes.

All she found under the tablecloth was a warm foot in a woolly sock, and it wasn't her own. She prodded it with her own stockinged toes. At first it retreated. Then it came back seeking out her foot again, found it, tickled the bridge, then slowly and seductively tickled its way up towards her knee. The foot inside the sock was very warm, and, oh boy, did it feel good caressing her leg. Now hang on! Whoa, tiger! The toe passed her knee heading for where no one had been for a very long time. Vera pulled back as the toes increased speed going up inside her thigh. Instinctively, she clamped her knees together and the foot pulled out of the way to safety.

As it did, she shot upright to see where it had gone. What? And Who? Across the table Andrew, the insurance broker, moved his chair closer so he could whisper intently into the ear of Erich, the German banker. Erich delicately stroked Andrew's face as he listened, both men blissfully unaware she was even there. Surely, it wasn't one of them, but the woolly sock was back again tickling around her ankle, so it had to be someone.

She peered up and down the table. Without her specs and with so much booze on board, her vision was less than perfect. In a blur she tried to guess who had legs so long that they could have reached that far. She could see no one; so instead, she edged back her chair, lifted the tablecloth, stuck her head underneath and peeked at the foot as it dropped to the floor. She wasn't dreaming. That warm foot was most definitely wearing a sock which was also most definitely attached to the end of a long leg trousered in pin-striped worsted. As she watched, the toes wiggled a little dance mischievously as if to taunt her. She let out a piggy-wiggy snort of joy, then turned her focus as, to her left, two neatly crossed ankles with feet encased in silver sparkly ballet slippers shuffled into a more comfortable position.

She knew those feet! She came back up and checked out Debbie, sitting beside her. Debbie's eyes were now closed. Her shoulders slumped. Debbie couldn't take her booze, but Vera was sure she'd noticed her shoes when she arrived, so there was no mystery there. Ah-ha! So whoever owned the woolly sock must be directly opposite to Debbie. She peered blearily across the table again but she got her left and her right muddled up. She peered the wrong way and found Andrew and Erich, though Andrew sat twisted sideways, his arm around his German friend.

Could he really be that much of a contortionist that one of his feet could reach out and touch her? Would he even want to? It couldn't be Andrew. So, it had to be Erich!

Bemused, Vera went back under the tablecloth. The woolly-socked toes danced a little dance teasingly. Now there were two matching feet there. She snorted even louder in amusement, and scrabbled the dragging end of the tablecloth further out of the way so she could reach out and catch one of them. Screams of 'Stoppit' and 'What're you doing?' rang out from her fellow diners. Glasses were lifted high once again, candles wobbled, dipped and reignited, and finally the three feet high pepper grinder fell with such a loud crash, she shot up and banged the back of her head hard on the underside of the table.

Dragging strands of her hair from her mouth and eyes with one hand, she re-emerged rubbing the bump with the other. 'There's ... whose ...?' she attempted.

Andrew and Erich stared directly at her. 'It's you, isn't it?' snorted Vera pointing and waggling an accusing finger at Erich.

'Me? What? WhatisitIamdoin'?' asked Erich, his normally subdued German accent stronger than usual due to the high volume of his alcohol intake.

'They're yours,' sing-songed Vera.

'My what?' asked Erich.

'They're your toe-toes snigg ... sniggling ... snuggling in their little woolly socks,' she accused as if teasing a toddler.

'I do not wear any socks,' protested Erich, who leant back, brought both bare feet up on the table and pointed two soft pink soles at her.

Vera let out a rattling growl of frustration, leant across and tentatively touched them. Erich jumped. 'Tickles,' he said and groaned as she grabbed both big toes and waggled them hard.

'Where they gone?' she said, investigating his feet closely across the table, but she never got an answer.

The bang to the back of her head, combined with the alcohol, took over and the rest of Vera's evening became a complete and utter blank.

Chapter Two
Dreamland

She woke with a jolt, fighting the bedcovers. She was dreaming she was crawling over an immense bed on all-fours, wearing basque and suspenders, with long tawny hair all over her face, heading towards the largest male erection she had ever seen. In all her married life, which had lasted twenty-eight very happy years, she had never seen an erection like that on her husband, and even before that, when she was still happily single and attempting to prove to her coterie of female friends she was the most liberated feminist by bedding any man who passed her way, she had similarly never elicited such a response to her raging pheromones. Now here on waking, forefront of her mind, paraded an erect male member of the most magnificent kind, ready to pleasure and to be pleasured.

Wow! Was it impressive! It almost brought tears to her eyes. How had she ever made that happen?

Screwing those very same eyes tightly shut again, she patted her now silver-streaked tangled hair back from her sweating brow and eased the duvet slowly away from over her face. Only then did she try to peep out to face the daylight. The throbbing in her head was unbearable. Her mouth was dry. Nausea rose and made her weak and shaky, yet still, like a damned impression indelibly imprinted, the enormous erection assaulted her awakening with impertinence.

Dammit! Vera, dammit! Whatever made you drink that much?

'Can I come in?' a voice questioned softly. Olivia carefully opened the bedroom door. 'Cuppa?'

Even from that distance, Vera could smell the tea. Her stomach did a somersault and bile rose. She shot out of bed heading for the bathroom, but where was it? This wasn't her house!

Olivia retreated swiftly back out of the doorway and pointed across the landing to where the bathroom door hung open. The smell and sounds coming from inside were not pleasant. She pinched her nose in disgust and left Vera to it. Her bare feet were cold anyway. When Vera finally came back to the bedroom, a damp flannel clutched to her forehead, she found Olivia sitting up on the other side of the double bed drinking the tea she had offered.

'Haven't you got a hot man in your own warm

bed you want to annoy?' groaned Vera, crawling in beside her.

'Jez? Don't be stupid. He's my personal trainer.'

'Who knows every inch of you intimately!'

Olivia smiled to herself and sipped more tea.

'Where is he anyway?'

'He went home in the taxi while Ambrose, Andrew and Erich took you up to bed. That was some blackout you did. You went down spectacularly, sort of slowly, grinning manically, with a sort of … ecstasy all over your face. I told 'em we should have called an ambulance, but they said if you were grinning like that you must be okay and then the bastards did a runner. Do you know, they said it was all my fault so I should be the one to look after you?'

Vera lifted the flannel to stare at her. 'You should! It was all your fault!'

'I didn't force you to keep knocking the PG back! I did tell you to be careful.'

Vera tried to put some words together, but the throbbing behind her eyes was too insistent to allow her to protest with any eloquence. 'Is that my tea?' she asked instead.

Olivia looked into the half-empty mug. 'Sorry. I didn't think you wanted it,' she said proffering what was left. 'I could make you another,' she added, but made no move to get out of bed. 'I'd forgotten how pretty this room is in the morning light,' she said instead.

Vera grabbed the mug and sipped at the nearly cold tea. It tasted awful. 'Why did you insist we carried on drinking that ghastly pink PG?' she asked eventually. 'Did you get it cheap or something?'

It was obvious Olivia had. 'I can't afford to crack open that case of red I bought for Christmas, can I?' said Olivia. 'It's not ready yet, and that lot wouldn't know the good stuff from the rubbish, anyway.'

Vera finished the cold tea and spread the flannel over her face as she lay back on the pillows trying to decide if she needed to run to the bathroom again.

'You should have known not to hit it too hard, though. You really know your wine,' Olivia said, without either apology or malice.

Vera groaned. How long had she been friends with Olivia now? Was it getting on for twenty years? It must be. And had she ever really liked her? At this moment, Vera couldn't remember. All she knew was that with her cold feet taking up the warm spot in the bed, and by denying her the tea, Olivia had become the single most irritating person she currently knew. She felt like ordering her out of the house, but as this was Olivia's house unless she could actually crawl out of bed, get dressed and get herself back to her own home, Vera was stuck. 'Your feet are bloody freezing,' she moaned plaintively and kicked them over towards the other side of the bed.

'No need to get narky just cos you've got a bit of a hangover,' said Olivia.

'I'm going back to sleep.' Vera threw the duvet back over her head.

'Good idea,' said Olivia and snuggled down beside her.

It was three in the afternoon before Vera was woken again by Olivia snoring loudly. For several seconds she was certain she had woken up beside Richard, and she very nearly rolled over into the middle so she could face and cuddle him, until another loud snore and a 'wha's'at!' from a female voice brought her to with a massive lurch. She sat bolt upright and stared at the body beside her. Olivia opened her eyes as if she sensed Vera was staring ashen-faced at her.

'What's wrong?'

'I thought you were Richard,' Vera whispered and promptly burst into tears. Olivia's arms were around her instantly, clutching her so tight that Vera could hardly breathe. 'Can you let me go?' she mumbled eventually with her mouth and nose pressed hard against Olivia's shoulder.

'Sorry,' said Olivia and pulled back looking at her intently. 'I know how hard last night was for you...'

'I'd better go home now,' said Vera, cutting off any further discussion. She stared around the room for her clothes, then checked out what she was already wearing. Under the bedclothes she lay in her bra, tights and knickers. She could see none of the other clothes she had been wearing last night at dinner.

'They're here,' said Olivia, reading her mind and reaching down beside her side of the bed to retrieve Vera's discarded satin skirt and lacy top. 'You wouldn't let us take anything else off.'

'Us?' asked Vera, shocked.

'Ambrose, Andrew, Erich and me,' Olivia confirmed.

Vera looked down at her underwear and blushed furiously. 'I couldn't undress you on my own,' Olivia spluttered. 'I was too drunk'.

'And I was out for the count!' protested Vera.

'Neither Ambrose, Andrew and Erich would have minded,' said Olivia, avoiding stating the obvious. 'They're good blokes,' she said vaguely.

Vera knew Andrew and Erich were gay and together as a couple, but who the hell was Ambrose?

'Will you stop repeating Ambrose, Andrew and Erich as if they're The Three Musketeers!' snapped Vera. 'Olivia! You let them undress me!'

'So? Ambrose, Andrew and Erich wouldn't have minded.'

Vera looked at her friend as if she was an alien. Olivia's lack of any kind of concern was mind-blowing. 'And who undressed you?' she countered.

'Me. I think,' said Olivia, checking out the ancient nightie she wore with a rueful look. 'Must have been. I can't imagine any man, whatever his persuasion, would have sought out this old thing for me to wear, do you?'

Vera staring at it blankly, saw that it had some of its

trimming hanging off and that it had been through more washes than a dishcloth. The absurdity of the situation suddenly hit her. She threw her face into her hands and chuckled hysterically until Olivia asked her if she was feeling all right. 'No,' she whined in between giggles. 'What sort of a stupid night have we just had?'

'One to remember?' attempted Olivia and burst into giggles, too.

Olivia wouldn't let her call a taxi until she had eaten the scrambled eggs that Olivia prepared while Vera took a shower. She found Vera tracky bottoms and a sweater to borrow. As they ate, Olivia played back messages on her phone. There were four similar ones, all saying 'fantastic evening, let's do it again,' from Etta, Ian, Hen and Suzette. Debbie's message asked if Olivia could check if she'd left one of her shoes anywhere. 'Didn't she notice she hadn't got it on when she went outside?' asked Vera.

'That's Debbie,' answered Olivia. 'She's always half-asleep.'

Jez left a message so lewd, even Olivia blushed. 'And you tell me there's nothing going on between you two!' Vera shook her head in disbelief.

'There isn't. Honest. He is just my personal trainer.'

Vera didn't believe a word of it, except, when she thought about it later, what better chance would he have had than staying with Olivia last night, so probably she was telling the truth and there was nothing going on yet. Had she got in the way of something that was developing? Perhaps now wasn't the time to ask if it was at that sensitive stage.

Erich's message was the last, delivered this time in his normal, very correct, and almost more British than the British accent with only the slightest hint of his German upbringing. 'Thank you for a delightful and most entertaining evening last night, Olivia. Ambrose, Andrew and I had a very good time, and hope you and Vera did, too.'

'Ah, isn't that nice?' said Olivia, playing it again. 'Ever the gentleman. He'd never mention what he'd seen.'

Vera listened to it in silence, staring at the screen of the mobile phone. When it finished, she looked up at Olivia, frowning. 'Which one was Ambrose?'

'The man sitting the other side of Debbie. Took my place near the head of the table when I started pouring the brandy.'

Vera closed her eyes, trying to visualise who had been sitting where around the table. She could remember most people, even though before that evening she had only ever met Olivia. They were all much younger than her, more Olivia's age. Most of the others seemed to have met at least some of the others before, so it hadn't struck her as unusual that somewhere during the course of the dinner, some people swapped seats to speak with old friends. Perhaps it was this that had confused her. Ian had been one of them. She'd spoken with him all the way through the first course, and then he'd started talking across the table to the very pretty black girl in the red dress with a red flower behind her ear. She was probably Etta, though Vera couldn't remember for certain as they'd only been introduced at the beginning and never spoke again. Vera remembered having a long conversation with Debbie and Erich about whether they were dog or cat people and had laughed at Erich who declared himself neither. He'd said he'd rather take an alligator for a walk. For a while after that she'd sat talking to no one, so surely she must have looked around then, but she remembered no other man sitting at her end of the table.

No. She definitely remembered no man other than Jez, Ian, Andrew and Erich. 'I don't remember any Ambrose,' she said.

'I introduced you when you came in. Tall, greying, still wearing his business suit because he'd come straight off the train from London.'

It meant nothing. Vera simply couldn't remember him.

And then a dreadful thought struck her. 'Please don't tell me he saw me in my underwear, too?' she pleaded, horrified.

Chapter Three

'I'm never, ever, going to drink alcohol again.'

There were eleven urgent messages on her answerphone when Vera eventually got home. Or, at least, they said they were urgent, but when she diligently wrote them down, all of them could wait until Monday. There were none from her children, so she presumed all her family were still alive and not too bothered about what she was getting up to. Nor was there one from her mother, Rosie, currently at her villa in Majorca.

Typical, thought Vera. I'm the one who always religiously calls. When she hasn't got a man she's on the phone a minute after I usually ring on a Saturday. Vera suspected that Rosie was doing something to that damned boat she'd got involved in with Benjamin, her latest man. She'd ring when she wanted something or finally got around to thinking about her family at home. She always did and, when she did, she would always complain that it was the family's fault that they hadn't been in touch with her, never the other way around.

I can't handle her today anyway, thought Vera, and made coffee, drinking it flopped on the settee, shoes kicked off as she nursed her thumping head. Her body felt as if it had been in a boxing match. She dozed off again.

By then, the whole of Saturday, which she had planned to use catching up on chores, was lost. She hadn't gone to the shops to stock up. Nor had any washing been put on. Eventually, she tugged herself off the settee, changed out of Olivia's clothes and dragged on her old jeans and sneakers, but when she picked up her car keys, she paused, held her palm up, breathed into it and smelt her breath. There was still a strong smell of alcohol. Perhaps it was wisest if she didn't drive until tomorrow.

Takeaway curry then? Her stomach lurched at the thought of a spicy meal. Pizza? Nah. Chinese? Ugh, no! Pasta? Too much effort. Instead, she made herself a toasted cheese sandwich with stale bread and managed to eat half of it lolling in front of the telly. Whatever she watched made no impression on her. By eight-thirty, she was back in bed swearing that she was never, ever, going to drink any alcohol again. From this moment on, she was going to be teetotal. Being run over by a ten-tonne truck would surely leave her aching less than she did at present.

When she woke needing a pee at five-thirty the next morning, she was again dreaming of the enormous erection. She swore, rushed to the loo, did what she needed to do, and raced back to her warm bed. That damned erection! Why was the image of it haunting her? Go back to sleep and it will go away, she thought, but she was too cold. The early April promise of longer and lighter days with a good bit of sunshine hadn't lasted and an Arctic breeze was blowing in from the north. The chill in her bedroom had woken her completely and as she'd slept so deeply, she knew there was no chance she could doze back to sleep again. Instead, she lay and forced herself to think about what the erection meant. She could come to only one conclusion. Surely it meant exactly the same in the dream world as it did in waking hours. She was craving sex. Her sex drive was re-awakening again.

The realisation made her terribly sad. She'd thought, and had prayed, her sex drive had left her for good and, in truth, she was heartily glad it seemed to have deserted her. That made it easier to live in her self-imposed little bubble of grief. It was two years and seven months since she had last experienced making love and as that last time had been one of the loveliest, but also perhaps the quickest, she'd ever enjoyed, she didn't want ever to lose sight of it.

That morning, Richard had been due to tee-off at

golf at ten minutes past eight. He woke horny and insistent and had deftly woken her by nuzzling the nape of her neck, his hand reaching round stroking her nipple. His penis was already hard and pushing into the small of her back. She'd rolled over, he'd kissed her a little more, came on top of her, and before she was even fully awake they had both peaked and were satisfied. Their lovemaking, so familiar and well-practised, needed no help. When one asked, the other still responded, two bodies coming together, conjoining to imitate a well-oiled machine working at full capacity. He had left her sated, telling her to go back to sleep and have a lie-in. She'd done as he'd said and never saw him alive again. The aneurysm was massive, instantaneous and fatal. He died on the golf course, the cold of the day turning his body into human marble even before she knew he was gone, the warmth of their last lovemaking consigned now to a precious memory.

She'd been enraged when the bereavement counsellor asked if they'd enjoyed a full marriage. It felt cheapening and disloyal for it to be in doubt. To her it was nobody else's business and she refused to reply. Instead she'd turned away so the woman couldn't see the fury on her face. Friends consoled her that she'd had one of the closest and loving marriages they had ever witnessed, but it was no consolation knowing her marriage to Richard was now a thing of the past and that their physical closeness could be no more. That, of anything, was the hardest grief to bear.

Rosie, her mother, was understanding at first. She'd been a widow a long time. She loved Vera and was gentle in the first few weeks, but Rosie wasn't one to let dust settle. Her philosophy in life was that you met it head on; that's how she'd tackled her own bereavement and she expected Vera to do the same. The gentleness quickly evaporated. Her tone became firmer, until the day she told Vera she must get on with her life now she was on her own, that she was still a young women with the rest of her life before her and now that there was no risk of her getting pregnant, she should start 'having fun again'.

Vera had been so incensed that her mother wouldn't accept how much she was still grieving she'd turned on her to deflect the conversation away from the terrifying thought of starting over. Retaliating, she'd spat, 'Well, if I'm a young woman now, why did you give me the godawful old-fashioned name of Vera? It makes me sound like I should be in a museum.'

'You know you were named after my Italian aunt, the one with the flashing eyes and the sexiest stare. You've turned out to be a beauty, just like her. Anyway, Vera means truth. And we wanted you always to be truthful.'

'Well, the truth is, Mother, that my heart is completely broken and I never want to think about getting involved with another man ever again.'

'That'll change as soon as you meet the next one,' Rosie responded pragmatically, pouring enough brandy into two glasses to fill them half full and then forcing Vera to drink hers in one go. It had helped her sleep that night, and, for once, it left her with no hangover, but by then both were entrenched in their own attitudes. A gulf appeared between them. After that, neither mother nor daughter broached the subject of Vera meeting anyone else again. Her mother very quickly went back to Majorca to get on with her own life, leaving her daughter with one last piece of advice, that she should accept every invitation that came her way, no matter how small, keep herself busy and if she wanted to drink on her own, to do it without any hesitation because the whole family had a great capacity for holding their liquor.

The trouble was, Vera knew she wasn't like the rest of the family. She knew how quickly alcohol affected her and so she normally avoided drinking to excess. It impaired her judgement and broke down her resistance to impossible men. It made her sexy and compliant, and she knew she was still too fragile to have to deal with the fallout that could come from any misguided alliances. She knew from her life before Richard that alcohol got her into carnal trouble, and that scared her.

So, if my sex drive is re-awakening again, she

mused as she warmed up in bed, I am definitely never drinking alcohol. I cannot handle its messes. I'm too old for all that. Leave it to the youngsters. They can make their mistakes and have fun making them, but not me. That's all behind me. Anyway, why do I need another man? I had the best. I don't need any of the rest.

With that certainty settling her troubled mind, she showered, went to the convenience store as soon as it opened, shopped for the day, bought the Sunday newspapers and went home feeling much happier with herself. Status quo returning to normal, she settled in for a lazy day on her own.

Chapter Four

'Can Ian have your number?'

Her resolve was broken when Olivia rang at midday. 'What're you doing?' she asked without preamble.

'Reading the papers. What're you doing?'

'I've had a phone call.'

'Bully for you.'

'Are you still being narky?'

Vera did not deign to answer. This conversation was going nowhere. Olivia ignored the silence and wittered on. Vera stared at the bright light streaming in through her kitchen windows and told herself she really must clean them as soon as she could get Olivia off the phone. She watched dust particles dancing in the sunrays. With eyes half-closed, she started seeking out the shapes of animals and even found what looked like a vase of flowers in the smudges on the glass. Happy mind-drifting turned to disgust when she noticed how black the window frame had gone. That needed a good bleach!

'… so he asked if he could have your number.'

Vera had stopped listening. Her mind had drifted off long ago.

'Can he have it?' Olivia asked, raising her voice and speaking very slowly.

'Can who have what?' asked Vera, coming back with a jolt.

'I knew it. You haven't been listening to a word I said, have you? Listen! This is important.' Olivia launched again into some story about how Ian had rung her late last night from a wine bar when he'd bumped into Etta and had frozen. 'She was with a group of friends,' Olivia repeated Ian's story, 'and, sober, and in front of them he hadn't had the nerve to ask her out. But he thought you, Vera, were right. He really, really liked her, even though she wasn't his obvious type. He'd never normally be attracted to a girl like Etta who he thought was out of his league because she is so beautiful, so now he wants to know what you think he should he do?'

'How was I right?' Vera interrupted Olivia's excited flow. 'What have I got to do with all of this?'

'It was you who persuaded him to go and sit beside her at the dinner party. You told him she looked kind and even if she didn't fancy him, she wouldn't be nasty to him. Don't you remember?'

Vera remembered him moving. She also remembered how later she'd watched him sitting beside the poor girl with his hand hovering over her bra fastener. How could he be so predatory one night, then not able to ask her out the next? Young men! Sometimes they needed a boot up their backsides.

'So! Can I give him your number?'

'Who?'

'Ian! He wants to talk it through with you. Wants to ask what he should do next.'

Vera sagged. She'd been really enjoying her quiet Sunday. What had all this got to do with her? 'No,' she said.

'Go on. You're really good at all this relationship advice and stuff. You spot couples that should be together. Look at your Christy and Annie. You introduced them after you met Annie at pottery and thought she'd be perfect for him. You wouldn't have Mickey and Wyeth if you hadn't got Annie and Christy together.'

Vera thought about her son and his wife. Christy had been so quiet and self-contained, so unlike his father, that she had despaired he would ever settle down with anyone. He was completely happy playing rugby, drinking with his mates and working for Richard. Annie needed a calming influence. With her tattoos and Mohican, her bovva boots and chains, she was as far away as any mother could look for a future daughter-in-law, but then Vera noticed that when Annie talked about her motorbike a glazed look of adoration came over her face. She was in awe of the power of her bike and Vera had lived long enough with Christy to know that he felt the same way about his. All she'd said was, 'You should meet my son. He rides the same bike as you,' and the rest was history. Now they rode their bikes, both with sidecars on the side for their two little boys, and were as content as ever Vera could hope.

'I never thought she'd be perfect,' Vera said. 'I just thought Annie was a sweet girl underneath all that grunge she used to wear.'

'Then, what about Nigel and Monica?'

'I had nothing to do with Nigel and Monica getting together.'

'You did. You sent her to that meeting when you could have gone yourself.'

Vera chuckled. She had indeed; but then, anyone could have spotted how her assistant went glassy-eyed and weak at the knees whenever the architect's assistant delivered plans. It hadn't taken a genius to see there was a mutual attraction and that all that was needed was a little push so they could spend time alone together.

'So! Can Ian have your number?'

Vera let out an enormous sigh. She didn't want to get involved in anyone else's love life. 'No!'

'That's a yes, then,' she heard Olivia respond forcefully.

'Didn't you hear me say no? N O spells NO, Olivia. He's a nice enough young man, but he's old enough to be handling his own affairs. He's a solicitor, for heaven's sake. If he can't ask a woman out, how's he got the courage to deal with his clients?'

Olivia harrumphed in that sort of 'I'm not interesting in all that tosh/I've got my teeth into a juicy bit of meddling and nothing is going to stop me now,' kind of way she always harrumphed when she was on a mission. 'He does conveyancing, Vera!' she said, intoning very clearly as if Vera were three pence short of a pound. 'His clients come to him. He doesn't have to draw them in. People buy and sell houses every day of the week.' She stressed her point, but then she overstepped the mark. 'Look at you. It's made you a tidy living and you'll make a packet when you eventually buy us out.'

That was a constant bone of contention and Olivia knew it. On the other end of the line, she went silent.

With her sister, Olivia owned and ran a clothes shop which was how she knew and was known by so many very different people. It was located in two adjacent buildings in the oldest and most desirable part of town. One building was for 'hers' clothing, the other building for 'his', and they were connected by an elegant conservatory running the full length behind the two shops. Here, male and female shoppers could gather and share a coffee or a glass of champagne overlooking the copiously stocked gardens which ran down to the river. There was even an old boathouse on the riverbank alongside which was moored a sleek, highly polished Edwardian rowing boat complete with oars which nowadays never moved. Recently though, with cheap imports and growing competition, combined with an out-of-town retail park opening, the business had seen a serious downturn in profit and Olivia had been trying to persuade Vera to take the premises off their hands.

Vera, who with Christy still ran the family building renovation business alongside the building merchants Richard's father had started, blankly refused to even consider buying them out. With three more stories above, the double-frontage building backing on one of the prettiest bends in the river would certainly make a perfect project to alter into executive apartments, but Vera was no asset stripper. She saw enormous potential, but she also saw a much greater disaster in the loss of a good friend who would only live to regret her short-term decision. If ever word got out that the Claremont sisters were thinking of selling, then there would be a scramble amongst the more unscrupulous property developers to acquire the shops, so Vera had been telling Olivia that the property market was due for an upturn and she should wait, praying instead that Claremonts' business might turn a corner and her friend would change her mind.

I can't deal with this today, Vera thought, as she tried to think up yet another excuse as to why she shouldn't talk to Ian about dating. What good would it do? He was a grown man and should be perfectly capable of looking after himself. She didn't know Etta, but she had seen with her own eyes how attractive the girl was. No! This was a recipe for disaster, but she knew without question that Olivia was not going to give up. She was like a dog with a bone. Vera was going to have to let the stupid young solicitor down gently herself.

'Oh, give him my number then. But I honestly can't see what I can say that will make anything change that girl's mind. Tell him to ring me in a couple of days.'

'I knew you would. I'll ring him now. Expect a phone call. You're not going out, are you?'

'No. I was planning to bleach the grime from behind my kitchen sink!'

Olivia snorted with derision. 'Vera. You're so funny. It's Sunday,' she said and promptly put the phone down without even saying goodbye.

Vera, irritated that she'd been forced into a corner, actually did get out her rubber gloves and the bleach and by the time the phone call from Ian came, there was not a spot of black remaining on the tiles or the grouting. There was also a long gap where she'd scrubbed so hard that some grouting came away. She threw off the rubber gloves in fury. They fell to the floor, knocking over the open bottle of bleach as they went.

'Yes!' she snapped, picking up the house phone.

'Am I speaking to Vera?' a timid voice asked, obviously sensing the person on the other end of the line was not in the mood to be interrupted.

Ian! Vera recognised his voice instantly. Damn Olivia! She'd only gone and rung him straight back. And even if she'd thought to tell him to wait a while, he hadn't. Why did the damned woman have to be so impetuous? As soon as any new idea popped into her head, Olivia could be trusted to act on it. No careful thinking. No sensitivity to others' feelings. No, Olivia Claremont had not one cautious gene in her biological make-up, and she didn't expect anyone else to have one either. She was a risk-taker and a meddler. She delighted in making other people squirm. She was the human equivalent of a concrete mixer and right now Vera could have strangled her.

'Hello, Ian,' said Vera softening her tone and putting on what she hoped was a sweeter voice. 'How are you?' It wasn't this poor young man's fault.

Even so, while Ian told her he was very well, thank you, that he'd just left lunch with his parents, that he thought he might have a walk along the river bank, Vera held the phone away from her ear and pulled faces at it.

'That's nice, Ian,' she interrupted eventually.

'Are you doing anything nice?'

Vera looked at the rubber gloves on the floor, the bottle of bleach lying on its side with drizzles of the pungent-smelling cleaner dribbling on the draining board, the different kinds of marks appearing on the kitchen windows, more cleaning streaks now than smudges and nowhere near as artistic as before, and answered blandly, 'You know, a bit of this and that.'

'I'm not intruding, am I?' he asked.

She mouthed: of course you bloody well are at the phone, but caught herself saying, 'Of course not. It's lovely to speak to you, Ian'.

'I … er … um, I just … er.'

For God's sake, spit it out, man! thought Vera.

'Vera?'

'Yes?'

There was a long pause, and if she hadn't heard shuffling and someone breathing on the other end of the phone, Vera could have been persuaded that the young man had expired through anxiety, which the nastier part of her truly wished he had, but eventually he got his thoughts around words which came out in one great big stream.

'Vera, I was hoping that you could give me some more advice because you were really, really great at giving me advice at Olivia's party on Friday and I seemed to be getting somewhere with Etta, but when I bumped in to her on Saturday at Oysters and she was with all those other girls I couldn't go over and speak to her and I got all worked up and I just couldn't do it so I …'

'Ian! Take a deep breath and start all over again!'

Vera raised her voice, interrupting him in full flow.

She heard his deep intake of breath. She heard three more deep rasps, and then, eventually, she heard him say: 'Vera, I'm awful at this romantic stuff. Is there any way you can tell me how to get a date with Etta?'

Chapter Five
Meeting Men (and Women)

It took Vera forty-five minutes to get Ian off the phone, by which time the sun had moved lower on the horizon, its rays had stopped coming in through her kitchen window and she was starting to feel cold.

She filled the kettle to make herself a mug of tea, and as it came up to the boil, she cleared away the bleach and rubber gloves. She hadn't meant to stay on the phone for so long to the young man, but as they got talking, his dilemma also started her thinking. How come a perfectly acceptable, upright and honest man, educated, in well-paid employment, with a good future ahead of him, was finding it so hard to find himself a girlfriend?

Okay, in social terms, Ian was a bit of wimp. There was no brashness in him. He was a gentle man who clearly only wanted to meet a gentle woman and settle down. The more he told her, the more she started to feel really sorry for him. 'It's so hard meeting nice girls these days,' he'd said at one point. 'It was easier when I was at school and Uni, but nowadays I'm so busy and I have so many commitments, I don't have the time to waste clubbing or going to bars. I go to the gym, but as soon as I've worked out, I go straight to the next thing. I'm trying to build up my business. I'm still studying. It's taking all my energy and time.'

What Vera didn't know, because there was no way she would have ever been told, was that later that day, her own daughter, Felicity, would be standing outside La Taverna, an Italian restaurant on the other side of town, drumming up the courage to walk inside. She was due to meet for the first time a man called Steve who she had found on an internet dating site and she was as nervous tonight as her mother had been about dinner on Friday at Olivia's.

This wasn't her first internet date. There had been others. None had been successful, but Fliss had surprisingly high hopes of this one. There had been a long exchange of chats between them and she'd liked the caution he'd shown in giving out his personal information. She'd checked him out as best she could using Mr Google's services and what he told her about himself had been corroborated on Facebook and Twitter, though there wasn't that much other than basic information on any of the sites. She was really looking forward to seeing if he was as nice in real life as he had sounded in their written chats. She'd already built up her own image of him: that he was well-presented, well-spoken and easy-going. Something was telling her that this evening was going to be very important to her future.

So, all that was left to do now was to walk through that door with its steamed-up windows, through the cramped and very full tables, ask at the bar for a reservation in the name of Steve, and she'd finally find out whether he actually was as handsome in the flesh as he looked in his profile photo. Although there was something ordinary about the image he'd chosen to share, there was a fineness in his features she found attractive. His hair was mousy and cut in an average fashion. She recognised his polo shirt as one that was sold in M&S. He wore a gold signet ring on his little finger and a smart, but not flashy watch. He looked just the sort of man she was looking for: solid, reliable and, above all, unscary.

What was there to be frightened of? All she had to do was walk in and be pleasant.

The problem was, however, that she was more frightened than usual. This wasn't a simple case of excitement or nerves. Fliss was always in some way frightened, experiencing the many various shades of fear ranging from mild self-consciousness to all-out panic with regular monotony. It was why she was so terribly thin. Whenever she got anxious, her appetite drifted away. Her beloved dad had told her when she was a teenager that, because she constantly shook so much, she would never need to do exercise. The gym wasn't for her and she believed him. Her slight frame made her contemporarily fashionable and she was adept at dressing to show it off to perfection, but she could never quite do away with the large spectacles and heavy make-up she chose to hide behind. As long as Fliss had her glasses and her face on, and the other person could not see directly into her eyes, she was able to cope. For Fliss was one of life's truly shy people and that made life hard for her.

Right now, it felt exceptionally hard. Just do it! Just do it, she willed herself, but would never have walked through the restaurant door unless another couple had walked up behind her and the man had politely held the door open for her to go in before them. There was no room to bolt. She was forced to walk in first, and then there was the confusion of the waiter asking if they wanted a table for three, which meant she had to say, 'No, I'm meeting someone else. His name is Steve.' All of it proved incredibly hard.

The waiter looked around. Immediately behind him, just inside the door, a man sat by himself. 'I'm Steve,' he said, and half stood up, holding out his hand to her. Fliss caught the knowing smile that passed between the couple with whom she'd walked in. They had clearly guessed instantly this was an internet date! It couldn't possibly be anything else on a Sunday evening between two people who had never met before.

Fliss blushed from the tips of her toes to the roots of her hair. Steve indicated for her to sit down. The table was tight against the windows. There wasn't much room. She squeezed her feet around its legs, then fell on her chair, dropped her handbag and set the glass of lager he'd already ordered spinning on its base. He caught it before it spilled, saying, 'Ain't goin' to miss a mouthful of that. Expensive 'ere, in't it?'

The local dialect 'in't it' did it. She instantly disliked him! Not that Fliss was in any way a snob, or so she liked to think. She was born and bred in this town, too, but she already knew that as soon as he heard her surname, he would assume he knew everything about her. Once he knew who her family was, she'd be judged by them, by her parents and her grandparents, not for herself. It always happened. That was the problem of coming from a well-known family. Not that they were so very wealthy. It was just that they'd been established in the town a very long time and there were even streets named after their predecessors who had been mayors and headmasters. Worse, there was the builders' merchants her great-grandfather had started which still dominated the corner of the most congested junction in town, one where everyone read their name in big letters every day as they sat in traffic queues. People still made a joke of the name painted in twenty-foot-high letters on its frontage because their surname was Father and the sign announced Father and Sons.

Fliss's full name was Felicity Mary Father and if she could have changed it without offending her family, she would have done it yesterday. The only way to get rid of it that she could see was to marry, but finding a boyfriend, let alone a husband to take her out of her misery, was proving a mountainous struggle.

'Laugh it off,' Christy told her in his lovely gentle way. 'I'm always going to be Christy Father. People think I'm a dyslexic Catholic priest.'

'Which would make me a sin in the eyes of the Church,' sniggered Annie. 'Hey, look, I'm Annie Father. Makes me sound like a steward on a route march. I'm thinking of adding Isit to the front of my name!'

Fliss did laugh with them and calm down a little, but here she was now, knowing she was going to have to lie through her teeth to avoid giving Steve too much information too soon, or otherwise it was going to be yet another miserable evening of rib-taking about her name.

She peered across at her internet date. He didn't

look much like his photo. The hair was curlier, with early flecks of grey. He was sturdier and shorter than she had imagined. Hadn't he said he was six foot two? More like five foot eight, she thought and grimaced. That was her height, so that would make it difficult to wear the four-inch heels she loved so much. There was still something about a man being taller than the woman. Fliss was old-fashioned enough to want a man to tower over her. She had dreams of her beau being able to kiss the top of her forehead, or to cuddle her from behind, his arms wrapped around her to keep her warm, and still watch a rugby match over the top of her head.

She tried to smile at him across the table. He reached across and touched her hand. 'Glad you could make it finally,' he told her. Finally? This was the first date they'd arranged. Ah well, just a slip of the tongue perhaps. She eased her hand back as she stared around the crowded restaurant. 'Busy in here tonight,' she whispered.

'Sorry?' he said, trying to hold her hand again. She put it firmly on her lap under her side of the table.

'I said, it's busy in here tonight.'

They both looked around the restaurant. It was a modern Italian, with glass containers of different shapes of pasta on the bar. Spotlights in green and red picked out artistic photos of the famous sights of Italy, the Colosseum, the Arno Bridge, the Leaning

Tower of Pisa, a woman sitting on the back of a Vespa being driven at top speed by her lover and the ubiquitous still from the film, *Roman Holiday*, of Audrey Hepburn laughing, shocked and delighted, as Gregory Peck withdrew his empty sleeve from the carved mouth of a stone lion. The owners must have come from Turin because there was a display akin to a shrine to Torino FC alongside the tiny bar, the club's dark red shield emblem with the rearing bull, its front hooves held upright like the hands of a dancer, centre front, pride of place. Behind it was an aging framed photograph of a fair-haired man with the dates 1939-1976 underneath his name, Giorgio Ferrini. It meant nothing to Fliss. She didn't even like football.

The noise level from customers chatting around them was high. The atmosphere was warm, almost steamy, and the smell of garlic and herbs, tomatoes and baking bread intoxicating. The waiter asked if she would like anything to drink and she asked weakly for water. He handed her a menu and walked away without urging her to have something stronger, even though it must have been obvious to him that was what she needed. Before her, all Fliss could see was a sea of letters swimming in front of her eyes. The thought of food was making her gag. She pulled at the collar of her shirt. She needed air.

'Wanna share some garlic bread?' her date asked without looking up from his menu.

She shook her head, but he didn't notice. ''ey, mate,' he called across to the waiter. 'Bring us some garlic bread on yer way back, will yer?'

And then he turned back to Fliss and said, 'Now that's sorted, 'ang on a mo while I go and take a slash. I had three glasses of these piss-weak lagers before you come. I thought you weren't gonna make it.'

Other customers turned to look their way as he noisily pushed his chair back and clumsily made his way to the toilet. Fliss stared out from under the safety of her glasses and baulked at the look of amusement on their faces. Well, nearly all of them looked amused; all, that was, apart from one man sitting alone on a table for two closer to the bar. She'd noticed him earlier checking the time. He was very much taller than everyone else, with nicely cut hair and a freshly pressed shirt with creases in exactly the right place down the outside of the sleeves.

Their eyes met. Fliss's stomach did a pirouette.

She felt herself flush even redder. Could this evening turn out to be even more awkward with a drunk for a date and another man staring her out? She needed to leave, but how? And then she had a brainwave. She speed-dialled her mother, who picked up on the first ring. 'Don't speak, Mum. Just listen. Look, I'm in a sticky situation. Can you ring back in a couple of minutes and make it look as if you've called me urgently home? I need an excuse,' and just as quickly she ended the call, ramming the mobile back in her handbag.

Across the room the man sitting on his own was still staring straight at her. Why, exactly, was he looking at her so oddly? Instinctively, she looked down, then quickly back up to see if he was still looking. He was. He was even standing up now. Then he sat down again when her dining companion pushed him out of the way as he banged out of the toilet wiping his hands on his trousers. 'There's no paper in the bog,' Steve said as he sat down and finished drying them on the table cloth.

Hold tight! Mum will ring back in a minute and then this will be all over, Fliss thought, mentally preparing herself to run out full of apologies but determined to go. She rummaged in her bag for a tissue and surreptitiously found the couple of twenty-pound notes she kept for emergencies and slipped them into her trouser pocket. She couldn't leave without paying her share towards this evening, even though she'd had nothing to eat or drink yet. Where was that waiter with her water? God, she needed a drink.

Oh no! The staring man was staring her way again. He was even standing up, but he hadn't noticed the waiter returning from behind the kitchens behind him, the plate of garlic bread Steve had ordered in one hand, a carafe of water in the other. Too late! The man stepped out, straight in the way of the waiter.

To avoid him, the waiter deftly lifted the plate high above the man's head, did a dance on the spot, plonked the carafe on the nearest table and steadied himself by grabbing the back of someone's chair. The man seemed oblivious to what had just nearly happened. He dropped a couple of bank notes on his table, grabbed his mobile phone and jacket and headed towards the door.

He's been stood up, realised Fliss. He's paying for what he's not had and I'm planning to do the same. Well, at least we're both honest, she thought.

Looking quickly back down at her menu in case he thought she was staring, she resisted the urge to get a better look at him as he left through the door behind her. But the door stayed shut. He wasn't leaving. She peeked up to see him heading their way instead. Her eyes shot back down to her menu as he came to a halt right alongside their table.

'Can I help you, mate?' asked Steve, his tone stressing his displeasure.

'Is your name Steve?' asked the man.

'Yeah. Wot of it?'

Fliss plucked up the courage to look up at the man now. She'd been right before. She thought she'd spotted the most beautiful pale blue eyes. She could see them clearly now because he was bending over her, his face close to hers, staring her straight in her own eyes.

'Well, my name's Steve, too,' the man said,

without moving his head, anger making his words sharp. 'And I think you're sitting with my date.'

'Hang on, mate,' protested the Steve she was sitting with, half rising, but failing because there just was not enough room. Every inch of Fliss went cold. She could sense, even though the two men were blocking her view, that many other customers had stopped talking, homing in to watch the potential entertainment of the brewing argument.

'You're Steve, too?' whispered Fliss, laying her hand over the seated Steve's to stop him getting nasty.

'I am,' said the Steve with the beautiful pale blue eyes. How Fliss wished those eyes would stop flashing so menacingly at her. 'And you're Felicity.'

'Felicity!' gasped seated Steve. 'Ain't you Carly?'

Felicity looked down at the hands on the table. Seated Steve had both of his reaching out towards her. Her own were clutching the rim of the table. Steve with the beautiful blue eyes was leaning on the table his hands spread wide to support him. Oh Lor! There was the gold signet ring on the little finger of his left hand and the nice watch was peeping out from under his very nicely pressed shirt sleeve, exactly the same ones she had spotted in the profile photo of the Steve she was supposed to be meeting.

What had she done!

But, before she could answer, her phone noisily started playing Minuet, the ringtone that announced a call from her mother. She scrabbled in her handbag, extracted her phone and turned away from both men so she was facing the window. Against the blackened backdrop of the street scene outside she could see her own image reflected back at her. Whether it was a trick of the light, or a true reflection, she looked as blanched as a ghost.

'Mum!' she said, far too brightly, then listened intently.

'Well, I'm doing what you asked me,' she heard Vera panicking, 'but what's happening? Do you need me to come and get you or something? You are somewhere safe, aren't you, Felicity?'

'Can't you find the spare key?' Fliss said back, much louder than she needed.

'What key? I'm in my house! What's going on, Felicity?'

'Yes. I've got my spare with me. Stay in the warm in the garden shed. I'll come straight over.'

'I'm nowhere near the garden shed,' protested Vera. 'I'm in the sitting room.'

'It's no trouble. I'm on my way, Mum,' and with that she grabbed her things, pulled the two twenty-pound notes from her pocket, slammed them on the table and pushed her way out, whispering, 'Sorry. My mistake. I really am sorry. But I have to go'.

And with that, she was gone, out the restaurant door, running for the taxi rank and leaving two very bemused men, both called Steve, behind her.

Chapter Six

Olivia Never Listens!

Vera was not best pleased. 'Felicity Mary Father! How many times have I told you internet dating is dangerous?'

Fliss sat wrapped in a blanket, her legs curled up beneath her on the sofa, seemingly obsessed with the contents of a mug of hot chocolate. She chose not to look up.

'Do you want anything to eat?' her mother added, knowing she wasn't going to get an answer. 'You must be starving.'

The last thing Fliss wanted was food. Even the hot chocolate was giving her mental indigestion. She stared into her mug and watched a spiral of lighter-coloured liquid whirl round at the surface from where her mother had stirred it viciously. 'It was Sunday evening. In La Taverna, Mum. There were people everywhere.'

'And did you tell anyone you were going there?'

At first Fliss didn't want to answer. She already knew what the reaction would be and she didn't want to face it. This evening had already been traumatic enough.

'Did you?'

'I told Olivia,' Fliss finally admitted.

All she got in return was a sniff of derision and a hard slap on the coffee table. Fliss stared even more mournfully into her mug. 'You'd have told me not to go,' she said quietly.

Vera was still angry with Olivia for lumbering her with Ian earlier, but this was different. This was a coincidence in a million and Fliss had fallen victim to it. The look on Fliss's face said everything. She'd had a horrible evening and she didn't need her mother to tell her. Richard would have told Vera it was time to back off and cool down. He had always been the one who accepted Fliss's shyness and was prepared to wait while she worked her own way around it. Vera, on the other hand, had always been overprotective of her sensitive daughter. She would go into battle even when it wasn't needed. Many a time, Richard had had to put a stop to an argument caused by the two women in his life approaching problems in their own, very different, ways.

'When did you tell Olivia?'

'Yesterday. I popped into the shop to pick up that repair her sewing lady did for me.'

'And you didn't think to tell me?'

Fliss didn't answer. Oh yes, Vera guessed, turning it over in her mind. You talked it over with Olivia and she told you not to say anything to me, didn't she! The sheepish look Fliss cast her way confirmed her suspicions.

'It's a waste of time telling Olivia. Olivia never listens!' Vera said, so spitefully it made Fliss look up.

'We talked it over. I was excited, Mum. I liked the sound of this man. I didn't want to spoil it by making too big a thing of it. You'd have guessed. You'd have told me what to wear, what to say, what to do.'

'Okay!' answered Vera, showing Fliss the palm of her hand to stop her saying more, stung because it was true. She would have, but that didn't mean she liked being deliberately kept out of the picture. Her own daughter choosing Olivia's opinion over her own was bad enough, but this was serious. Fliss could have got herself into real trouble. 'Fliss,' she commanded, 'you must tell me next time you see this man because Olivia never remembers details and I don't want to be the one who has a couple of policeman at my door telling me they need to come in and I should sit down.'

'Mum! I'm not that stupid! Give me some credit.'

They glared at one another. Fliss backed down first. 'Anyway, there's not going to be a next time with this one, is there? Oh Mum, he looked so angry.'

'He was probably disappointed,' Vera said.

'What do you mean?'

'Well, look at you. You're so beautiful. What man wouldn't be disappointed when he's expecting to be going on an evening out with you and he doesn't get it?'

Fliss looked at Vera askance. 'Are you sure you're Mum, and not Dad?' she asked.

Vera realised that was exactly what Richard would have said to Fliss if he'd been here. 'Your dad was a wise old owl, wasn't he?' she said, softening. 'I must have picked a thing or two up from him. I didn't mean you'd fall into bed straight away with him, Fliss. But you are so beautiful.'

'I miss Dad,' said Fliss.

Mother and daughter smiled sadly at one another. 'So you really liked this man, did you?' asked Vera.

'How do I know? I never got to really speak to him. He was so angry at me for being so stupid, Mum.'

'But did you like the look of him?'

Vera watched Fliss shiver as she remembered how the pair of beautiful pale blue eyes sparkling with energy and passion had so impressed her. 'He was very tall. Nicely dressed. Spoke with the nicest accent. I wish I'd sat at his table, not the other poor drongo's. He was awful, Mum. Sounded like he came off the council estate up The Heights.'

Vera, who was no snob, scowled. Fliss didn't notice. 'Wasn't that one nice then?' Vera asked.

'Probably. But I wouldn't have liked to spend too much time with him. He was too nervous. Been drinking before I got there. Thought he was meeting a girl called Carly, so he's gone home tonight pretty hacked off, too, I expect.' She sighed. 'I'll just have to write the right Steve off now, I suppose.'

'Couldn't you send this right Steve a message saying you were sorry it had all been a real muddle?'

'Do you reckon he'd even read it! Oh, this internet dating is so damned hard. I wish I could just meet someone nice, at work, or through friends. Where have all the nice men gone, Mum? Was it as bad as this in your day?'

Vera knew her answer without even thinking about it. No. In her day there had been dances and get-togethers. No one worked miles away from where they lived, but then again no one had flashy jobs that meant they had to travel. So they had time to take things more slowly. Life was simpler somehow, and it had been a natural part of their lives looking for partners, for marriage, never expecting to go to university or to have gap years which took them away. Vera's friends were still friends she had gone to school with. She couldn't name one of Fliss's school friends who still lived in the town. Everyone else had moved away. Fliss didn't even have that many female friends that she could share a night out with.

How strange that Fliss was asking this question! It was exactly what she had discussed with Ian at length this afternoon. 'Do you know, I've already had this conversation once today,' Vera said. 'Stay the night and I'll drive you into work tomorrow morning. We can talk more about what you can do to say sorry to this nice young man with the beautiful blue eyes.'

'Sounds lovely,' said Fliss, relieved, 'but I'm bushed after all that excitement. Can we talk over an early breakfast instead? I need to go to bed.' With that she took herself off to her old bedroom.

Her light was still on and the door ajar when Vera finally followed her up, so she wasn't surprised when Fliss called out for her to come in. Fliss was lying in bed wearing one of Vera's nighties, just looking around. 'I love how you've decorated my old room,' she said. 'You're so clever with colours, Mum.'

Once, the room had been a riot of pink and purple with fairy lights suspended around the bedhead and feather boas hanging from the curtain rails and light fittings. All that had now been replaced by soft furnishings in a watercolour colourwash of lilac, pale turquoise and stone, offsetting the plain painted walls of the palest peacock blue. 'It always makes me think of the Caribbean when I sleep in here,' said Fliss.

'These aren't the hot colours of the Caribbean,' said Vera.

'No. They're its sunrises through blinding light,' said Fliss, which surprised her mother who hadn't heard Fliss say anything so romantic since she was a teenager. Her once artistic little girl had turned her back on painting and photography after she went to the local college to do a business course. Suddenly the stock market filled her days and she'd proved a good study. Nowadays she was working her way up through the ranks of the local stockbroker's. She hadn't wanted to join the family firm like Christy, so Richard had encouraged her to forge her own path, hoping it would give her the confidence she lacked. At work, Fliss showed no shyness. That only appeared in her social life, but Vera had been sorry to see her put down her paint brushes and camera in favour of a computer and copies of the FT.

'Mum?' Fliss brought Vera's musings to a halt. 'Who's this Ambrose?'

Vera frowned. 'I don't know any Ambrose,' she replied, thinking, I'm going to kill Olivia.

'Olivia said he was at the dinner party on Friday night.'

Okay! So Olivia had been talking about her business again, but if this is what she had told Fliss, then this Ambrose must be real. Yet Vera still could not remember this man who everyone swore was there. Even Ian had spoken about him today, but try as she might, Vera had absolutely no recollection of anyone called Ambrose.

This was starting to worry her. Not only had she forgotten him, she was even more deeply embarrassed that Olivia had blithely told her that he had helped half-undress her when she was at her worst for drink and he had helped put her in to bed in her underwear. Pray God she hadn't told Fliss what had happened. Why had he made not one little impression on her at all? There was only one answer. Damn the demon drink!

'Olivia says Ambrose thinks you're lovely,' said Fliss with a secretive smile. 'And she's got something to tell you when she next sees you.'

Worry turned to angry embarrassment. Oh, she has, has she! I am most definitely going to kill Olivia, slowly, painfully, torturing her, roasting her savaged flesh, thought Vera, whose imagination had gone into overdrive as to what she was going to do to her friend when she next clapped eyes on her. Talking to Vera herself was one thing. Talking about her to her daughter behind her back was completely out of order.

'Mum,' started Fliss, taken aback by the black cloud of anger turning her mother's face to a nasty shade of purple. 'Now you don't have Dad around to keep an eye on you any more, you do know neither Christy nor I will ever mind if you meet someone else. We don't want you to always live on your own. But it is early days. You will be careful who you get involved with, won't you?'

Although Vera was still roasting Olivia in her imagination, Fliss thought she was listening to her, so she added what she had been churning in her mind since Olivia told her all about Friday evening's dinner party. 'Mum, you will make sure you use precautions, won't you? You do know you're still terribly vulnerable, don't you?'

Chapter Seven
The Dancing Sea

Sleep eluded Vera until dawn. Throughout the troubled night she'd tossed and turned with too much going through her mind. Finally waking with the alarm from a light doze, she felt woozy. She rolled over and promptly fell back into a deep sleep.

'Mum.' A little voice penetrated some part of her consciousness some time later. She came to with a jolt. 'I'm off now. I've called a cab. Here's some tea.'

Vera could smell it, but couldn't bring herself to reach out for it. She muttered something incomprehensible, felt a feather-light kiss on her brow, and was instantly back asleep. The next time she woke she felt totally relaxed and refreshed. She lay half looking up at the ceiling, her mind still drifting somewhere between an urgent nagging to wake up and an enticing place where she had been extra warm, deeply relaxed and entwined with another person's body. Entwined with another person's body! Her eyes opened with a jolt. Her hand reached out and patted around the empty side of her double bed. Nothing! Phew! She squeezed her eyes shut again, and there it was again at the forefront of her imagination. The bloody enormous erection!

What was going on in her mind?

Fighting the bedclothes to sit up, she reached for the alarm clock. Ten past ten. Oh no! She had a meeting with her solicitor at eleven to sign the contracts of sale of the latest project, and then she was due for a board meeting at Father and Sons at midday. She raced for the bathroom, dressed haphazardly and, without even brushing her hair, ran for her car.

The rush-hour congestion had long passed, but now was the doddery hour when the less able drivers ventured out for their newspapers and fresh bread or for their weekly trip to the doctors to pick up their pills. She got stuck behind an old chap in a brand new Lexus doing twelve miles an hour and found herself shouting at him to 'turn left, turn right, turn anywhere, but get out of my way, you old prick.' When he finally pulled in, bouncing new tyres hard over a kerbstone, she calmed down. One day, she would be one of those old drivers and how would she like it if someone told her she had to move out of the way? It was a salutary thought. She slowed down and drove more carefully.

She was only ten minutes late for the solicitor,

who wasn't ready for her anyway, so she had time to slap on a little make-up in their toilets and brush her hair. His secretary had a pot of coffee and two cups waiting for her return, which she carried through as her boss came out of his office to collect her. 'Vera,' he greeted her, kissing her on both cheeks. 'As serene and beautiful as ever,' which made her snort and his secretary smile.

'What?' he asked with dancing eyes.

'You're an old flatterer, Martin Rosser, but I do like you.' She squeezed his upper arm. He led her in, his hand firmly keeping that hand on his arm as they walked in together. They waited for his secretary to leave.

'How are you?' he asked, holding out the chair for her to sit.

'I'm fine,' she answered. 'Particularly now I've got the full asking price for Number Forty. What on earth ever made them do that U-turn last week? I thought we were going to lose the sale when we couldn't agree on a price, and now it's all happening so quickly.'

'Snap their hands off, Vera. Full price and a quick sale. Deals like that don't happen every day. And I'm not flattering,' he said, changing the subject as if he wanted to say more. 'You do look better, you know. You are looking your old self again. What's happened to make the change?'

'Obviously, getting Number Forty off my hands

has been like lifting a noose from around my neck, but mainly I think it's time. And having to get on with things. I don't know, Martin. It's two and a half years now, you know, since we lost him.'

'And it still seems like yesterday,' said Martin, who had been a good friend to Richard. 'I still miss him at Rotary and the rowing club. Did you hear Alan Weyland was elected president last weekend? Roy's already completed his first full term since he took over from Richard. Time flies and you don't even notice it. We're getting old, Vera, and I, for one, don't like it.'

'Me neither,' agreed Vera, throwing back her coffee in one go. 'Come on, where are these papers you've got for me to sign? I've got to be at the merchant's for a board meeting midday.'

'Never ends, does it? Do you want another of those?' he asked as she put her cup back into her saucer with a clatter.

'Yes please,' she said, helping herself.

That meeting was easy. The board meeting that followed was not. A major supplier had increased its delivery charges overnight. There was a change in taxation coming in which was going to create difficulties for their existing computer software. The union had sent a letter demanding a pay increase for the staff.

'Shall we sell up?' asked Christy in a loud whisper

as he walked his mother back to his office. 'Or do we just give it away?'

'Give it away!' agreed Vera, linking arms with him and giving him a little cuddle. 'And we'll all go to live on a desert island. You, Annie and the boys can have the biggest palm hut and Fliss and I'll make do with the swamp grove. By the way, I signed the sale contract for Number Forty just before I came in. The monies for that should be through by the twenty-fifth.'

'Then what're you going to do, Mum? Start looking around for a new project to get your teeth into now you've got that big wodge of money in your bank account?'

Suddenly, a ghostly mirage of the enormous erection momentarily swam before her eyes. She squeezed them tight and shook her head to dispel it.

'You all right, Mum?'

She gritted her teeth, and nodded her head. Good! It had gone!

'Something just walked over my grave,' she said and pecked him on the cheek. 'And to answer your question, Christy, I haven't got a clue, but to be honest, I'm glad to see the back of Number Forty. I haven't enjoyed doing it. Your dad chose it, and he chose badly. We've made a good profit on it, but not as much as Dad expected. I lost both your dad and Bill Hughes just after we started it, and without Bill managing the lads, it's been hard work. I don't think

I want to get involved in another renovation just yet. I don't need to. There's enough money for me to not do anything for a while. I might just take my time and really sit down and think about what I want to do with the rest of my life.'

Christy pulled his mother into a bear hug. He was much taller than Richard had been, and certainly more beefy, but as she buried her face against his chest, his smell reminded her so vividly of his father, it brought tears to her eyes. She buried her face deeper so he didn't see her crying, but it was pointless. Her quiet, diffident, ponderous son was also highly aware of the emotions of others. He tightened his grip and held her tight until he felt her breathing return to normal.

She pulled back, a little shamefaced, and reached up her sleeve for a tissue.

'Annie says we need an au pair,' Christy said. 'Fancy the job?' to which she cuffed him so hard that even through his thick-knit sweater, he felt a bruise starting. 'I'll take that as a no then. Fancy a slice of coffee and walnut at the Café in the Park instead?'

Christy knew exactly what to say and when to say it as far as his mother was concerned. Her tears ceased. She wiped smudged mascara away from under them and turned her face upwards for him to check. 'You'll do,' he told her, holding the back door open high up so that she could pass through under his outreached arm.

'Solaire,' he shouted. 'I'll be back in an hour.'

A female voice called back from somewhere in the cavernous depths of the building. 'Okay, boss.'

'I keep wanting to call that new girl of yours Amber,' said Vera.

'Don't! Since you put that idea in my head, it's as much as I can do not to call her that. I'm sure she knows what I'm thinking.'

'Her parents didn't think that one through, did they!'

'Could be worse,' Christy said, chuckling. 'I told her she's passed her probation last week. She's finally got to grips with the printer and the customers love her. She talks the same language as some of them.'

'She can eff and blind then, can she?'

Christy grinned. 'With the best of them!'

They found a table at the café overlooking the empty paddling pool. 'Council cutbacks, they say,' said Christy, anticipating his mother's amazement. 'Elf and safety, cos they can't afford a lifeguard.'

'For a kiddies' paddling pool!'

All Vera got in return was a raising of Christy's eyebrows and a downward smile of derision. She tucked into her cake, realising how hungry she was. No breakfast and only mugs of tea as they were having the board meeting weren't going to sustain her. It had been a long day already and she still had to tackle Olivia. As she'd tried to listen to their financial accountant whine on about the computer system and the additional costs of a pay rise for the staff, her mind had wandered back to her most pressing problem. She was still as angry as hell with Olivia and she wasn't going to go to bed until she had had it out with her. That made her even more ravenous. Would Christy think she was menopausal if she went and got herself another slice of cake?

'I could eat that again,' she zoned back in to hear him say.

'Me too,' she said, problem solved, and let him go back to the counter to order it.

When he came back, Christy was whistling to himself. She heard him humming *The Birdie Song* and a smile spread wide across her face. 'Thinking of Dad?' she asked, because Richard had always whistled that tune when he was relaxed and happy.

'All the time. Particularly when I have problems at work. I try to think what Dad would have done.' Christy picked at a loose thread on his jumper. 'I was thinking about him the other day when I was playing with Mickey in the garden. I was trying to teach Mickey how to weave when he came to kick a ball. Remember the dancing sea?'

Vera did, only too well. She settled back in her chair, a mouthful of cake poised on the end of her fork waiting to go in to her mouth. 'Jersey,' she said. 'That most perfect holiday.'

'Annie had the radio on in the garden. I was playing with Mickey. Wyeth was crashed out in his pushchair. And then they were playing that old song about a wanderer, and I started singing along, and Annie asked me how I knew all the words.'

'Your dad loved that song.'

'Remember how he convinced me and Fliss it was the sea's theme song, and we believed him!'

Vera burst out laughing. 'And he'd do that silly dance of his to it.'

'It was such a brilliant evening. The tide was high on that surfing bay.'

'St Ouen's,' Vera interrupted.

Christy nodded. 'The sun was setting in those sort of horizontal stripes, glowing all dark red, and pale pink and purple. The water was right up to the sea wall, and that song was playing on the car radio. Dad made us get out to look at the water and the stupid thing was, the sea was swishing in little waves in exactly the same time as the song. And then Dad started doing that daft dance. He sort of dropped his bum, bent his knees like Elvis and wiggled, and Fliss fell over trying to do it with him, and you tried to take a photo, but you were laughing so much when the print came back all you'd got was a shot of the sky and we had little dark heads cut off at the bottom. I was trying to explain it all to Annie, but I suppose you just had to be there. You can't explain that kind of thing, unless someone has seen it for themselves.'

'No. You can't,' agreed Vera. 'But at least we four were there and we can remember.'

'Do you think Fliss remembers?'

Vera heard his change of tone. She put down the uneaten forkful of cake and put her hand over his. Sorrow had suddenly clouded his face. 'I'm sure she does.'

'She's getting worse, Mum. More shaky by the day. Her confidence has completely gone since she started thinking she is never going to get a boyfriend and that she's got left on the shelf. We've got to do something, Mum.'

Chapter Eight

Olivia Never Listens – Part Two

Claremont's had been a feature in the town for nearly two hundred years. It started trading first as a haberdashery shop selling ribbons and cottons from the front parlour of a well-respected family who had lost money in a financial scandal and fallen on harder times. Later generations added a dressmaker's in the back parlour and the family moved to the upper floors to reside. After the Second World War, it began to sell ready-made clothes for the working woman, and then, when the shop next door came up for sale and the Claremonts found they could afford to buy it, they expanded into selling clothes for all the family. Olivia now ran it along with her elder sister, Angelina, a smaller but less showy version of herself, and they had taken the shop upmarket. It had been a mistake. They had committed themselves to selling ranges of very expensive clothes just at the same time as the country had gone into recession. Claremont's, as a result, was struggling to stay open.

Angelina, the stable sister, calm under pressure, usually sunny by nature, today was feeling anything but. Thunderous could more aptly describe her mood.

When Vera entered the shop, it was Angelina who greeted her. 'She's done something to you, too!' she said before even greeting Vera.

'Am I that easy to read?'

'You came in through that door like you wanted to take it off its hinges. She must have done something. My bloody sister is a bloody minx!'

Vera took a step back and gave Angelina kisses of sympathy on both cheeks. 'When I get my hands on her, I am going to break every bone in her body,' Vera agreed. 'And then, I'm going to kill her.'

'Step in line,' Angelina suggested. 'She's gone missing. I had an appointment at the bank this afternoon to discuss extending our overdraft. She went off late morning saying she had an idea and needed to explore it urgently. She swore she'd be back at lunchtime. Have I seen her? Have I hell! She's not answering her phone. No one knows where she is. I've had to ring the bank and re-arrange for tomorrow. They're going to think we're not capable of running the business, and then what are they going to do? Banks don't work for their customers.'

Vera went silent. This was serious. Her argument

with Olivia could wait. 'Have things got that bad?' she asked. Angelina shrugged.

'I could see if I could lend you something to tide you over,' ventured Vera, already regretting offering as she doubted she would ever get the money back.

'Nah. If we go down, we'll go down fighting. I just wish Mum hadn't left us the business fifty-fifty. I can never get Olivia to see sense.'

Vera held out her arms for Angelina, who stepped in for a consoling hug. 'She's going to bankrupt us, Vera,' she said, pulling back. 'She's driving me to drink.'

The memory of waking up at Olivia's house in her spare bedroom after drinking so much alcohol she couldn't remember how she'd got there and, then dreaming of the enormous erection, shot across Vera's memory. She shivered. 'I vowed to give up the drink after dinner at her house last Friday,' she told Angelina.

'You don't want to share an Angosec with me, then?'

They look at each other and smirked. 'Oh, go on, then. Lead on, MacDuff.'

'Look after the shop, will you?' Angelina said to her assistant who was sitting cross-legged on the floor marking up a pile of stock due to go into yet another sale.

'Any bargains I might like in that lot?' Vera asked, peering over at the mountainous pile.

'Silk evening trousers down to fifty quid,' answered Angelina, taking her by the hand and leading her towards the conservatory. 'But they're too young for you. You need a bum the size of a flea's to do them up.'

Involuntarily, Vera checked out her bum in a mirror. It wobbled as she walked. She chose to say nothing, but deeply regretted having the second piece of cake with Christy. 'She's been interfering again,' she told Angelina.

Angelina looked up from opening a bottle of prosecco. At one point nothing but real French champagne was ever served in Claremont's. Nowadays, customers were lucky to be offered anything, no matter how much they'd spent in the store. Angelina poured a mouthful into a glass. It tasted pretty good to Vera. 'Where did you get this?' she asked.

'Discount store. £3.99 a bottle.'

'Blimey. I'd better call in and get some.'

'Don't bother. I cornered the whole of their meagre stock,' she said, filling the glass, adding a small drop of Angostura bitters to the méthode champanoise and topping it with a glacé cherry. It turned it into a pretty swanky-looking glass of pink fizz. 'Now try that for a good Angosec,' Angelina said.

'Wow. That's special. Planning to have a party, are you?'

'That, or a wake at somebody's funeral.'

The two women snorted, and took deeper draughts. 'What's she done to you, then?' Angelina asked.

'Been putting ideas in Fliss's head and then Fliss repeats them to me. Last night, my beloved daughter had the cheek to warn me to be careful. She asked me if I was using precautions.'

'Well, are you?'

'Angelina! I haven't even looked at a man since Richard died.'

'Perhaps, it's about time you started again. You're not getting any younger,' Angelina said.

'Speak for yourself. Who are you jumping in to bed with, then?'

'Dah! My husband. Peter! The one I've been with since I was seventeen.'

Vera grimaced. 'Sorry. Forgot which sister I was talking to for a minute.'

'Do you really want a bang on the nose, or are you getting addled?'

'Sorry,' said Vera, taking a big slug and emptying her glass. She held it out to be refilled.

'Oh! What the hell!' said Angelina, and topped hers up, too. 'I haven't told Pete we're in deep trouble yet,' she confided. 'I have absolutely no idea how he's going to take it. He's not a worrier, but he's going to think this is the end of the world as we currently know it.'

'You've always got this building as equity,' Vera said, pointing around. 'Have you considered selling up?' she added without thinking.

Angelina froze, wondering what else Olivia had told Vera. 'This is our home,' she said, quietly looking up at the ceiling. She and Pete lived on the upper floors. 'Has Olivia asked you to buy it?' she asked in a very quiet voice.

'Every single time we're together,' Vera said. 'But don't fret. I'm not going to buy it. Anyway, I don't think I could afford to. You're sitting on a fortune here, Angelina, but for God's sake don't let word get out. There are some pretty unscrupulous people out there.'

'Yes. And we can't even afford to buy Olivia out to ensure she doesn't drop us in it. I really could kill her, Vera.'

Before Vera could reply, the shop door banged shut as someone came rushing through. Both Angelina and Vera looked over in that direction. Seeing Olivia striding towards them, they turned and looked back at one another, lips pursed.

'Oh, yummy. Angosecs,' declared Olivia, slinging her coat and handbag towards a chair in the corner. 'I'm parched! I've had such a lovely, productive day.' She took a glass from the cabinet and reached for the wine bottle.

Neither of the other women spoke. Olivia stopped midway between pouring her wine and drinking it. 'What? What's up with you two?'

Vera sat back and listened delighted as Angelina gave her younger sister both barrels. She left nothing unsaid. She brought the wrath of every single one of their ancestors down on Olivia's head. To give Olivia her due, she sat and took it without interruption, all the time maintaining eye contact with her raging sister.

Running out of steam, Angelina ended close to tears.

'You're going to love what I'm about to tell you,' Olivia said blithely, appearing to have appreciated not one word her sister had hurled at her.

Vera had to admire her buoyancy. That lambasting would have sunk even the strongest of sailors.

'We're saved!' Olivia announced. 'The idea came to me yesterday. I checked it out today and tomorrow we're going to make our fortune. Oh, and it all revolves around you, Vera. It's all going to be down to you.'

Chapter Nine
The New Business

Vera's jaw dropped in sheer astonishment. She was shocked to the core. What level of gall did Olivia possess to take such a fierce rollicking from Angelina, and still be able to blindly turn the attention straight back to someone else? Anyone else would have been mortified, or quivering. At least a few tears would have been shed.

Olivia, however, calmly sipped her wine. 'Don't fret, big sis,' she said. 'Vera knows what to do. She's our trump card.'

Vera leant forward, came up close and personal to Olivia's face like an angry mother to a misbehaving child and said very slowly, 'I cannot afford to buy out Claremont's, Olivia!'

Olivia had the impertinence to giggle, and even tried to push her away with one index finger on the tip of Vera's nose. Vera's fury rose as fast as the mercury in a barometer placed alongside a hot furnace.

She stood her ground, moved not one inch, took Olivia's wrist, and held her so firmly that she couldn't pull a millimetre away. Olivia stopped giggling, but continued to return her stare through heavily mascaraed, unblinking false eyelashes as Vera slowly, firmly pronounced each word. 'Even if you begged me, I cannot raise that kind of money. Nor would I want to. I'm telling you the truth, Olivia!'

Finally dropping her eyes, making Vera let go. Olivia hid her smirking face behind palms held up towards Vera as if she was calming a raging bull. Her voice changed to that of a tiny child. 'Stop it, you silly person. No, no, no, no no.'

Vera and Angelina exchanged exasperated glances. Could Olivia really be taking note of what someone else said for once? They doubted it, and she wasn't. Olivia would always be Olivia and they had to accept this was the very same Olivia that they had both come to know and love and be frustrated by in equal measure. 'We don't need you to buy us out.' Her protestation rushed out breathlessly in her usual voice. 'We're going to open a new business.' She sat back, smiling triumphantly.

'She's finally gone mad,' groaned Angelina, raising her hands high in the air.

'No, I haven't', said Olivia. 'I've just had THE most brilliant idea for a new business.'

'Another one?' asked Angelina sarcastically. 'How many is that now?'

'I know some of the others have been a bit random.'

'A bit random!' squeaked Angelina.

'But this is a good one. This one's THE one!' Olivia insisted.

'THE one what?'

'The one that's going to save our bacon.'

Vera had heard enough. She drained her glass, put it on the table, then started gathering her coat and bag as she stood up.

'Where are you going?' asked Olivia.

'Home,' Vera said, all anger at Olivia dispersed as she finally accepted that this was one friend to whom she would never be able to talk reason. Angelina was right. Olivia had gone mad, and Vera did not have the strength to deal with it. Angelina was going to have to handle it all on her own.

'Sit down!' Olivia commanded. 'You can't go without hearing my brilliant idea.'

Vera humoured her. She sat back down, but only on the edge of her seat, clutching her belongings, ready to stand back up again. 'And what is your brilliant idea, Olivia?' she asked flatly, dreading what the response would be.

'You're going to start a dating agency in our boathouse.'

Angelina's hands dropped. Slowly, she lifted her eyes and looked quizzically at Olivia. Vera, completely and utterly stunned, tried to say something. Her mouth opened. Her head moved to one side like a duck's. Then she closed her mouth again. Words had completely deserted her. Her lips pursed in a kind of death twist as she tried to find even one suitable utterance in response to what Olivia had just said. She had to be having a joke.

'Nice one, Olivia. You got me there,' she said eventually, and grinned, nodding like a cartoon character.

'Don't you want to open a dating agency?'

'I don't even want to date! Why would I want to open a dating agency? And why would I open it in your boathouse?'

Olivia acted as if only she knew something that Vera didn't. She smiled a slowly widening, totally beatific smile, her eyes gleaming. The smile never left her face. 'Ian said you'd been brilliant. He was so impressed by what you advised him. So did Fliss. And Ambrose said he'd never met anyone as wise as you ever before. He said you really could read people.' All this was delivered with the sugary-sweet confidence of an Amazon executing a death blow.

Vera had had enough. She stood up, shaking with fury. 'Who the fuck is bloody Ambrose!' she exploded, only just stopping herself from hitting Olivia over the head with the wine bottle.

Chapter Ten
Friends Divided

Even Angelina had never seen such a passionate reaction from Olivia, even though everything Olivia did, she did with passion. Her younger sister burst into tears and flew to the toilet where she locked herself in and then proceeded to kick and pound the door while she wailed like a banshee. Angelina left her to it, and instead went into the shop to check that they had no customers. She found Toni still sitting cross-legged on the floor gawping in amazement in the direction of the conservatory.

It was nearly five o'clock. Angelina turned the sign on the door to show closed and told her assistant she could go home early. Toni raced out of the side door without saying a word, looking fearful. The pile of clothing she had been pricing remained scattered where she had knocked it over on the floor.

Vera went in the opposite direction to Olivia. As Angelina strode through the conservatory to speak to the assistants in the adjoining shop, she spotted her pacing the garden. It looked as if she was berating herself. Her mouth was certainly moving and she was holding her hands up to the sky as if she was praying for heaven's assistance. 'We've had a little accident,' Angelina told the manager of the menswear section. Luckily, there were no customers in that side of the shop either, only two astonished men who didn't know what to say. 'We've closed early. Why don't you do the same?'

Like runners off the starting blocks, the men swung into action. 'I've just cashed up,' said the manager. 'It's been really quiet again.' He handed her a practically empty cloth banking bag. Angelina weighed it in her hand and sighed. She was very close to crying, but, biting her lip to stop herself, she picked up the telephone. 'Christy?' she said when she connected with him. 'Your mum's a bit distraught, and she's had too much to drink. Is there any chance you could drive her home?'

'Thanks. She can leave her car in our parking space overnight,' she confirmed when he answered in the affirmative.

Checking all the assistants had left, she then went over to the toilet where Olivia was still working herself up into a real state. Angelina raised her clenched hand to rap on the door, and then something came over her. She'd had enough! She kicked the door so forcibly she left black rubber marks from the sole of her shoe on the white paintwork. 'Oh, for God's sake. Put a sock in it, Olivia. You are not a five-year-old having a tantrum.'

Inside the toilet, Olivia went quiet.

'I never thought you even knew the f-word,' Angelina told Vera, touching her shoulder as she came up behind her in the garden.

'Of course I do! But that is the very first time I've ever, ever, used it,' answered Vera, horribly ashamed of herself. She turned towards the shop to listen. All was now silent; the only noise that could be heard in the garden was the constant drone of slow-moving traffic on the other side of the building and the put-put of a tourist boat on the river. 'Has she calmed down?' she asked. She hated scenes.

'More importantly, have you?' asked Angelina.

Vera shrugged. Anger spent, worry about one of her closest friends took its place. Anxiety swept over her. 'Do you think she's having some kind of a breakdown?' she asked.

'Olivia's always having some sort of a breakdown. I've got past caring.'

That was news to Vera, who had only ever seen the buoyant, fun-filled side of Olivia.

'Don't you know she's bi-polar?' asked Angelina.

'No!' gasped Vera, guiltily thinking she would never have pushed Olivia so far had she known. The only negative she'd ever heard from Angelina before was that she described Olivia as having too much energy, and she'd always taken that as a grudging compliment.

'Her meds usually keep her on an even keel, but I'm worried now that the stress of the business has tipped her over the edge. She shouldn't drink. She shouldn't smoke weed. But what do I do, Vera? I'm not her keeper.'

'She smokes weed?' said Vera, not knowing that either.

'She does everything she shouldn't do, Vera,' said Angelina, biting the quick at the edge of a finger nail. 'But, it's also what makes her so loving, and funny, such a sociable thing. She really is good at bringing in the business when people have money, and at times some of her ideas are absolutely brilliant.'

'Does she ever see things?' asked Vera, her thoughts suddenly going in another direction.

'What do you mean?'

'She doesn't have any imaginary friends, does she? You know, friends like Harvey?'

'That big white rabbit James Stewart saw in that black and white film?'

Vera nodded.

Angelina shook her head. 'No. Well, I hope not. Why do you ask?'

'Do you know someone called Ambrose?' asked Vera, but at that moment Christy walked through the side gate into the garden and interrupted them.

It needed all his strength to open the gate, it had been closed for so long. 'Sorry. I couldn't get anyone to hear when I banged on the shop door and I've left my phone at the merchant's,' he apologised. Left open, the gate twisted on its rusty hinges.

Then he saw Vera. 'You all right, Mum?' he asked. Vera nodded as he took her coat and handbag from her.

'Olivia and I have just had a nasty spat,' she said, quickly hugging Angelina goodbye and following him to the car.

As they passed the window from the toilet looking over the garden, it opened and Olivia stuck out her head. 'Hi, Christy,' she called over and leant further out so that he could kiss her. 'How are you doing?'

'Fine, Olivia,' he answered, politely stopping to speak to her as if there was nothing wrong in talking to an older woman leaning out of a toilet window. 'Kids are good. I'll tell Annie I've seen you.'

Vera couldn't believe that Olivia now looked as if absolutely nothing had happened. She turned to walk away, but Olivia called after her. 'Have a good think about that business proposal,' Olivia shouted. 'It'd be absolutely ideal for you to get your teeth into something different now you've sold Number Forty.'

'How did Olivia know the sale for Number Forty had gone through?' asked Christy later as they sat in the car in traffic on the way to Vera's house.

'I have absolutely no idea. I only signed the

contract with Martin Rosser this morning,' answered Vera, thinking exactly the same thing. 'I wonder if she's sleeping with my solicitor.'

Christy burst into fits of laughter, but it was a question Vera returned to as she lay in a hot bath later that evening. Surely not! Martin was happily married to his flame-haired Irish lass called Deirdre. He was even older than Vera and that made him old enough to be Olivia's father.

Vera's mind turned to how much older she actually was than Olivia. What was there between them? Eight years? Ten? She wasn't sure and she definitely wasn't going to ask because Olivia would then want to know how old Vera was.

Vera shook her head, knowing she would never admit it to someone who was such a blabbermouth. Olivia was the most dreadful gossip and Vera loathed being gossiped about. Why give her any more ammunition than was needed? Vera wondered whether she wanted to remain friends with a woman who got her so wound up? Was she just too much trouble to be friends with? Then her thoughts turned to about how much fun she'd always had when Olivia was around. Did she want to give that up? She didn't think so, and she certainly didn't want to stop going into the shop. She bought most of her clothes from there. And if she fell out with Olivia, what would Fliss or Angelina say? Would she lose Angelina's friendship? That would be awful, and really, now she knew Olivia was bi-polar, could she really hold any of the manic ideas Olivia had against her? That would be just too cruel.

Vera's anger started to disperse. She couldn't take any more loss and she certainly didn't want to lose the one friend who could make her laugh either.

Angelina had been careful to stress that the illness made Olivia brilliant, too. That started Vera thinking about the many clever things Olivia had managed to do. There had been that wacky idea of reviving the alternative boat race, the one that used to be contested on the river at August Bank Holiday. The Health and Safety supremos at the council offices had poo-poohed the idea, shown her regulations from every piece of legislation they could find, and tried everything they could to stop it, but Olivia had done her research, arranged an impressive level of insurance coverage, taken it to the media and now it was the most attended charity event of the year. It drew coachloads of visitors into the town centre and with them loads of revenue for the town's traders.

She'd also been instrumental in raising enough funds in a week to send a child with breathing difficulties to a clinic somewhere in Eastern Europe for treatment. Where Olivia saw a need, she could usually dream up a solution. Angelina was right. Olivia did have some absolutely brilliant ideas. She cared about people and she would always do what she could to help them. She made contacts and friends easily. She would work tirelessly. Vera realised she liked having Olivia as a friend because she truly liked her.

She got out of the bath, drying herself and starting to think about this latest idea of Olivia's. Where on earth had it come from? What had made her think of starting a dating agency?

Suddenly, it was obvious. Olivia had thrown the dinner party to which she had invited friends who only knew her but did not necessarily know one another. Possibly only Andrew and Erich, who Vera assumed were already a couple, had arrived together. Even Vera had come alone, and had happily been plied with as much of Olivia's cheap wine as the others had drunk until she made a fool of herself by knocking herself out.

Vera went to bed thinking about what she'd been told first by Ian, and then within a short space of time by her very own daughter. They'd both told her how hard it was for the young to find a romantic partner nowadays. Their lives were busy, their time short, but resorting to internet dating was giving few of them satisfaction, though to hear them talk it was also causing a great deal of hilarity. Vera wondered if internet dating was making a fool of their desperation because it amounted to no more than buying a partner for life from an old-fashioned catalogue. *Caveat emptor* should be written in whacking great letters over every photograph. The buyer definitely had to be beware by being aware that they were likely to have to waste a lot of time on finding out from the few things the person chose to reveal about themselves whether they were going to believe it or not enough to trust the other person with their emotions.

She went to sleep with only one thought uppermost in her mind. Perhaps Olivia was right, after all. Perhaps there was a better way of finding a life partner. But could it possibly be done by someone like Vera, working out of a boathouse at the bottom of the garden of Claremont's clothes shop?

Chapter Eleven
A Seed Change

An unexpected break in the weather the next morning was a welcome diversion from the restless night Vera had endured. The rain stopped and the temperature soared as a warm front arrived. There had been no more disturbing dreams that she could remember, so she concluded her restlessness had to be due to her mind being so stimulated with the revelations of the past few days that it needed to put them into mental boxes ready for her to deal with. It must have been working overtime as she slept.

Mug of tea in one hand, she drew open the double doors from her kitchen to the garden and wandered out in her housecoat and slippers. The recent chilly spell of rain had done damage. Certain plants were flopping over. Those needed tidying. Others were just starting to show signs of fresh blooms as if they knew a long spell of warmth was imminent. On one side of the long garden, before Richard died, she'd erected an archway leading to nowhere which he'd nicknamed 'Vera's folly'. The intention had been to obscure an awkward area with plants all called Vera. She'd found a clematis called Vera. There were lavenders called Vera, too. There was even a hybrid tea rose called Vera Johns which produced large, pale orange blooms which she'd really like, but since losing Richard the job had never got done. Without him, the project they had once shared lost its meaning.

It had always been such a wasted space in the garden and it made her heart sink. Now she stood contemplating it again. For years the rough area beyond had remained partially hidden; hidden from view from the kitchen by a butt catching precious rainwater from the roof, but when a heavy storm brought down the roof guttering and its downpipe and that had, in turn, caused damp in the dining room on the inside wall, she'd decided to do away with it all.

Now, the area just looked a mess. It was an eyesore which defeated all her efforts to tidy it up and for the past two and a half years, she had studiously ignored it. 'Stick in a big bush,' Richard had once unhelpfully advised. 'Root penetration,' she'd countered. 'What about an enormous statue then?' 'You've been trying to get an ugly Venus de Milo into my garden for too many years,' she'd protested.

'My garden, is it?' he'd laughed. 'What happened to the concept of ours?'

'Okay, the grass can be yours,' she'd conceded, lifting his arm and wrapping it around her shoulders as they surveyed the area, comfortable together in each other's warmth. 'Mowing the lawn is all the work in the garden you ever do.'

He hadn't argued. Gardening was never his thing. Hard surfaces, bricks and mortar excited him. Renovating, repairing the worn-out, putting new ideas into older properties, satisfied his need for all to be neat and tidy. The 'pretty stuff' he left to Vera. 'You've got a much better eye for colour,' he'd always said, seamlessly handing over the jobs he hated to her. In truth, she did have a more artistic eye, so happily accepted being the one who chose decorations and soft furnishing, tidying up outdoor spaces with plants. The way they'd worked together, he doing the hard building graft after seeing the potential, she doing the finishing touches, had been highly successful. They'd made a good living out of it over the years.

Number Forty had been the last project they'd started together, and Richard had died almost before it had begun. It had been a struggle for her to complete it ready for sale, particularly after his long-standing foreman, Bill Hughes, also died early in the project. Vera wasn't certain of much for her future, but one thing she was sure of – she did not want to repeat that experience again. It had been simply too challenging at a time when she was emotionally drained. The only reason it got completed at all was because there was so much money tied up in it. Within days, that money the sale released would be sitting in cash form available for its next use, but she had absolutely no idea what that was going to be. There was nothing at all left in the 'to do' list that she wanted to do now she was alone.

What, exactly, was she going to do with herself now it was all over? The enormity of the thought suddenly terrified her.

As if felled by a fatal shock from a bolt of lightning, she realised she had absolutely no idea. Number Forty had been the last of her shared commitments with Richard. Probate was complete. The children were doing their own things. Their own house needed little doing to it. Christy was making a success of stepping into Richard's shoes at the builders' merchants. With the sale of Number Forty, she had effectively made herself redundant.

The dawning realisation made her physically wobble. She reached for a garden chair and fell over one of its wicker arms, landing so heavily on its cushion she spilled the full mug of tea all over her housecoat. Its cloying wet seeped against her bare thighs.

My God, she thought. This is it! This is what I've been dreading. What am I going to do with the rest of my life?

It was a daunting prospect. Suddenly, the only way she could see was in a blur, only think clearly with supreme effort; only breathe by physically forcing herself to overcome the compression that knotted her chest. So, this was actually IT! Her past had effectively come to an end, her present was empty and her future was, as yet, unwritten; but who or what was going to write it?

When no answer came, her anger rose to a crescendo. 'Damn you for dying, Richard!' she screamed to the open sky and slung her mug at the archway that seemed to be taunting her. The mug sailed through the opening, smashed into the plastered wall beyond it and shattered into a thousand pieces which fell back to the ground, leaving what little remained of her undrunk tea as a stain on the dirty cream paint of the wall. Her vision cleared. She stared at the stain unblinking. And then she saw it.

She threw back her head and she roared with laughter.

Before her, from the wet, murky brown splodge, an indistinct shape emerged. The more she stared at it, the more she could make out the rough outline of a semi-clothed woman, head in profile, half a broken arm dangling by her naked breasts, the other arm completely torn off. Below the nakedness of her upper body, the impression of drapery faded away where wasn't enough tea left to complete it.

'You bastard, Richard Father!' Vera giggled

uncontrollably to herself amongst a mixture of tears and laughter. 'You got your bloody Venus de Milo in the bloody end!'

She knew now that she would face her future. She had few tangible ideas what it actually contained, but she knew instantly how she was going to face it. She would take baby steps. She would do nothing big or impetuous. Instead she would wait, and look, and listen out for any opportunities. The first had just presented itself. Stripping off her wet nightie and housecoat in frustration, she strode back into the house to find a thick stick of charcoal from her painting box. Kicking off her slippers, she went back in to the garden. Completely naked, with wet soil caking around her toes, she clambered through the archway, cursing as tendrils caught painfully in her hair. She wiped away any rough bits and rubbish from the Venus de Milo stain on the wall, then drew around it carefully to give it solid form.

When she was satisfied she was finished, she clambered back through the archway heading for the kitchen. Neither knew who was the most shocked as she strode back in through the double doors naked and they came face to face with one another: Christy, who had let himself in with his own door key when she hadn't answered the doorbell, or Vera, who, on seeing her son, grabbed for a tea-towel with which she unsuccessfully tried to hide her nudity.

Christy instinctively turned his back. 'Mum! What the hell are you doing?'

'Don't look! Don't look!' answered Vera, crouching behind the central counter.

'I'm not looking. Honest, I'm not looking. Look, I'm going into the lounge and I'm shutting the door,' he promised as he sprinted for safety, hands shielding his eyes.

Only when the door slammed behind him, did Vera bolt for the staircase, but as she passed the shut door, she heard him snort with a burst of amazed laughter, at which, she, too, suddenly saw the funny side. She romped, two at a time, up the stairs heading for her bathroom, leaving a trail of muddy footprints on the beige carpet as she went. She was giggling so hard when she slammed the bathroom door behind her, she was shaking. Only then did she catch sight of herself in the mirror. Her body was scratched and dirt-stained. Her feet were black with dirt. Her fiery cheeks were framed by a wild bird's nest of tendrils of undergrowth tangled into silver-streaked, curly hair. What did she look like! What had she done? Her poor boy was never going to get this image of her out of his mind!

Hurling herself under the shower, she washed her hair and body, then wrapped herself in a bath sheet and wound a towel around her hair. 'Make some coffee,' she ordered, shouting down the stairs to Christy, and as she creamed her face and limbs, then dressed, she heard the lounge door open, footsteps crossing the hall, then eventually the rising squeal of the kettle coming to the boil.

She decided the only way to handle the embarrassment was to brazen it out. When she strode into the kitchen fully dressed and accepted the proffered mug of coffee from her tight-lipped son, she firmly told him, 'Don't you ever dare say a word to anyone, not even Annie. Do you hear me, Christy Father!'

'Me! Not one word!' he squeaked, barely able to contain his laughter.

'Good!' she said and took a deep slug of her coffee. It was scalding hot. She had to spit it into the sink.

'You all right?' asked Christy and exploded again into fits of laughter.

Vera splashed handfuls of water from the cold tap into her mouth, then, dabbing her face on kitchen towel, turned sternly towards him. 'You are never, ever, to tell anyone about what you just saw,' she commanded. 'Promise!'

Christy raised his palms in mock capitulation, but his face told a very different story. 'Christy!' Vera warned.

Christy bit his lips and shook his head in the sort of agreement he would never be able to keep; and then he noticed how his mother's bottom lip started quivering as an unchecked tear escaped and slid slowly down her cheek. He pulled her into his arms and held as tightly as he could as the floodgates opened.

In her son's arms, Vera wept over the death of Richard like she had never been able to weep before.

Chapter Twelve
Germinating Ideas

'It had to come some time,' Annie told her husband when they fell into bed that evening and were finally able to talk about Vera's breakdown. 'It's been long overdue.'

Christy said nothing. His mother's distress had deeply affected him. He settled himself in bed, stretching his long limbs almost to the end of the mattress. He pulled his wife in tight towards him. They lay for a long time luxuriating, appreciating bodily rest. The boys had gone to bed overtired and fractious. It had taken a long time to get them off to sleep. Eventually, alongside him, Annie's breathing changed and her own sleep started to overcome her. Christy was so deep in his own thoughts, he hardly noticed.

'I don't think too much about Dad being dead, and me not able to speak to him nowadays,' he mused out loud to himself. 'It's still as if he's in another room and he'll walk in and start telling me something, or like he's somewhere out there checking I'm doing the right thing,' and then, as he contemplated whether he needed to do anything more for his mother, sleep overcame him, too. The very next thing he knew was when he was woken at the crack of dawn by his younger son, Wyeth, howling from his cot in the bedroom next door, and his elder son, Mickey, launching himself at his chest earnestly telling him, 'Dada, Whyiff's pooed his nappy.'

'Tell Mumma,' Christy mumbled, desperately hanging onto the last vestiges of sleep.

'Mumma!' screeched Mickey directly in his ear as he thumped Annie hard on her shoulder, waking her with a jolt, denying both of them any more sleep.

Breakfast over, Annie tried to put on Mickey's shoes as Wyeth spread spilt oatmeal over the tray of his high chair, his pudgy baby hands slapping it before he licked his fingers and spread the mess in his hair. Mickey resisted her efforts to put on shoes and insisted on putting on his welly-boots instead. 'Sure you've got enough time to drop him off to nursery?' she asked Christy, who was checking out prices on his laptop. Christy nodded absentmindedly as he copied costs down on a handwritten estimate.

'Then I'll take this little'un over and check out if Vera's okay this morning,' she said, lifting her younger son's hands from a milky porridge puddle and wiping both of them, his face and hair and the tray with wet wipes. Wyeth screeched in protest and slapped her hand away. She stood back and frowned at him. He stared back at her unblinking. 'If I take you to see NanaVera, will you promise to be good?' she asked and got a shrill chimpanzee-like holler in reply.

'I come,' said Mickey, pulling at the pocket of her trousers.

'You're going to nursery,' said Annie without thinking and got a sharp stamp on her bare foot from a tiny welly-boot. 'Mickey!' she protested, grabbing him by the knee. 'That's not nice.'

Christy snapped his laptop shut ready to speed the irritated little boy away from more confrontation.

'What's that plant that sounds like NanaVera?' he asked as he rammed the laptop in his man-bag. He had to raise his voice over the sounds of Mickey striding around the kitchen slapping his welly-boots on the tiles.

'What plant?' asked Annie, scooping Wyeth from his chair.

'When Mum stopped crying, she said she was finally going to plant up that archway thing in the corner. Said she wanted plants named Vera. I couldn't think of one,' said Christy, lifting Mickey by one arm from where he now flopped on the floor trying to get one of his boots off. 'Leave that, Mickey! You're going puddle-jumping today.'

Annie and Christy stared out of the window at a cloudless, sun-filled, sky and shrugged at each other. 'Aloe Vera?' asked Annie, trying to wipe Wyeth's grubby face.

'That's the one.'

'Aloe Vera won't grow over an archway,' said Annie, sniffing Wyeth's nappied bum from behind. 'Poo, you've done another one. No wonder you're grizzly.'

'I'll see if I can pick up one for her at lunchtime from Robin Redbreast's.' The name of the garden shop in town made him think again of his mother's nakedness. He shook his head, trying to dispel the thought as he pecked his wife on the cheek. 'Say bye-bye to Mumma,' he told his son and Mickey obediently blew palm-wet kisses.

'Do you know, I never expected it, but Mum's still got a cracking figure,' Christy said as he opened the door for Mickey. All he heard as he strode out to the car was his wife protesting 'Christy!' as she took their younger son upstairs to change his poo-filled nappy.

'I don't know why you're getting so embarrassed,' Annie told her mother-in-law later that morning. Wyeth had fallen asleep in his pushchair, his head lolling to one side. The two women shared coffee on the patio and sat watching him snooze. 'We all have the same. It just comes in different shapes and sizes.'

Vera took a deep intake of breath.

'Didn't you worry someone might see you, though?' went on Annie, taking another biscuit from the tin. 'I know I shouldn't,' she said cupping a minuscule amount of fat from around her waist in the other hand, 'but the boys are wearing me out. I need the energy.'

Today she wore a t-shirt top skimming her bare midriff to show off her latest tattoo, two Chinese dragons which went all the way around her waist, chasing each other's tail, one's mouth open to catch the pearl the other held in its back claws. It was certainly a work of art, but one Vera wished Annie hadn't chosen to wear on her body. What on earth was it going to look like when the ink faded or she put on so much weight the nifty dragons became extinct dinosaurs? Vera dreaded to think, but there was no way she would ever challenge Annie. Her daughter-in-law, this week sporting spiky black hair streaked with indigo blue, was stubborn and could well resort to having even more tattoos if she thought they might be a serious source of provocation.

'It never crossed my mind,' Vera answered honestly, looking around her garden. 'Who's going to see me out here?'

'People on the top deck of the bus!' Annie reminded her. 'They can see over the wall.'

Vera flushed and chewed a piece of loose skin on a finger. It hadn't even occurred to her. She had been too wound up. Annie saw her distress and softened. 'You've never really had a good cry since Richard died, Vera. You've been so brave. And we have been worried.' Gently, she pulled Vera's hand towards her, stopping her from chewing at the skin, and then sat stroking her mother-in-law's hand as they both stared, deep in thought but silent, at the child sleeping peacefully in his pushchair.

'I have absolutely no idea what I'm going to do next,' Vera whispered eventually.

Annie waited. Vera said nothing more. Instead she stared into the distance, biting her lip. Annie looked around for inspiration; and then her eyes lighted on the archway with the Venus de Milo drawing behind. 'What about that for a starter?' she asked.

Vera followed Annie's gaze as Annie went on, 'You're right. A statue wouldn't work in there. It'd be too big. I'd do what you've done. Paint that goddess woman on the wall like you've pencilled her in. You're great with a paintbrush. Make her funny. Then put your Vera flowers in all around her. That'd look good. It's a start.'

Vera peered at the charcoal sketch on the wall. Annie was right. The area did need a focus. A mural would make it look like an arbour. 'Venus de Milo's arbour.' Her thoughts came out loud.

'Vera's harbour in any storm,' teased Annie, and they both smiled. 'And if you don't do it, I'll get a tattoo of Venus done on me instead,' she threatened, checking out her bare arm, knowing exactly what Vera's reaction would be. 'It'd be the right shape to go just about there.'

'Don't have any more!' Vera pleaded without thinking. 'Let me paint Venus on the wall instead and we'll call her Annie de Milo.'

'Nah. Vera de Milo'll do,' said Annie, sounding satisfied. 'Paint yourself,' popped out of her mouth before she could stop it. 'Christy says you've still got a cracking figure.'

Vera blushed profusely at the thought of how much of her son had actually seen.

Chapter Thirteen
Vera de Milo

Vera was intently sorting through paint tester pots at Father and Sons when her mobile rang. She still felt highly sensitive. It was making her weepy and she found she could only concentrate on one thing at a time. Life, for the moment, felt very, very difficult indeed. 'Hello?' she answered, automatically putting the phone straight to speaker, distracted between one paint called Midnight White and another simply called White. Perhaps the marketing men had run out of unnecessary soubriquets by the time they got to name a paint which purported to have no colour. That led to wondering whether or not she needed flesh colour or the colour of alabaster. Thinking about the job in hand was taking her mind off far more unsettling thoughts.

'What colour is marble?' she said aloud.

'Any colour,' answered a voice from her mobile. 'Why?'

'What colour's that marble that Michelangelo used? You know, for that Madonna and child in Rome?'

'You're odd, Vera! Why are you wittering on about marble?'

Vera came to abruptly. That was Olivia's voice! Oh no! She hadn't checked the caller ID when she answered. She suddenly remembered she didn't want to speak to Olivia and promptly ended the call.

Her mobile rang again within a matter of seconds. Fumbling to silence the phone, it rang until it went to voicemail. She really couldn't handle Olivia today. Her emotions were still too raw. Probably she was never going to speak to Olivia ever again. Her friend had upset her just too much. The third time the phone vibrated and lit up, Vera switched the phone off. Surely, Olivia would get the message and leave her alone now.

'Carrara,' came a man's voice from the other side of the shelving, making her jump. She peered between the paint pots, but could only see a man's chest in a blue and white checked shirt.

'Sorry?'

'I couldn't help overhearing,' the voice in the shirt said. 'The Piéta is made from Carrara marble.'

'That's white, right?'

The shirt moved as if the man was walking around the shelving to speak to her. 'It didn't look very white when I last saw it in St Peter's. It was more a kind of taupe.'

Taupe! Vera shook her head as if she was hearing something alien from outside a bubble. It was so unusual for a man to use the word taupe. She put down both tiny pots of paint and started looking at the grey section. 'You don't happen to know what the Venus de Milo is made from?' she asked speaking to the shelves as she scanned the range. She couldn't see a paint tester called taupe. Might Norwegian Skies be a shade near to it?

'She's Greek, so she won't be made of Carrara marble.'

'Is she?'

'Yes. From a much earlier period. She's a fine old bird and still very white.' The voice was refined, the accent bordering on posh. Vera was peering through the shelving to see who it belonged to, so she never heard its owner walk up behind her. A hand passed her shoulder, picked up the pot of Midnight White she'd been considering and put it into her hand. 'Try that one,' the man said. 'That should be just about right.'

Stupidly, she looked down at it and not up at him. It was only as he walked away, saying, 'Say hello to Olivia next time you speak to her,' did she turn around to see the back of an upright, very tall, thin man with silver flecks in his hair, wearing a blue and white checked shirt tucked into well-worn jeans, striding away from her carrying a two-litre pot of fence paint.

'Why did I take more notice of the pot of paint, than I did of him?' she wondered later after Fliss arrived to join her for supper.

'Whoever he is, he knows Olivia,' replied Fliss, trying to be helpful.

Vera thought about it, and shook her head like a snorting horse petulantly refusing oats. It wasn't important and she certainly wasn't going to contact Olivia Claremont to find out something she didn't need to know. The man had been nice enough to help her out, and she would probably recognise his voice again if ever she met him, but that was enough for now. She couldn't handle any more.

'You didn't fancy him, did you, Mum?' asked Fliss bemused and struggling to find an explanation for why her mother was obsessing with this chance encounter. The mind machinations contorting her mother's face only usually happened when she was perturbed or angry.

'It wasn't at all like that, Fliss!' Vera protested, and then wondered if she had actually fancied the man. She couldn't have, could she? All she'd seen was the back of him. How could you fancy a man from the back? 'What about your love life?' She changed the subject and pulled her daughter in close for a cuddle.

'Dire,' said Fliss, dipping out from under her arm and picking up a slice of celery before it went into the pot. 'What're we having?'

'Hotchpotch risotto,' said Vera, who could make a speciality out of leftovers when she couldn't be bothered to shop. Fliss knew the signs. Mum was having a bit of a hard time.

They ate their dinner quickly so they could go through to the sitting room to watch the News. Vera felt she'd heard it all before. Energy prices were going up again. A man had murdered his estranged wife and children and then committed suicide before the police knew anything about the atrocity. A warlord had been committed to life imprisonment, but his wife and all the riches he had squirrelled away from his country had disappeared. There was more about the NHS. Some other hospital had failed to balance its books. Some minor sporting hero had returned from some nondescript tournament to be feted by his home town. How many evenings had Richard insisted they eat in time so they could watch the News? He was obsessed with it and could never understand why Vera often chose to load the dishwasher whilst it was on. Fliss had inherited her father's keen interest in social issues. Christy, like Vera, would only take an interest when it made a real impact on his day-to-day life.

Life's too short, Vera thought dispassionately and left Fliss to watch the telly, her attention unswerving as she listened intently. 'Ice cream?' Vera asked and got a brief nod in response. When she returned with two bowls of mint choc chip, Fliss ate hers without saying a word, but as soon as the programme finished, she remembered her manners and thanked her mother for a lovely meal.

'How do you do that?' asked Vera.

'Do what?'

'Concentrate so hard, then slip straight back in to what you were doing before. I'd have forgotten what we'd even had for dinner if I'd watched the telly for three-quarters of an hour.'

Fliss shrugged. 'Dunno,' she agreed. 'Come on. Tell me all about Vera de Milo. Have you done any drawings yet? Is she going to look like you?'

'You've been talking to Annie!'

'Christy, actually,' Fliss conceded. 'It's good you've taken on a project, Mum.'

Vera protested it was hardly a project, just a bit of tidying up, as she found and brought the plans she'd drawn up for Fliss to see. 'You do still have a great figure, Mum,' Fliss said without looking up as she checked them over.

Vera looked at the plans in horror. How much had Christy told his sister? 'That's not me! Well, the face might be, but the body's not.'

Fliss looked her mother up and down. Tonight Vera had made a real effort with her appearance, even if she hadn't with her cooking. That said everything about her state of mind. She was covering how dreadful she must be feeling. Fliss checked out the tailored pale grey trousers under a complementary silk shirt in shades of apricot and lime. She saw how Vera's hair was freshly washed and dried to wave softly around her face. There were wrinkles. What mother of two children in their twenties didn't have some wrinkles, but Fliss was glad her mother never disguised them. Vera wore her wrinkles with pride, particularly the laughter lines at the corners of her eyes and around her generous mouth. A little bulge around her midriff implied a life well lived. Her bum was still neat enough, her ankles and wrists tiny. It was painful watching her go through this latest emotional setback. She hated seeing Vera look so unhappy.

'I've had a message from that Steve,' Fliss ventured after a while.

'And ...?' hedged Vera.

'He's not at all happy.' Fliss pulled her mobile out of her pocket, found the dating site app, opened it and showed her mother the message.

Vera read: **'My profile photo was accurate. Shame you couldn't recognise me. I recognised you.'** Harsh!

Vera's first thoughts were: what a stupid bastard, quickly changing to: he doesn't sound nice enough for my Fliss, running on to: she's had a lucky escape, and then: poor bloke, he was obviously really disappointed.

What a mess, she finally decided, then couldn't think of anything tactful enough to say to Fliss who was obviously waiting for her to say something. 'I've never seen one of these dating websites,' she said instead.

'App, Mum. It's an app.'

'Okay. So show me how it works.' Vera handed her back the mobile. Fliss patted the space beside her on the settee and her mother slipped into it. Together they both peered at the tiny screen as Fliss gave her a rapid run-down on how it all worked.

'So, you flick to the right if you like them and to the left if you don't?'

Fliss nodded. Vera watched as Fliss started slowly, then sped up, hardly looking at the profile photos of many men. Every one was flicked to the left, even though Vera thought some of them looked pretty nice from their photos. Either Fliss was terribly choosy or she wasn't really interested in going down this route.

'Bit … precious … don't you think?'

'It's how it works, Mum. No one who goes on these sites expects it to be any different.' Fliss suddenly sounded defensive.

'But, it all seems so … callous … somehow.' Vera took the mobile from her daughter and slowly flicked through a few. 'He looks nice,' she ventured. Fliss grimaced. 'Well, what about him?'

'Not interested,' said Fliss.

'So you've been in touch with him?'

Fliss looked down at her hands. She obviously

had and had been given the brush-off. Vera saw red. What was wrong with these young men! Her daughter was beautiful, and talented. She didn't deserve to be treated like a piece of meat.

'Most of these guys only want a blonde with big boobs.' Fliss laughed, but so sharply it was hardly convincing.

Vera started flicking through again. 'So, tell me again how you get in touch with someone you like.'

Fliss repeated more slowly what she had said before. It appeared that if a woman liked the look of one of the men, she put him in a group of favourites. Once there, provided she had paid a subscription, the woman could send the man a message. By being chosen as a favourite, the man could check from his end and instantly decide if he wanted to respond to the message. If he didn't, he simply ignored it. It was a form of instant rejection without any guarantees.

'How many of these have you sent messages to?' Vera asked.

Fliss obviously didn't want to say. 'A few,' she answered, not very convincingly.

'And what do you look like on your ... what do you call it?'

'Profile.' Fliss took back the mobile and found her own entry on the site. She looked pretty in her photo with her dark hair with its heavy fringe. It was a natural pose against a backdrop of roses. She was holding her spectacles in her hand and squinting against the sun looking tanned and relaxed. Vera remembered Christy taking the shot at a barbecue at home on an evening when Richard had been teasing her. They'd all had fun. She was half-smiling, perhaps a little too shyly, but it was a nice smile, which could perhaps have been a little more showy, but one that said she was a nice girl from a nice family.

Perhaps that was what was wrong! Perhaps the kind of men who went on these sites didn't want a nice girl from a nice family. Perhaps all they wanted was sex so they went for girls that gave the promise of a good time.

Perhaps that was what was wrong with this Steve bloke who had been so nasty to Fliss!

'Show me Steve again,' said Vera wanting to check him out now. Fliss quickly brought his profile up and handed Vera the mobile so she could read it. So he was thirty-three, a professional man, though it didn't say what he did for a living, he'd never been married, he was looking for someone and didn't specify whether it was for a friendship, a short-term relationship or marriage. He looked like Mr Average from his photograph. Vera noticed the same neatly ironed polo shirt. She spotted the good watch. The photo showed him sitting behind a desk in what looked like an old-fashioned office. There was a rather pleasant seascape hanging on the blue-painted wall behind him.

'Did he look like this in the flesh?' asked Vera, wondering what was wrong with him. It had to be his personality.

'Exactly,' confirmed Fliss. 'Oh, and Mum, he had the most beautiful pale blue eyes. I'm such a fool for getting so flustered. I would have really liked to meet up with him.'

The amount of pain Vera heard in her daughter's voice brought her up sharply. She had been about to say that he was a fool who didn't deserve a date with Fliss, but then she thought better of it. Instead she took another good look at Steve's profile photograph. She enlarged it, and when she did, she spotted something very, very interesting.

Chapter Fourteen
On The Case

Vera knew immediately where the photograph of Steve had been taken. As she enlarged it on the screen of Fliss's mobile, the side of an ornate ormolu clock appeared behind his left shoulder. She could see clearly now that the seascape she had first spotted was hanging over a mantelpiece before which Steve was sitting and which was mostly obscured behind him. On that mantelpiece sat a clock Vera instantly recognised. She knew it because she had once bought it by mistake when she left an absent bid at an auction. She'd wanted an art deco piece, but had muddled up their lot numbers and ended up with this ugly ormolu monstrosity. But what had seemed an awful mistake, turned out to be extremely profitable. Wanting to get rid of it before Richard got wind of her stupidity, she'd hid it in the garage, put an advert in a trade magazine and within days of its publication had sold the clock on again for a very good profit. Only then did she confess to Richard what she had done, and he'd been so amused he said the mega-rich woman he'd married could take him out to dinner.

If she was right, and the people who had bought it from her still owned it, she guessed that the grown-up man in this photo was probably the tiny boy who had been running around the house when Vera had delivered it to them. Somewhere in the mountain of back paperwork in boxes in the attic would be an invoice and receipt. Surely the family still lived in the house if this up-to-date photograph was anything to go by? Find the receipt and she could track them down.

But should she tell Fliss?

Definitely not! Fliss was still too raw from the bungled date at La Taverna. 'I would have chosen him, too,' she said, trying to encourage her daughter to cheer up.

'Too late now,' moaned Fliss, making Vera squeeze her daughter's hand in sympathy.

'Couldn't you try again? What about saying sorry?'

Fliss grimaced. 'I don't think he wants to hear me say sorry, Mum.' She went to the exchange of messages and handed her again that last one which had come through only that morning: **'My profile photo was accurate. Shame you couldn't recognise me.'** Vera read it again slowly. It was a petulant thing to say. Had there really been any need to say anything? God, he needed to grow a pair of balls.

Vera's hackles rose. If only she could give the young man a piece of her mind. Well, she could if she tracked him down. She'd look through those old boxes tomorrow, find the address and she'd do it! And then, another idea shot through her mind. She didn't need to put in all that effort. The answer lay sitting in her hand. He was contactable through this dating app. She had his messaging page open. If Fliss wasn't going to say sorry, why didn't she do it for her? It would be so easy to give them both a little shove. What more could go wrong? If he chose never to reply, Fliss would never know. If he came back with another angry reply, Fliss would surely see he wasn't worth bothering about? So, their first meeting had gone a bit haywire. Lots of meetings end up way different to how people expected. That's the whole point of the meeting: to see if you want to meet up again. Vera could see nothing to lose, and everything to gain. What was wrong with Fliss saying sorry? Or more accurately, what was wrong with her saying she was sorry pretending she was Fliss?

The theme tune for the News blasted out from the television. Fliss instantly turned towards it, unable to resist finding out if anything had changed since she had watched the last bulletin. Vera shifted in her seat and brought the mobile down by her side. She pressed the reply button and a small box appeared above the virtual keyboard. If she was quick, she could send him a message. He would never know it wasn't from Fliss. She used one thumb to press out: **'Kicking myself. Try again?'** Before she could change her mind, she pressed send and shut down the app so that she didn't do anything else silly.

By the time she went to bed, a mixture of anxiety and excitement had overcome her and interrupted her sleep. When she did drop off in the early hours, her dreams were rapidly moving and incomprehensible. Text messages flashed through them mixed in with splashes of white paint as she floated amongst it all in a garden she didn't recognise. The archway she had in her own garden appeared and through it she could clearly see the ormolu clock sitting on the mantelpiece now attached to the back wall. The clock fell and she lunged and caught it just as it started striking. She counted each strike, getting up to twenty-eight, then she saw herself talking to a couple with a child threading in and out of their legs as they spoke. 'I bought it for twenty-eight quid,' in her dreams she watched herself saying, 'but I'll sell it to you for eight hundred and fifty,' and the man reached into his pocket, took out a wad of notes which he threw at her laughing so hard his double chin wobbled and peeled away from his face. Fliss appeared and caught his chin in her hand, then expertly reattached it, patting it back into place as if it was Play-Doh, at which point Vera woke with a snort, sweaty and thrashing the pillow away from her face.

She turned the digital clock towards her so she could see the time. Its phosphorescent green glow showed it was nineteen minutes past three. She was exhausted, but try as she might, she was unable to drift off to sleep again. At five in the morning she gave up and went downstairs to make herself a hot drink. What have I done? she thought, as she sat sipping at the steaming tea, half-listening to the song of the blackbird that nested at the far end of her garden.

Her life was in such a muddle. Waking up drunk after dinner at Olivia's, then falling out with her, was bad enough; but then there had been the dreams of the enormous erection, stripping off naked in the garden and not even noticing what she was doing, Christy walking in and seeing her in the buff and then telling Annie and Fliss when she'd pleaded with him not to after she'd wept so profusely in his arms. Now this disaster! Sending an online dating message to a man making out she was Fliss purely because, as her mother, she thought she could make things better for her unhappy daughter. Everything was insane. The only thing that had gone easily in the past few days was when the unknown man sorted out the tester pot of Midnight White paint for her. Even then she'd only talked through a set of shelving to him and she'd only seen the back of him. Why hadn't he stopped to speak to her directly? She started doubting that the encounter had even happened. Had he been a figment of her imagination, too?

She shook her head as another memory appeared in the centre of her mind. It replaced the image of the back view of the man in the blue and white checked shirt and it was even more random. She suddenly remembered the toe in the woolly sock under Olivia's dinner table creeping up the inside of her leg, reaching under the table trying to catch it, then coming back up and cracking her skull sharply. Perhaps that was what had gone wrong? Perhaps she was suffering from a brain injury because what else could make her think she could make anyone happy again when she was so damned miserable and out of control herself?

Damn Olivia and her suggestion that Vera start a dating agency!

'And where the hell did that stupid thought come from?' she shouted, shocking herself rigid and promptly bursting into floods of uncontrollable tears again.

Chapter Fifteen
Out Of The Frying Pan

Angelina retrieved a loose strand of Olivia's long red hair from her linen jacket, and then patted her to indicate she now looked perfect. Olivia took a deep intake of breath. 'I'm scared,' she confided.

'I know, but it's got to be done. You did give Vera a hard time. You need to apologise, Olivia.'

Olivia picked up a magnificent bouquet of cut flowers from where they lay on a chair. Wrapped in cellophane, the heads of the blooms hung over her arm, the stems were so long. 'Too much?' she asked her sister.

'Perhaps a tad,' conceded Angelina. 'Did you take your meds this morning?' Olivia nodded like a child. 'And no booze last night?'

'Not a drop since Monday,' Olivia confirmed. 'What if she won't answer the door?' She panicked, her face blanching.

'Vera's our friend, Olivia. She's not a monster.'

Angelina pushed Olivia towards the door. Olivia looked back into the shop as if she was desperate to find something to stop her leaving. Angelina pushed her more firmly. 'Will you please go! I need to open up the shop and you're more likely to catch her at this time of the morning.'

Olivia stood on Vera's doorstep for a full ten minutes before she plucked up the courage to ring the doorbell. She'd parked in the street so that Vera couldn't hear her car tyres crunching over the gravel of the drive. She'd even tip-toed along the edge of the damp lawn, keeping her stilettos well elevated, so that her friend wouldn't hear her approach and have the chance to ignore her when she rang the doorbell. Eventually, straightening her dress, tidying her hair again, and taking the deepest of breaths, she reached out to press the bell.

Even from outside, the chime sounded extraordinarily loud. Olivia took a step backwards and composed herself.

Nothing happened. The door didn't open. There was no sound of footsteps coming up the hall. Olivia peered through the side bar of glass on the door. She could see lights were on in the kitchen. Similarly, the landing and stair lights were on. Upstairs, Vera's bedroom curtains were drawn and the blind in her en-suite bathroom was down completely, obscuring the already obscured glass pane.

What should she do? Olivia shifted the bouquet

of flowers from one arm to the next. They were heavy, and the bottom felt wet. She feared any sap that leaked out would mark her mint-coloured linen jacket. Should she leave them on the doorstep? Had Vera just popped down the shops for her newspaper? Olivia stepped back on the drive meaning to check if Vera's car was in the garage, forgot her stilettos and felt one heel sink in deeply between the sharp-edged gravel. She cursed under her breath and bent her leg up to see if she'd scraped the leather away from the metal underneath.

As she did, the front door opened. The two women stared at each other open-mouthed, neither expecting to see the other. Olivia's first thought was that Vera looked truly awful, whilst Vera's heart sank knowing she was going to have to deal with a confrontation for which she had no stomach this morning.

'Well, don't stand there posing like a bloody flamingo,' said Vera, more sharply than even she expected. 'I suppose you want to come in.'

Olivia obeyed without demur. Her stomach was in her boots. All bravado had deserted her. Every fibre in her body told her to run, but something made her follow Vera meekly inside the door. She took off her stilettos and carried them in her spare hand, trying not to drop them as she negotiated the bouquet through the narrow part of the hall following Vera to the kitchen. 'These are for you,' she said, placing the bouquet carefully on the counter and lining up her shoes precisely below them on the floor. A drip finally fell from the cellophane and landed on one of her stockinged feet. She wiped it away with the toes of her other foot, twisting it as if she wanted to hide even that small source of contention.

Vera offered neither a seat, nor any indication that she was pleased to see Olivia. She clung to the edge of the counter and stared into the middle distance. Olivia felt she had walked into the middle of a television thriller where the victim is so overwrought they can't explain to the policeman what atrocity has happened to them. She had never seen Vera look so completely wiped out. There were dark bags under her eyes. Her hair was a mess. She was still wearing her nightie, quite a nice one Olivia noted, but not one she'd bought from Claremont's. Olivia waited for an opening, but none came.

And then Olivia recognised exactly what was happening. This was abject grief and Vera was in the clutches of it.

Olivia rushed around the counter, wrapped her arms around her friend from behind and clutched her as Vera's legs gave way and she buckled forwards. The howls of pain came next, then the tears until Vera was sobbing so hard she was choking on her own spittle. Olivia held her as if her life depended on it. She wasn't going to let Vera fall because she knew if she did let Vera go, Vera might never get back up again. Olivia recognised the grief, because it was exactly what she felt on occasions; and each time it had happened to her either her mother or Angelina had been there to clutch her close until composure was regained and the worst was past. Falling meant no coming back. Not letting go of grief meant constant pain. Trying to hide it created madness.

Olivia would never let her friend go down any of those routes. No one had ever let her go down them, so now it was her turn to help her friend in her time of need.

And so she stayed wrapped tightly around Vera and let her cry until she was spent. It took a long time. There were many tears to be shed, but eventually, along with the howls, they subsided. Only then did Vera turn to face Olivia. She reached out and when Olivia's arms were offered, Vera clung to her for strength.

The chirrup of Vera's mobile phone broke the impasse. The two friends pulled away from each other, embarrassed now. The mobile lit up and flashed the name of the caller – Fliss. Vera shook her head. Olivia understood and reached out to answer the call.

'Hi, Fliss!' Her voice sounded reedy and high-pitched. 'No, I'm fine, thanks. Just got a bit of a frog in my throat.' She coughed, even though she didn't need to. 'No. Your mum's upstairs. I was just making coffee while she got changed. Shall I get her to call you back as soon as she comes down?'

Vera could hear Fliss start to ask what Olivia was doing there, and was deeply relieved when Olivia ended the call, saying, 'Let her think we lost the connection.'

'Sorry,' said Vera, and hung her head.

Olivia lifted her chin so that Vera had to look into her eyes. 'What for?'

'I …' Vera started.

'It's me. I called at a bad time,' interrupted Olivia. 'I'm sorry. I just wanted to bring you some flowers. They're to tell you how very sorry I am about how I've been. I'm an idiot. I got carried away. I should never have pushed you so hard … oh Vera, I am very, very sorry.'

Vera's eyes slid to the flowers. She fingered the cellophane wrapping around them. 'They're beautiful,' she whispered so softly Olivia thought she might be about to burst into tears again.

Whenever Olivia was troubled, the only thing she could really think to do was to burst into action. 'Coffee,' she said, grabbing the kettle and filling it from the cold tap. 'Why don't I make coffee while you go upstairs and get a shower?' Then she thought better of being bossy. Vera obviously didn't need it. 'Or should I go?' Olivia scooped up her stilettos. 'Yes. That's what I'll do. I'll go.' Then she changed tack again. She couldn't leave Vera in this state. What if she did something stupid? 'But, then again ... do you want me to go? Do you want company? Have you eaten? Should I make breakfast? Yes! That's it. I haven't had breakfast. We could both have breakfast. What would you like? Anything! I can cook anything ... or just toast ... do you even eat breakfast?'

Olivia's anxiety brought Vera back to a state of being able to cope. She suddenly felt terribly cold. She looked down at herself and saw she was only wearing a flimsy nightie. Her feet were bare. 'If I go and have a shower, could you manage to make some tea?' she asked Olivia, who jumped as the kettle came to the boil and started whistling behind her. She lifted it. It was over-full. Some of the scalding water splashed on the work surface.

'Go. Quickly! Go ... and get some warm clothes on,' she commanded. 'There'll be a fresh brew on the table as soon as you come down,' and with that she started opening and closing cupboards and drawers looking for teabags and mugs, spoons and milk.

Chapter Sixteen
Into The Fire

Vera and Olivia talked until late in the morning before Olivia suddenly remembered Fliss's phone call. 'I'll go, then you can ring her back,' she offered. 'I think you ought to ask her to call in this evening. You shouldn't be alone.'

'I'll be all right,' said Vera who, although exhausted, felt lighter for having talked so much and so frankly. 'Olivia. I am grateful. Thank you for listening.' She touched her friend's hand. 'You're a good listener.'

Olivia snorted in derision. 'That's the first time anyone's ever told me that,' she said. 'Everyone tells me I never listen.'

Vera pulled a wry face in agreement. 'You never do usually,' she concurred. 'But you've earned a lifetime of brownie points this morning. I honestly am grateful.'

Olivia was rather pleased with herself. She gave

herself a little pat on the back and preened. 'It'll never last,' she said honestly.

Both women knew it was hardly likely to, but this morning, exactly when Vera had needed it, Olivia had been the right person to act as listener. There was something inherently comforting in letting go of some of the pain to someone who knew why it was necessary themselves. She told Vera Angelina had warned her that she'd had to tell her that she was bipolar after her recent meltdown.

Olivia spoke honestly about her cocktail of medications, how she had counselling and therapy weekly, that her episodes could hit without warning, at any time, and she never knew how long they would last. 'I rely on other people to tell me when they're happening,' she confessed. 'But I rarely take their advice. Even after all these years, I still try to soldier on on my own.'

Vera told her she'd had no idea and that made her an awful friend.

'Don't worry,' Olivia reassured her. 'What's the point in me telling people unless they need to know? Would you want anyone to know you are mentally ill? I'd rather people just think I'm rather wacky and interesting and that I'm fun to be with.'

'You are!'

'Yes, and quite frequently I'm a pain in the arse, too, but I honestly try not to be.'

Vera had hugged her then. There were no words

she could think of that might be of comfort. Olivia had lived with her erratic mental state so long she had seen every reaction possible from people when it revealed itself. Very little surprised her nowadays.

'But yours is a different kind of grief, Vera,' Olivia had said wisely. 'Losing Richard in the way you did was horrid. He was such a nice man. Is it any wonder you feel so wretched without him? He was such an enormous part of your life. I think you've done brilliantly to get this far without a total collapse. We all do, and actually, that's what's kind of fooled us. We took our eye off the ball because we thought you were getting over losing him and moving on with your life.'

'So did I,' said Vera. 'I just don't know where this has all come from.'

'Take your time,' Olivia advised. 'All you can do ...' but she never finished her sentence because Vera's mobile rang and interrupted them. They both looked at the display. It was Fliss again. Vera spread her hands in apology. She needed to take the call otherwise Fliss would get worried.

'Darling!' answered Vera. 'I was just about to ring you. Olivia was just leaving.'

'Don't let her go,' urged Fliss. 'Put the speaker on so you can both hear.' She sounded very excited. Vera and Olivia exchanged frowns.

'Are you there, Olivia?' they heard Fliss ask.

'Yes. Why?'

'Because he's been in touch again. You said he would. You said he'd have second thoughts and he'd message me again.'

Vera and Olivia exchanged a nod with arched brows. 'Steve,' mouthed Olivia, but when Vera frowned, she had to turn away as the frown was one of genuine worry that her part in causing his change of heart might be revealed.

'Mum. You know you told me to tell him I was sorry. Well, I haven't had to. He sent me a long email this morning. I'd given him that new address you suggested I set up, Olivia, so he didn't know my real one, and he used that one. He apologised for being curt, and he said when he'd seen how nice I looked, he'd been terribly disappointed at La Taverna, and then he'd bumped into that waiter and that had made him embarrassed and it all came out wrong when he came up to us and the other Steve was so shirty and he was sorry and could we try another date?'

'Are you going to go?' asked Vera.

'Of course I am, Mum!'

'Well, be careful.'

'Vera!' reprimanded Olivia. 'Fliss is always careful. You should be telling her to be care-free and go for it.'

Vera gave Olivia a warning glare, reminding her whose daughter she was giving advice to. Olivia smiled a sickly smile of supplication, quickly realising she'd overstepped the mark again. She knew only too well mothers always liked to think they knew what was best for their daughters and woe betide anyone who told them otherwise. Olivia might disagree, but she daren't say so for risk of offending her friend.

'Mum! I've suggested we start with coffee at Robin Redbreast's Saturday morning,' they heard Fliss say. 'Everyone will be in there buying their bedding plants, so I'm hardly putting myself in danger, now, am I?'

The garden centre was a good idea. Vera relaxed a little. Olivia gave a thumbs-up and was clearly delighted Fliss hadn't been put off from agreeing to meet up with him again. 'I can be a bit sensitive, too,' Fliss rambled on. 'I can't blame him for getting upset at me, can I? And over coffee, I can tell him how sorry I am that I made such a mess, can't I? He will understand, won't he?'

'Sounds like he wants the chance to find out, darling,' Vera said, hoping against all hope that he never mentioned the internet dating message she had sent on Fliss's behalf. It sounded as if Fliss hadn't checked, and he hadn't said anything about it in his email. Best it stayed that way.

'Pop into the shop late afternoon, Fliss, and we'll find you something new to wear. That'll give you a bit of confidence if you make a big effort,' Olivia said.

When Fliss agreed, Olivia turned to Vera. 'And why don't you come? There are some things in the sale you'd like. That'll be good for you, too.'

At first, Vera refused, but after Olivia left and as the afternoon wore on, she started to feel aimless. It had helped enormously to cry so hard and then to tell someone how deeply she was still grieving, but one thing Olivia said several times stuck in her mind. She had said, 'You can't bring him back, but that doesn't mean you've lost him. You still have wonderful memories, and two amazing children to share those memories with. I wish I'd had that in my life, but I've never even got close once to finding someone who wanted to share their life with me. Richard wanted to share his with you.'

She tried to eat, but the food tasted like cardboard. She threw her sandwich in the bin, and put the kettle on again. All she seemed to want was tea, and copious amounts of it. Perhaps losing so much fluid in the form of tears meant she needed to replace it and the craving for tea was the method her brain chose. Once upon a time, if she'd been in this amount of shock, Richard would have poured her a stiff brandy and made her drink it. Gin and tonic had been their favourite aperitif, one they shared every evening before dinner. Whisky and wine were for dining out. Beer was for home and the pub, or for sharing with friends. Cocktails were for holidays. She thought about pouring herself a brandy. There were enough bottles of it in the drinks cupboard, but drinking in the middle of the day felt like failure.

Alcohol was going to solve nothing, but some company might make her feel better, and the company of her daughter seemed the best company she could seek out today. Late afternoon, she reversed her car out of the garage and made her way downtown to join Fliss at Claremont's.

They met each other when they took adjoining parking spaces in the street. Vera's mood lifted when she saw how upbeat and smiley Fliss looked, so when Fliss came to kiss her, Vera threw her arms around her daughter and clutched her in an unending hug.

'You all right, Mum?' Fliss asked, knowing her only too well.

'I'm fine,' she lied.

'Made it up with Olivia, have you?'

Vera threaded her arm through her daughter's and waited for a car to pass so they could run across the road before another one came. 'Getting there,' she said and swept Fliss in through the doors of Claremont Ladies before Fliss could ask any more. 'So what are we going to buy you for this date?'

'Buy me?' quizzed Fliss, grinning.

'I'm treating,' said Vera. 'I'm flush since I sold Number Forty. Take advantage whilst you can!' Her daughter smiled even more broadly before being swept into a hug by Olivia, closely followed by kisses on each cheek from Angelina.

'Everything all right?' whispered Angelina as she similarly welcomed Vera with kisses.

'Don't mention my meltdown,' Vera whispered back, and then, spreading out the skirt of a silk dress asked, 'What do you think of this Fliss?'

They opened a bottle of good champagne after the shop had been closed for other customers and Fliss had tried on every shape and style because she could find nothing she found perfect. In the end she apologised and said she'd feel better anyway in her jeans and a nice t-shirt. 'I don't want him to think I've made too big an effort,' she said wisely. 'I want him to see the real me, and the real me is happiest in jeans and t-shirts or my business suits. I'm not really that dressy.'

'But you looked lovely in that denim dress,' Vera prompted and was delighted when Fliss stared across to where it hung ready to be replaced on its rail. A neat shirtwaister, with short sleeves and side pockets, the dress was given a stylish edge because it was cut from many different weights and shades of denim. Classy, but something that could be worn every day, it had given Fliss's slender frame more definition and made her look more of a woman than a boy. It was obvious she liked it, but the price was horrendous. She'd taken one look at the price ticket and her cost-conscious mind had rejected it. The dress would need to be worn a very great many times to justify that amount of expenditure.

'What if we gave you a bit of a discount?' asked Olivia, following her gaze as behind Fliss's back Vera gave Olivia the thumbs-up.

'How much of a discount?' jumped in Fliss quickly.

'Ten per cent?' said Olivia.

'Make it fifteen and Mum will buy it for me,' said Fliss.

'Don't you dare discount any of the other sizes,' hissed Angelina to Olivia as she passed her with the dress ready to pack it into tissue and one of the Claremont glossy bags.

Olivia smiled serenely. Instead she refilled every one's glasses, emptying the bottle. 'And that's the last of the good stuff,' continued Angelina. 'Don't you dare order any more of that either!' Olivia thrust the champagne glass into her hand and hissed back, 'Well you'd better enjoy that while you can, hadn't you!' which got a full-on glare from her big sister.

Fliss left first, proudly clutching the Claremont's bag containing her new dress as if it was made of precious metal rather than glossy paper, leaving Vera to wait while Olivia totted up her own purchases. She'd found a lightweight sweater and a white blouse on the bargain rail and after trying them on decided that a treat in the form of new clothes was better than sitting at home alone drinking brandy.

'Thank God that young man decided to email

Fliss,' Olivia said, handing her the bag.

'I just hope to God she doesn't go back over their internet messages and find the one I sent that made him do it,' said Vera thoughtlessly.

Olivia pounced on her mis-speak straight away. 'That you sent ...?' she queried.

There was no point in trying to cover her tracks. 'I sent him a message from her phone last night,' she confided, looking out towards the street and watching Fliss drive out of the parking space. 'Don't you dare tell her.'

'What did you put?'

'I didn't have much time. She was sitting right beside me. I said something like ... I'm kicking myself. Try again?'

'But it worked!'

'Yes. But she doesn't know why!'

'She doesn't know why what?' asked Angelina, homing into their conversation.

'Steve's got in touch with Fliss because he thought she'd sent him a message, but it was Vera not Fliss that sent it,' Olivia explained, over-excited.

'Vera! You didn't!' gasped Angelina.

Vera had the grace to look shamefaced. 'I couldn't bear seeing her so down in the dumps,' she explained. 'I thought it could make any worse, so I sent it, and then I got all worried about it, and that's the part of the reason I got myself so upset last night. I shouldn't have done it.'

'But it worked!' said Olivia, as excited as a giddy kitten. 'Vera, you're a genius when it comes to this stuff.'

'What stuff? I just did what any good mum would do'

Angelina looked at Vera askance. 'You've got more courage than I have. I wouldn't have even thought of doing it.'

Vera blanched. 'Please don't tell her. Please don't let her think her mother has to find her a boyfriend. What if it all goes wrong?' Angelina pulled a concerned face. Vera looked at Olivia who was now pacing around the shop floor. It was obvious she was thinking something through, and the something was something very big. Her face contorted with each thought. Her hands moved as if she was arguing with herself and pointing out both sides of the argument. Vera and Angelina watched her. Neither wanted to interrupt.

Eventually she turned around and faced both of them, arms crossed in front of her waist. 'Vera!' she said with absolute certainty. 'You are brilliant. You are a genius at this love-matching stuff.'

Vera opened her mouth to protest, but was stopped by Olivia showing her the palm of her hand to quieten her. 'And that's why I was right when I said you should run Claremont's Dating Agency. But we aren't going to call it that, are we? No! We're going to be calling it the Normal Dating Agency.

because that's what we're going to offer – normal dating. And you're going to be the genius who gets the right, normal, people together.'

'We're going to make a fortune once word gets out,' she said and strode through to the office leaving Vera and Angelina dumbstruck.

Chapter Seventeen
Typical Rosie!

Rosie Blane was very angry. Even if she'd tried to cover her rage, her crimson face would have given away the depth of her emotion. Her eyes popped. Her breathing was shallow and rapid. Her words came out as high-pitched squeaks. She quivered with pent-up fury, so much so that her legs felt like they were set in concrete and her palms dripped with sweat. 'You've done what!' she expostulated, spit flying towards Benjamin's face.

Benjamin wiped it from his cheek, his eyes locked on hers in total defiance. 'It was my boat,' he said.

'And my money that refurbished it! How could you, Benji?'

'It was just a boat,' he said, and went to turn his back. Rosie grabbed his arm firmly. He shrugged her off and walked away, but Rosie was fast. She bolted round, bare feet sliding on the tiled floor, and slid to a halt to face him. When he tried to push past her,

her fury broke. She lifted her fist and she punched him hard, square between the eyes. For a woman in her seventies, she packed one hell of a punch.

Benjamin buckled, holding his broken nose. Blood spurted splattering the floor, his clothes and even hitting her bare legs. Rosie, wearing only a bathing costume, looked down at her highly-tanned but wrinkled and thread-veined saggy skin, saw the crimson of fresh blood dripping down her thigh, and was promptly sick. All she could think was that there was no fool like an old fool. That that was her now! A stupid, silly, old fool. Her stomach lurched. Her vomit joined Benjamin's blood on the white-tiled floor and formed a pool.

'What the hell was I ever thinking?' she moaned to Vera thirty minutes later. She couldn't wait to FaceTime her daughter and tell her what had happened. It was such a juicy story and she would dine out on it for a long time to come.

'Where is Benji now?' Vera ventured, bracing herself for the salacious gossip which was sure to follow. How come her mother always forgot that she was also a co-conspirator in these regular escapades? It was no good Vera reminding Rosie that this was not the first time she'd got herself involved with an unsavoury man. To Rosie's mind, new love was true love; that was until she found the flaws and she moved on.

'Don't call him that! My Benji's gone and the real

Benjamin has taken his place,' she wept, her tears more self-pitying than angry.

Here we go again, thought Vera. Another one bites the dust. When will she ever learn?

'... asked Henrique next door to take him to the clinic,' Vera zoned back in to listen to her mother's moaning, 'and I haven't seen hide nor hair of him for the last five days. Henrique's horrible wife, you know that bit of a girl he bought in Thailand and married within months of Judy dying, came over, asked if she could pick up some of Benjamin's things and cleared the place out. She's nothing but a tart. Far too young for him. She'll be off with someone else as soon as she's got all his money out of his pockets.

'Anyway, I'd already put most of his stuff in black bags by the front door, but the little bitch must have come in and had a good look around. I should never have gone to the shops whilst she was carrying them out to the car, but I couldn't bear to be there. Do you know, she's even taken all my face creams, even that expensive suntan lotion I forked out a fortune for from the bathroom.'

'Perhaps she can't read English?' Vera fell again into the trap of encouraging more from her mother. Long ago, she'd learned the whole story always had to come out, otherwise Rosie wouldn't be satisfied. The best way to handle it was to go silent until the rant of gossip dribbled to a close.

'Spanish, darling. I'd bought them here in Majorca.'

'Spanish then. She didn't take anything valuable, did she? How much have you actually lost, Mum?' Vera suddenly panicked, trying to remember whether her mother had taken much of her jewellery with her or had left it in the safe at her English home. She peered at her mother on the computer screen to see if she was still wearing her enormous diamond ear studs and the wedding rings she never took off.

They were still there, plus an armful of jangling silver bracelets and a rather nice polished stone on a chain around her neck. Rosie looked just the same as usual, her mass of silver curls loosely held on the top of her head in a make-shift bun, her heavy boobs spilling over the top of an expensive bathing costume in a striking pattern of emerald fern leaves against a royal blue background. Her best asset, her vivid and penetrating blue eyes, were heavily outlined in black, making them even more prominent. Her lipstick was her usual shocking pink. She looked well, much better than Vera felt. She made no effort to cover up the fact she was an aging woman. Instead, Rosie revelled in it and showed off her figure with no shame at all.

'I'm not that stupid, Vera!' she retorted, interrupting Vera's perusal of her. 'Not that much. Just a bit of pride, that's all,' she said, trying to elicit sympathy and support.

Vera didn't answer. She looked down so her

mother couldn't clearly see her face or the thoughts that were going on beyond it. Now, what was she expected to do? Did she need to rush down to Majorca to sort her mother out? Should she try to persuade her to come home? Vera's head spun. She needed yet another problem like a hole in her head.

Vera couldn't help Rosie, not when she needed so much help herself.

For a long time now she had been waiting for something like this to happen. Since Vera's father, Christopher, died, Rosie's penchant for younger men had become an increasing worry to her family. She was taking so many risks, particularly when she preferred to hook up with men in Majorca rather than back at home. The family thought it was because Christopher had been adamant the family should never be subject to gossip in their own home town, and so it turned out, without having to live up to his exacting standards, Rosie wasn't as prim as she'd had to be when she was married. Her penchant for the exotic came to the fore. She'd gone through men like there was an everlasting supply. Her past liaisons had ranged from Majorcans, Italians and there had even been a Latvian that lasted just a matter of weeks. As long as they could dance, Rosie fell for them, and as she grew older, the men seemed to be getting increasingly younger, too.

At first, Vera was outraged. She was her father's daughter. She'd grown up thinking just like him and this new phase in her mother's life horrified her. 'So what if Granny wants to spend her time getting more and more tanned in the day, then dancing the night away in salsa clubs?' Christy had asked innocently one day. 'It's keeping her fit. She doesn't have a thing wrong with her and she hardly looks a day over sixty. She's no pushover, Mum. Most of her money is secure. She's not overspending. If it's making her happy, then let her do it. It's keeping her well out of your way and your hair. You're not having to look after her. She loves that villa in Majorca.'

'They're taking her for a ride,' Vera said, to which, Christy, uncharacteristically, smirked. Marriage to Annie had certainly brought out his cheeky sense of humour.

'Good one, Granny,' he said and received a stinging cuff on the upper arm from his mother, even if she had to agree her choice of words could have been better.

Then Rosie had met Benjamin, a late fifty-something, mixed-race yachtsman from The Netherlands when he delivered a newly-built expensive boat to a wealthy customer on the island and they'd all sighed a breath of relief. He seemed stable. This one stuck around, so none of the family had questioned it when Benjamin bought a run-down boat to renovate and had moved in with Rosie in her villa. To hear her talk, it seemed as if her aging mother was getting more bedroom action than anyone else in the family, certainly more than Vera who had got none at all since Richard died, and there was no way any of them were going to stop her. With this turn of events, seemingly they had all been wrong about Benjamin.

'What are you going to do?' Vera asked, her thoughts coming back to the present.

'Nothing,' answered Rosie pragmatically.

'Nothing?' replied Vera, truly shocked.

'Put it down to experience then,' said Rosie.

'Experience!'

'Yes experience, darling. What can I do? Benjamin and I were together long enough. We had plenty of good times. I put that money into his boat willingly because I enjoyed sailing on it. I knew he was a gambler, but I never thought he'd lose the boat on the turn of a card. He must have not one penny left. Let him rot in some pit somewhere. He sponged off me and gave up his flat back in Rotterdam to live here, so now he's lost his home, too. I'm not going to rescue him, and I'm certainly not going to chase after him. He wasn't that good in bed anyway! And he snored like a dying donkey.'

Vera was floored. Even if she could think of something to say, would her own mother listen to it? She had to admire her. Rosie had got herself in to this mess. She'd dealt with it in the way she thought best, and now she wasn't going to moan about it. 'Are you coming home?' she asked tentatively, but the way

Rosie took a gulp from the very full glass of wine she had poured herself before she made the call revealed how quickly she was bouncing back. There'd be another man in her life very soon, Vera was sure of it.

'Nah,' Rosie confirmed. 'The weather's too good here at the moment. What would I want to come back to the UK for? Now, there's a list of things I need you to do. Have you got something to write with?'

Nothing changed! Vera dutifully wrote down the list her mother gave her, most of it to do with her home down the road. Rosie wanted her to check that the gardeners had moved some shrubs. The little car she kept in the garage needed a good run. Did Vera think Annie would like to use it for the summer? Rosie's longstanding school-friend had asked if she could use the house to put up some guests coming to attend a family funeral, so Vera needed to put out fresh towels and leave them some milk. Perhaps the windows needed opening before they came. 'It's only for one night,' Rosie said imperiously, forgetting to ask Vera if she had time to do it before they came. She was so involved with living her own life, she also forgot to ask Vera how she was getting on until just before she ended the FaceTime conversation, and Vera, who wasn't at all inclined to give her mother anything to gossip about, didn't encourage the conversation turning to her own woes.

Vera thought she'd got away with it, until at the last moment, Rosie said, 'So, what are you doing with yourself, darling?'

Vera floundered. What should she tell Rosie? It certainly wouldn't be anything about her own meltdown. She was barely coping with the thought of what she'd done herself yet. Nor would it be about her fallout with Olivia. She didn't want to say a thing about Fliss's impending date next Saturday with the man from the internet until she was knew which way it had gone. Rosie would make too much of it and would ring Fliss with advice that would only unsettle the young woman. Business and Christy and his family were safe topics.

'Did I tell you the sale of Number Forty went through last week? Out of the blue, they accepted the asking price, and it's gone.' Rosie nodded as if she wasn't interested. 'I've been seeing a lot of Mickey and Wyeth,' tried Vera.

'Not baby-sitting, I hope. Don't you dare let them take advantage of them, Vera! It's the parents' job to bring up their children. Not the grandmother's.'

That hasn't changed then, thought Vera uncharitably. You always had other plans if I asked you to help out. Richard's mother did far more than you; but that was an old argument that Vera would never win. Instead her eyes lighted on the plans she was working on for the archway area in the garden. 'I have had a bit of a breakthrough,' she said, covering her less friendly thoughts. 'I've finally worked out what I'm going to do with that awkward patch in the garden. The bit where I put the archway up.' She lifted the laptop and started walking.

'Where're we going now?' asked Rosie petulantly.

'I thought you'd like to see it,' Vera said, turning the camera angle around so that it faced the garden.

Rosie took a while focussing on what she was seeing. Eventually she saw Vera had roughly sketched a comic figure of the Venus di Milo with her own face above it.

'Good God, Vera. Just look at your tits! You'll never get a new man with pimples as little as those!'

Chapter Eighteen
The Normal Dating Agency

Vera was cleaning the downstairs toilet, kneeling awkwardly in the confined space so she could give a good scrub behind the toilet pan. When the doorbell rang, she was still shaking her head in amazement at what her mother had told her. Creakily, she pulled herself up from kneeling. She looked at her watch. Eleven-thirty. Time had flown this morning, and here she was, still in jeans and baggy t-shirt, not yet washed. Who could this be now? She'd never get everything done this morning that she wanted to.

She opened the front door still wearing yellow rubber gloves and carrying the toilet brush.

'I'm not interrupting, am I?' asked Angelina, shyly pointing at Vera's rubber gloves and the toilet brush she carried.

Vera laughed. What a lovely way to welcome someone at the door! What had she been thinking? 'No. Course not. Come on in. It's lovely to see you out of the shop. How did you manage it?'

'I did have to shout and stamp my little foot,' agreed Angelina. 'I told Olivia it was either her taking a turn in the shop for a change or I'd shut up and stick a notice in the window saying we'd all gone mad and shot ourselves. I need a day off. I can't do every day while she swans off and does nothing. The boys are next door. They'll make sure she doesn't get up to too much mischief for a couple of hours.'

Vera's eyebrows rose and Angelina's responded with the same wry inflexion. They both knew that wasn't true. Olivia could get up to a great deal of mischief in a matter of minutes, let alone a couple of hours. 'Would you make me a coffee, Vera? I need to talk to you.' Angelina sighed. It was obvious she was close to the end of her tether.

Discarding the rubber gloves and toilet brush, Vera switched on the kettle and collected the cafetière. Angelina paced the room. 'I've just been speaking to my bloody mother,' Vera said trying to penetrate her friend's unease.

'How is she?' asked Angelina politely. Vera had never seen her so out of sorts. Neat and petite, Angelina was the prettier of the two sisters. Where Olivia took after their father, who had been a tall, wiry man, but had inherited their mother's auburn hair, Angelina was a mirror image of their mother with her father's hair colour. She was a strawberry blonde with pale skin and tiny features. Everything about her was in correct proportion. She wore her hair in a smooth bob which was always perfectly cut and coiffured. She loved high fashion as much as Olivia, but where Olivia wore wacky outfits which reflected her personality, Angelina always chose tailored clothing, with simple shapes in solid blocks of colour. Her only frippery was her shoes on which she spent a great deal of money, but today she looked quite unlike her usual self in cut-off trousers with an oversized blouse on top which needed a good press. On her feet she wore tatty trainers.

'I sort of borrowed next door's dog and took him for a walk,' she suddenly said and Vera realised she'd been staring. 'I needed an excuse.'

'What have you done with the dog?'

'He's outside in the car.' When Vera walked over to the window overlooking the drive, Angelina added, 'He'll be all right. I put the car in the shade, and I've left him his water with the window open. He's fallen asleep on the back seat.' Then she saw the look of concern on Vera's face. 'Should I bring him in instead?'

The dog was an affectionate young chap. He had a tan and brown coat with a white hairy underbelly. His face was white and fluffy with tan patches around his intelligent chocolate eyes. He had great big puffballs of greying eyebrows above which made him look as if he was constantly amazed.

'Aren't you a lovely boy?' said Vera, making a great fuss of him. 'I'd love another dog.'

'Why don't you have one?' asked Angelina.

Vera shrugged. She just hadn't gotten around to even thinking about it since Richard had died. The thought of training a new puppy was still a step too far. She'd put it into the something for a later date box in her brain. 'What's his name?'

'Benji. Benjamin,' replied Angelina not expecting the snort of surprise she got from Vera. Even the dog looked up enquiringly at Vera. 'What did I say wrong?' she asked.

'My ... bloody ... mother...' explained Vera, emphasising the words with juicy expression, 'has just kicked out the latest boyfriend and his name was Benjamin. You wouldn't happen to be a bit of a rogue, too, would you, Benji? Your namesake turned out to be a bit of one. Granny Rosie in Majorca would tell me off if she thought I was making this much fuss of any living being called Benjamin today.'

The dog turned around and sat on her feet, inviting her to scratch his back. He was soft and rubbed his neck against her knees. 'I'm in love,' said Vera, suddenly feeling more light-hearted than she had for ages. 'Why have I never met you before? Whose dog is he?'

'That new man's. Moved into the red brick house on the far side of the shop a couple of months ago. The one behind that fence that runs down to the river. He asked Pete if he could pop in and give Benji his dinner and top up his water today. He's been called to an urgent meeting up in town. Said he hadn't sorted doggy day care out yet. Benji's got a kennel the size of a Wendy house in the garden, so he'd be all right outside all day, but I just felt sorry for him being on his own for that long. So I sort of borrowed him. We've been all round the park, haven't we, Benji?'

Angelina was relaxing. The dog changed places, nuzzled up against his new best friend, then flopped down on the floor, covering Angelina's feet with his big head. She sipped at the coffee Vera offered her and stared around until her eyes fell on the archway and the drawing Vera was doing behind it. 'Is that it?' she asked. 'Is that the Vera di Milo?'

Vera considered the drawing which was still in its early stages. 'That's it,' admitted Vera. 'But my … bloody … mother has just said its tits are too small, and if they are mine, I'll never attract a man.'

'How old does she think you are!'

'How old does she think she is!' replied Vera. 'She's going backwards, and here I am lurching towards my dotage.'

At that, Angelina finally burst out laughing. 'You're not old!' she said. 'Now if you want to feel old, be me. Try having to deal with Olivia all the time.'

Vera waited. There could have only been two

reasons why Angelina had turned up so unexpectedly. Either Olivia had done something else, or Angelina was going to beg Vera to buy them out of Claremont's, and Vera dreaded having to turn her down. She simply did not want to take on that level of stress again, but it was so unusual for Angelina to come to Vera's house. Their friendship was based on Vera going into the shop, where, although they always chatted happily, Olivia would dominate the conversation and Angelina seemed content to let her do so. Olivia was good for making sales. Angelina was the background strength in the business.

'I'm not here to ask you to buy Claremont's from us,' Angelina started.

Vera exhaled a big sigh of relief. So, if Angelina wasn't here to try to sell the property, what had happened to Olivia? Dear God, don't let her have had a relapse, Vera thought. But hadn't Angelina said she'd left her in the shop? Surely, she'd never have done that if Olivia was in the clutches of an episode.

'I'm glad,' confirmed Vera. 'Because I really don't think you should sell up. You'd only end up regretting it.'

Angelina bit her lip. 'We are close to the edge, Vera. I'm not going to deny it. But I agree with you. What would we all do if there wasn't a job for us at Claremont's? It's all I've ever known. And Olivia, too! Pete and I live above the business. We don't want to lose our home, but unless we start making more money, we're in real trouble.'

Vera poured their coffee. Angelina was so agitated. Could she possibly be here to ask for a loan? 'Do you want me to invest, then?' Vera ventured.

Angelina took such a long time answering even Benji sensed the hiatus in the conversation. He opened his eyes and lifted his head to look up from one woman to the other. Angelina stroked his mane. 'That might be a possibility. Now that you've sold Number Forty. But, would you want to do that? Would you want to take the risk? You know things are bad. We might never be able to pay you back.'

Vera acknowledged the possibility. It would be a risk, but she didn't want to cut off another lifeline if that was what Angelina needed. She hesitated to say no, even though common sense said she should. Instead she added milk to their coffee and offered a biscuit from a tin. Angelina didn't want one. 'I've been meaning to ask,' Vera hedged. 'But how did you all know so quickly that I'd signed the contracts of sale for Number Forty? Even my family weren't sure when it was going through and I didn't tell them until it actually had.'

Angelina blanched. 'Wasn't anyone supposed to know? I'm sorry, Vera. Olivia told me and I assumed you'd told her,' she said anxiously.

Vera touched her hand to reassure her. She'd

suspected as much, but knowing Angelina would have told her if she had known, Vera let it go. Angelina was one of the most trustworthy people Vera knew. Like Vera, she hated gossip and how it spread like wildfire around town, particularly when her sister was often the person who spread it.

'Then where did she get it from?' Angelina asked.

Vera shook her head, obviously deeply displeased.

'Someone in the know must have spoken out of turn. Oh Vera. That's awful. Who can you trust nowadays? You don't think it's whoever she's been sleeping with lately, do you?'

Vera was angry enough to suspect even her own solicitor, but as he was an older and supposedly happily married man, she doubted it was him. Better all round if she kept her anger to herself and said nothing further. The news was out now. It would be old news very soon, so perhaps it wasn't that important to determine the source of the leak. It was damned disconcerting, though.

Both women took pensive sips of their coffee. Benji lumbered to his feet and, sensing the tension, stuck his big head between them, his tail swishing so much it hit both of their legs, and inviting them to stroke him. 'It's all right, Benji,' said Vera. 'No one's angry. We're just talking. Settle down, you lovely young man.'

The dog lay down again. Angelina stared out into

the garden trying to make up her mind if she really should say the next thing now, knowing that what she had come to tell Vera would only make everything ten times worse. Olivia was causing Angelina untold trouble, but how was she going to stop it unless she shared it with the person it affected the most. 'Now, I am going to have to talk out of turn about Olivia, Vera, and I don't think you're going to be very pleased when you hear what I've got to tell you,' she began.

She looked so scared, Vera went cold. Angelina couldn't even look her straight in the eye. 'She's gone off the deep end again, Vera,' she said, trying to conceal the trepidation she felt. 'She knows how seriously we're in financial trouble and she's panicking. We do need a new source of income double quick, but she's only gone and had flyers and business cards printed up. She's taken out terribly expensive adverts in the paper and she's already telling everyone who will listen. You know that idea she had for a dating agency? Well, she's set one up. She's applied for the licences. She's talked to the lawyer about forming the company. She's named you and me as co-directors.

'She's only gone and done it, Vera. She's set up the Normal Dating Agency and she has told everyone you are going to run it.'

Chapter Nineteen
Bad Idea

Olivia handed over the clutch of messages she had balled into her palm. As she opened her fingers to reveal them, they spread like a dandelion clock in the breeze, opening out, lifting, escaping on the air flow from the open conservatory door before they fluttered to the floor. The flimsy pieces of paper had been torn from a tiny message pad. They were no more than scraps, but each one held a name and a number.

Some of them started floating towards the door. 'Quick. Catch them. We mustn't lose any of them,' Olivia said in a panic, chasing them this way and that, but in her rush she only made them float further away on the draft she caused. Angelina helped her. Vera caught one and read the scrawled writing: *Toby Goodman 076 0583 2922 Man*

Vera knew Toby Goodman. He ran Breeches and Bridles, the equine supplies store in Dreningham.

He'd been an amateur jockey in his youth, riding in the county point-to-points, but his youth had been many decades ago. Toby Goodman was older than Methuselah. His wife had died last year and their three children all had children of their own.

'What does this mean?' Vera demanded, pointing to the word 'man'.

Olivia sheepishly looked up from where she knelt on the floor, reaching her full length to retrieve the precious pieces of paper. She'd already stuffed a lot into the breast pocket of her calf-length chiffon overshirt; making the pocket bulge like a third monster boob sitting above her own pert left one. As she leaned closer to take a look, her legs got tangled between palazzo pants and the overshirt.

'That he's looking for a man?' Olivia offered.

Vera exploded. This was just too much. 'Toby Goodman wants to meet a man!' she spat out incredulously.

'He's finally come out,' said Olivia as if it was the most normal thing to say. Beside her, Angelina, also on hands and knees and with just as many sheets of paper stuffed into her trouser pockets, twisted backwards to look at Vera, a worried look of apology scoured so permanently into her face she might never be able to find a different expression again.

'But he's got children and grandchildren, and there are rumours there are others, so no one knows how many are actually his.'

'He said he's been living a lie all his life and now he wants to settle down with someone who finally understands him,' Olivia said.

Vera fell down on a chair and buried her head in her hands. 'God, give me strength!' she moaned.

'He's only like everyone else, Vera. He just wants to be loved,' said Olivia, catching her foot in the excess chiffon material around her knees and lurching forward. She reached out, scraping her hands on the hard floor, but failed to stop herself from falling prone at Vera's feet with a clatter.

Motionless, Vera stared at her as Olivia rolled to one side trying to free the chiffon material but tangled herself in it more tightly. She awkwardly slipped first one arm, then the other out of the garment, leaving it on the floor, still with its pocket filled with papers, as she scrambled to her feet. She adjusted her palazzo pants and matching t-shirt until she was comfortable again, flicked her long red curls back from where they'd stuck against the foundation on her face, then retrieved the overshirt and wound it around so that the papers were firmly held within its material. Finally, tucking a loose piece of material inside the bundle, she placed it in Vera's lap with such deference it could have been the most precious of gifts.

Terrified what Vera was going to do next, Angelina got to her feet as inconspicuously as she could and stood hovering. She looked even more dishevelled than ever. Vera wore the jeans and baggy t-shirt she'd been wearing to clean her downstairs loo. Neither were a good look to be in the shop, but before Angelina could suggest going upstairs to her home, or even into the office, Vera had charged in and launched a tirade at Olivia, who had stood her ground with increasing difficulty. The furthest Angelina had been able to move either of them was into the conservatory where, behind them, she had sensibly closed the interior doors into the shop.

'This is such a bad idea, Olivia,' Vera eventually said, holding the bundle out towards Olivia. 'You're going to have to go back to all these people and tell them you've made a big mistake; that there can't be any dating agency. You jumped the gun and you are going to have to sort it out.'

'But I promised ...' pleaded Olivia.

Vera looked to Angelina for help. There was none coming. Angelina didn't know what to do, either. Vera started to feel like a headmistress reprimanding naughty pupils. 'What did you promise?' Vera asked so quietly it frightened Angelina. She turned to see if her sister was going to burst into tears.

Olivia certainly had wet cheeks, though the tears weren't yet flowing freely. 'That we'd find them someone nice to date,' she whimpered. 'I didn't mean to upset anybody. I thought I was doing the right thing.'

'But so many, Olivia! In such a short time. Is that what you've been doing when you haven't done your shifts in the shop?' asked Angelina.

'Once I told Becca and Jimmy, word just sort of got round.'

'Becca and Jimmy from Oysters?' asked Angelina, referring to the popular pub at the other end of town. People met up in Oysters before they went on to one of the two clubs on either side of it. Purr attracted the younger crowds. Daniella's closed earlier and was more expensive. 'Toby Goodman never goes in Oysters. Please don't tell me you got to him in Daniella's!'

Olivia grinned. 'He got that one wrong if he's looking for a man, didn't he? Should have gone to The Maid Marion. That's where the gay guys hang out now. All he'd have done at Daniella's was grab-a-granny.'

Astonished, Vera watched the two sisters slip back into their easy way of talking. Had they forgotten so quickly what a disaster this actually was? How was she going to extricate both them and herself from this mess and save all their good names? It beggared belief how many names and phone numbers Olivia had already collected. There must have been over one hundred and fifty. The only way she could have got so many in such a short space of time was to have touted for business, going around all the pubs and clubs and brazenly asking people if they wanted to join.

'You did tell them a fee would be involved, didn't you?' she asked.

'Yes. I told them all it wouldn't be cheap; that we set high standards.'

'Did you tell them how much?'

'No. I fudged on that one. I'd forgotten to have a look at what internet dating cost, so I thought they could all make their choice again once we contacted them to make appointments.'

Deep in thought, Vera turned to open the doors and walk from the conservatory, back in to the shop. 'Don't go ...' Olivia started to call after her, but Angelina hushed her sister when she saw Vera was simply going behind the counter to find one of the large Claremont bags. She snapped it open with a sharp flick, then balanced the open bag on the counter. There was no one other than the sales assistant in the shop and she was refolding clothes down the other end. Carefully, Vera undid the bundle of chiffon, found the pocket and dropped the pieces of paper from it into the bag, then, holding those down, she carefully shook the overshirt to see if any more fell out.

Angelina walked over, emptied her pockets and put the papers she had collected into the Claremont's bag along with them. 'Are you sure these are all of them?' Vera asked. The three friends searched again and found more. These were duly put into the same bag as the others.

Olivia went to take the bag from Vera, but Vera held its cord handles. 'No. Not you,' she said firmly. 'You don't touch these ever again.'

'But I thought you wanted me to ring and apologise to everyone.'

'Change of plan,' said Vera. 'Give me all the paperwork you've got already. I'll need to see the marketing leaflets you had printed. The flyers. The contracts from the lawyers. Everything.'

Olivia already had them in another glossy Claremont's bag. She rushed to the office and collected them, handing them over to Vera with as much relish as she had put the slips of paper in to her lap. 'What are you going to do with them?' she asked, her exuberance returning rapidly.

'Calm down!' Vera said sharply, and Olivia slightly raised her hands in apology. 'I want you to speak to no one else. I want you to take no more numbers. In fact, I want you to go off the radar, Olivia. I don't want anyone to know anything until I've done a great deal of thinking. Can you do that, Olivia? Can you keep your big mouth shut?'

Olivia, so excited now, indicated she could by pulling an imaginary zip on her lips closed.

Vera doubted she would be able to keep her hastily given promise. 'I'm warning you, Olivia! Not another word. Disappear for a while. I need you out of the way.'

'Why? What are you going to do?' asked Olivia.

'I'm going to see if there is some way we can get ourselves out of this great big mess without getting ourselves run out of town as undesirables,' said Vera. 'Do you have any idea at all how much people are going to hate us when we don't deliver what you've promised?'

Chapter Twenty
Ambrose's Spur Of The Moment Idea

Ambrose Hidrio stood back to let a heavily pregnant older mum get off the train before him. She was struggling to see the steps beneath her very large bump. Ambrose suggested she went down backwards, took her bags from her with one hand and offered his free hand for her to hold. Safely on the platform, she waited for him as he brought down her bag along with his own heavily laden briefcase. He then carried her bags for her to the ticket barrier where she told him her partner was waiting to meet her, treating her with great deference and politely asking when the baby was due. When she told him the given birth date was just a matter of weeks away, he wished her great joy because he truly meant it. He even shook her partner's hand when he handed her bags over to him.

'What a lovely man,' he heard the woman say as he walked away.

It had been a long day already and his workload wasn't yet finished. Ambrose would normally have speeded off amongst the surge of other half-running, speed-walking commuters eager to get home, but his natural courtesy had prevented him from leaving this woman, even though he felt dirty, hungry and he could kill for a pint or two of the earthy real ale he favoured. That would all have to wait, however, as first he had a far more important job. He needed to drive home as fast as he could to feed his dog.

Traffic was equally heavy between the train station and his new house on the river. Every traffic light was against him. He sat drumming his fingers on the steering wheel in frustration. Today's meetings hadn't gone well. Unexpected problems had been brought to his attention. He could have done with staying in town, but as he hadn't yet arranged doggy day care for Benji, or found anyone he could pay to look after the dog, he now had to come home, then go straight back up to London tomorrow, and that would mean asking the nice couple who lived above Claremont's if they could keep an eye on his beloved mutt again.

There were certain things he hadn't fully thought through when he moved so quickly from central London to this commuter belt town, and caring for Benji when he needed to be away was one of them.

The move had been a spur-of-the-moment decision after his soon to be ex-wife, Amanda, told him she no longer loved him because they no longer understood one another's desires. She moaned he needed to slow his life down to include her now and again, and asked him to retire early, suggesting he move to Italy with her. Italy was where she'd decided she would find herself. He wasn't at all certain what the term 'find herself' meant. They'd been married twenty-three years, she'd chosen not to have children so she could rise to the top of her career as a barrister and now she told him she wanted to throw it all in and retire to the back of beyond in a country they hardly knew, where they didn't speak the language well and where she expected to 'find herself'. When he finally calmed down enough for them to talk, she told him it was all about reconnecting with the real essence of their needs. He thought he was already pretty well connected to his own needs. Was he meant to 'find himself', too, just because she'd seemingly fallen out of love with her own life?

When he cautiously suggested that this felt like a mid-life whim, she'd blown a gasket and demanded Ambrose move out of their Canary Wharf penthouse. It was blindingly obvious then that she'd already made up her mind and that the new life she wanted didn't include him. There had been the inevitable blazing argument and, the very next day, he bought River House on the rebound.

It had all happened so quickly. Knowing he couldn't concentrate, he cancelled all his morning appointments, said he was doing a spot-check site visit and caught the next train to the Home Counties to see a block of flats halfway through refurbishment he was adding to his property portfolio. It was as good a way as any to get out of London. He needed to think. He couldn't do it in the office and he certainly did not want to go home. The sun was shining, but he hardly noticed. He had too much else on his mind. As soon as he saw the quality of work was good enough at the block of flats, he abandoned the rest of the visit and wandered down the High Street. It was then he saw a man putting up a For Sale sign on a lovely old property right at the end. Always on the lookout for good properties for his portfolio, he went up and asked how he could get details. The man was the estate agent and he was at the house with the owner now preparing the details. Ambrose persuaded them to give him an instant viewing.

He fell in love with the garden rather than the house. The slope to the river was broken into two terraces, with high fences on both sides. It would be perfect for Benji. The house was in dire need of updating, but when Ambrose found out the last owner had died a month ago in a nursing home and his daughter, who was over from South Africa, had already cleared the property wanting a quick sale, on a whim he put in an immediate offer for the asking price. He added a premium if the daughter would accept there and then and take the property off the market without letting other prospective buyers see it. When she accepted three hours later, River House was his. He knew instantly. This property would not go into his portfolio. This one was going to be his new home.

He'd expected to be back into the office in the afternoon, but he rang in and asked his PA to cancel all his afternoon commitments, too. Whilst waiting for an answer on River House, a plan was forming rapidly as to what he would do now his wife no longer wanted to be married to him. As he took a long walk around the town, he came around to agreeing with his wife. She was right. Their marriage had run its course. He'd given up many long years ago trying to persuade her to have children, but he acknowledged then that it was still the bone of contention between them that bugged him. He'd told himself he had stayed in their marriage because he truly loved her. She freely admitted she was so completely self-centred she'd be a neglectful mother. He'd laughed it off, persuading himself that the strength of his love was going to be enough, but she was right. It wasn't. She had been telling him the truth all along, and now she was forcing him to accept it.

He saw now that there her refusal to have children had always been the fault line threatening to tear them apart. He could never truly cast aside his deep disappointment of their marriage being childless. It wasn't how he believed marriage should be. When she asked him to have a vasectomy, he flatly refused, telling her he was never going to be castrated. She retaliated, saying it was only a matter of tying tubes and their sex life would improve, but he'd been adamant he would not put himself through the operation.

To assuage his fury, he'd gone straight out and bought himself Benji's predecessor, who he named Randy so that she was always reminded that she lived with a full-blooded man. Amanda, bitter that she hadn't got her own way, instantly hated the dog, telling their friends Randy was his kiddy-substitute. 'Of course he is,' Ambrose joked back through gritted teeth as he made a great fuss of the puppy. 'You're my one and only son, aren't you, Randy, and I'm going to leave the family fortune to you one day, aren't I? You're going to be one very wealthy dog when I'm gone.' Secretly, he still hoped that Amanda would forget to take the pill and fall pregnant so he would have the child and heir he deep down wanted, but she never did.

'Dogs live extremely short lives!' Amanda had retorted mutinously and laughed the brittle laugh she used to cover how displeased she actually was.

She must have known how equally displeased he was. Since then he'd never been without a dog. Amanda hated both Randy and Benji.

So his trip to quietly check out this latest acquisition proved timely in more ways than one. He was charmed immediately by the town. Old and long-established, the High Street was quaint, packed with shops selling upmarket goods to the rich visitors who flocked in to see and be seen. There were signs outside the Town Hall for concerts in the park and the world-famous rowing regatta. The independent bookshop had books in the window written by all the authors who had spoken at the literary festival the previous month. From the bundle of information he carried in his briefcase he already knew there were two enormous supermarkets on the edge of town erected on recently built industrial estates with plenty of parking. The block of flats his company was purchasing would be a small purchase for his business, one a more junior director could have handled, but he'd chosen this time to do a site visit himself, more as a check and balance as to how his business methods were running rather than in any great desire to see what was just another asset to be held until sold on for profit.

He'd met Olivia that day in The Maid Marion when he'd popped in for a pint and a ploughman's. 'Hello,' she'd said turning round at the bar and checking out who was in the pub for lunch. 'I haven't seen you in years. I thought you'd gone to live in Australia.'

There was no one else she could be addressing. Ambrose had taken a table at the far end of the bar and now sat with his back to the wall. 'I think you're mistaking me for someone else,' he answered, his mouth filled with the pickled onion he'd just popped into it.

The strikingly beautiful, but slightly scary-looking red-haired girl brought over her glass of pink Pinot Grigio, approached him, peered closely, stole the other pickled onion on his plate, and sat down opposite without asking permission. 'You're not, are you?'

'Not what?'

'No. It's not what, it's not who and you're not Richie Ryder's elder brother,' she said helping herself to some of his crisps.

'Are you hungry? Would you like me to order you a ploughman's?' he asked, amused and affronted in equal measure.

'Darling, I couldn't possibly eat a whole one. Too big for me at lunchtime. Got to look after my figure, you know,' she said and promptly took the piece of cheese he'd cut ready to go into his mouth after the pickled onion.

She had the porcelain complexion of the true redhead, sparkling deep blue eyes, spoke with the clipped accent of the Home Counties, and was wearing a beautiful, and very expensive-looking, outfit of sea-green trousers and matching tweed jacket that suited her colouring perfectly.

'I like Australia. Don't you?' Ambrose asked, thinking that chatting to a lovely young woman was not a bad way to while away some time.

'Never been,' she confessed, taking a huge slug of her wine. 'Full of Australians.'

'What on earth have you got against Australians?'

'Oh nothing, darling. Love 'em to bits, but if you live in this sleepy old town, you don't need to go all that way to meet them. We get them here by the coachload. They come in for the water. Training, you know.'

Ambrose mentally kicked himself. Of course they did. Rowers came here for the regatta. He'd have to remember that one. 'You're a local then, are you?'

'Yes. Born and bred. You?'

He took his time before answering. 'Considering moving here from London. I've just viewed a house.' The way her ears pricked up, he knew he needed to be careful what he said next. She was so open, she had no way to conceal her interest. Gossip, he thought. Good old gossip, the stuff that makes the world go around, and she loves to be the first to know something so she can be ahead of the game.

'Oh, which one?' she asked predictably, eyes sparkling as she leaned in, buttered a slice from his chunk of bread and popped it in her mouth. He bit his lip to stop himself laughing at her cheek, sliced another piece, buttered that and offered it to her first. When she pointed to her mouth to show she was still chewing and shook her head, he cut off a piece of cheese, put it on top of the bread and popped it in his own mouth instead, waggling his fingers before his full mouth, a ploy to delay his own answer. As he carried on his charade, a thought shot into his head so forcefully, he stopped chewing and gagged.

'Are you okay?' Olivia asked anxiously.

He choked, then swallowed, then took a deep draught of his real ale. How could he ever tell this woman that he had only just met that he had just considered whether the babies he made with her would also have bright red hair?

Chapter Twenty-One
Vera's Even Better Idea

In everyone's life, there comes a time of reckoning. Bad decisions have to be rescinded, or, at least, reversed. Big rethinks have to take place. Past demeanours need some form of punishment. Vera lay awake wondering exactly how much more punishment her life could take, because she felt as if she had passed the point of reckoning and was serving a life sentence, one she wasn't enjoying serving one little bit.

I can't take it if this agony goes on much longer, she thought as she tossed and turned, exhausted from worry, but with worry preventing her from rest. I'm still grieving. I don't need any more aggravation. I don't need to be made a laughing stock in my own home town. Why can't Olivia see that!

She'd taken a taxi home from Claremont's. The two glossy Claremont's carrier bags came with her.

She'd known the old boy who was driving her from when she was a child. He'd once taken out her elder sister. 'How many years is it now since you lost Onesta?' he asked, just as he asked every time he drove her. 'Whenever I see you, you still remind me of her. She was so very pretty, your sister.' He'd obviously been very smitten with her, but it had all been such a long time ago.

He was talking about her gentle, kind sister, Onesta, whose name meant honesty, whilst Vera's meant the truth. At least, Rosie had been consistent in her choice of the unusual for her typically English-rose girls, giving both of them Italian names. Onesta had died far too young, wanting desperately to be married and have children, but denied any more life than nineteen years when unexplained heart failure felled her in an instant. Vera still remembered the moment the family had been told. Inspired by Wimbledon, Onesta had gone off to play tennis early one evening. Vera, six years younger, turned down the offer to join her, preferring instead to finish watching a tennis match from the tournament on the television. Police had turned up at the door to fetch their parents whilst it was still going on. Onesta had been riding her bike, tennis racket under her arm, and had fallen off on the grass verge. At first they thought she'd lost control, clipped the kerb and hit her head, but a passer-by had said it was odd how she fell sideways for no apparent reason. She just toppled over. Her death would have been instantaneous, the coroner concluded.

'Over thirty,' Vera answered the taxi-driver. 'And I still miss her every day,' reflecting that was as near the truth at the moment as it could ever be.

'And how's your mum doing? Is she here or over in Majorca?'

'Spending a couple of months over there,' she answered carefully, unwilling to give too much information. 'She's okay, thanks,' she added, thinking that it would be people like this taxi driver who would gossip about her, Olivia and Angelina if they ever found out the mess Olivia had got them into. She'd lived in the town all her life and she had always lived up to her name. She had always been truthful. There was no way she was ever going to let the good name of Vera Father be besmirched for the sake of her idiotic friend and her random ideas.

Dammit, Olivia! I couldn't be more angry at you if I tried, she thought as she stared out of her bedroom window later, mulling over the problem. How was she ever going to get them out of this mess?

Because it was a mess!

Sleep eluding her, Vera went downstairs to make tea. She sipped it as she stared out at the garden slowly emerging from the gloom of night. There had been no further progress on the Vera di Milo. The charcoal outline was starting to fade. In this light she could no longer see the original tea stain that had started it all. Putting down the mug of tea, she went back upstairs and dressed in her oldest t-shirt and jeans. Without sleep she couldn't think straight but at least she could try painting in her wall art as if she was doing a painting by numbers. The plan lay on the coffee table. The paints were outside the door. It might just take her mind off things.

By seven-thirty she was chilled to the bone and hungry, but the Vera di Milo had started taking form. Steadily she worked paint into the old wall, spreading it thin at the edges as if the Venus like figure had broken through a film and was emerging fully formed to grace the garden. She'd decided that was an easier way to deal with the background rather than painting the entire length of the wall. It would be just too difficult pulling climbing plants away, or painting around them, so a stand-alone trompe l'oeil was needed, painted in such a way that it created depth and dimension.

She was pleased with what she'd achieved. There was plenty more to be done, but with the female form delineated it made a good start. The rest needed much more work, but first she needed more tea and to settle her grumbling stomach with toast. It was as she stood waiting for the kettle to boil and the toaster to pop that she started to see a way around the Normal Dating Agency problem.

Money!

Money was central to the problem. It was both the curse and the cure. Olivia had pursued the idea of setting up another business within a business simply because Claremont's was failing and she was right to be looking into every opportunity that might save it. That was sensible, not stupid. The fashion shop was close to going broke. It did need both a fresh injection of cash as well as a fresh group of customers coming in through its doors. The shop needed to be used in more than one way. So that made Olivia's idea of setting up the dating agency an inspired use of existing resources. If the agency operated from the boathouse at the bottom of the garden, clients would have to access it through the shop and that would create footfall. But was it the right kind of business to combine with a clothes shop?

What other kind of business could be put in there without disrupting the smooth running of the clothes shop? Vera ran through a multitude, but none was as good a fit. A clothes repair shop needed more space. Similarly, bringing in fresh ranges of stock would need space and display areas. A teashop would need the boathouse to be completely altered. A travel agency was unlikely to bring in many more customers buying clothes. Nor would renting out the boathouse guarantee any upturn in Claremont's original business.

If people came in to join a dating agency, Vera reasoned, then it was obvious that they wanted to change their lives as well; and when people changed their lives, they often updated their clothes. So, perhaps Olivia was actually on to a good idea. She'd already proved the need with the number of names she'd collected. Vera grabbed pen and paper and starting making a to-do list to see if it was actually feasible to start a dating agency in the boathouse, reasoning that all that was needed were limited resources, just a cosy and private place to meet, a small office area and a loo. Top of the list she put: *check out condition of boathouse. Is it suitable?* Then she added: *Could an upmarket agency be run from there?* followed by serious business questions like: *can registered address be main building?*

Vera had already dismissed Olivia's first idea of selling Claremont's. Angelina had told her it wouldn't sell as a going concern once any prospective buyer saw the accounts and how poor were the previous years' profits. They were running at a loss, so selling the building would only attract developers and Vera, with her expert knowledge, already knew that the historic building had development restrictions which would make it difficult to sell, making the price potentially far less than the building was actually worth. On top of that, Angelina and Pete would lose their home.

Vera thought about Olivia's home. When Angelina and Pete married, their parents had bought a new detached house up the hill from the river.

Olivia was still at school then and had moved with them. She'd lived there ever since. When both parents died within a short space of time, she and Angelina jointly inherited everything in equal shares. Vera wondered if that included the house, which could be being used as security for the bank facilities, so she wrote down on her to-do list: *If shop goes bankrupt does Olivia lose her house too?*

She couldn't, and definitely wouldn't, see both her friends lose their homes! There was another possibility which she added: *Do I buy into shop?* but by the time she'd finished both her tea and toast that idea had been firmly crossed through. Without an increase in business she, too, could lose money in a very short space of time, so it wouldn't solve the problem and Vera did not want to risk any of the money she and Richard had worked so many years to accumulate.

Very quickly afterwards she added another note to her list. *Town gossip!* It had to be avoided at all costs. If Vera got involved in a failed venture with Olivia and Angelina, it surely would have a knock-on effect for the Father and Son side of her business, and that could potentially put Christy out of work. Might it affect Fliss's job at the stockbroker's as well?

Fliss! What day was it? Vera thought, dropping everything. Friday! Tomorrow was the day Fliss was meeting the correct Steve at Robin Redbreast's and Vera had promised herself that she would ring the day before to wish her luck and also to remind Fliss to keep her phone on when she went to meet him. It had crossed her mind that she should turn up and lurk in the background of the garden centre, but its café overlooked the outside plant stands and there was only so much time Vera would be able to loiter without someone she knew spotting her. She'd also thought about sitting outside in her car in the car park. It would make her feel better, but Vera knew for certain it would also infuriate her daughter, who was already nervous enough.

Vera flicked on her mobile phone. The front display showed Friday. Vera added an enormous reminder to her list: *RING FLISS!!!*

Then another thought occurred to her. Would she be so concerned about her daughter's safety if she thought a real-life person, in a real-life dating agency, in a real-life place where people came to be interviewed and checked out, had set up the meeting with a man who had been thoroughly vetted and knew that the meeting was happening? Vera thought not. It was no different to arranged marriages where the parents know the background of the other family, but instead of the liaison being subject to financial gain, the two potential lovers made all the choices. They were in control of the outcome and could meet knowing someone else knew all about the other person. The first meeting could even happen within the safety of the dating agency offices, with the dating agency staff close by. *Could a room be made in the boathouse where the couple could meet for the first time in comfort and safety?* Vera added to the list.

Vera sat back on her chair chewing the end of her pen. A calm had descended within her. *COULD THIS ACTUALLY BE A GOOD IDEA?* she wrote at the bottom of her list.

She still refused to allow herself to be swayed too easily until that question was answered. She started thinking about the negatives. *People lie about themselves. How does anyone know they are being honest?* she wrote.

She switched back on the kettle for more tea, suddenly aware that what she needed was more a pro-and-con-list rather than a to-do list. She tore the top sheet off her pad, wrote PRO on one side and CON on the other with a line in between, then started rewriting all the points she had already considered, adding others as she thought of them.

As the morning wore on, and after she had spoken at length to Fliss, who, although at work, was too nervous to get much done and was lurking in the staff room, Vera finally came to a decision. It wasn't one she had expected at all, nor was it reached by all the points she had written down on her pad.

She'd accidently kicked over the Claremont's bag containing the slips of paper Olivia had collected with names, numbers and prospective partners' gender written on them and they had all spilled out again.

She counted each and every one. There were over one hundred and fifty slips of those details. That bag of names brought Vera to one incontrovertible conclusion: people wanted to join a dating agency.

At that point The Normal Dating Agency was finally born in her mind. The only decision now to be made was whether she should be the one to run it.

Chapter Twenty-Two
All Systems Go

The café at Robin Redbreast's was mobbed by eleven, Saturday morning. Fliss hadn't been able to find a space in the car park and had had to park in the yard at Father and Sons and walk. It wasn't a particularly warm day and she'd forgotten to bring a cardigan. She resorted to throwing the all-eventualities anorak she kept in the boot of her car over her shoulders, meaning to take it off and carry it over her arm when she got to the main entrance. She didn't want to arrive blue and shivering. It was hardly a good look.

As it turned out, it wouldn't have mattered. She walked up to the sliding doors, eyes turned down as usual, and never noticed that Steve was directly ahead of her. He stopped to allow a member of staff with a trolley overflowing with geraniums in boxes through ahead of him, and she walked slap bang into the back of him. The anorak fell off her shoulders.

Her spectacles fell off the bridge of her nose, and they banged heads as they both bent down at the same time to retrieve them.

She muttered 'sorry'. He picked up her specs saying, 'my fault', handing them back to her as they looked directly into each other's eyes.

'Felicity?' he asked, blue eyes boring directly into her melting brown ones no longer hidden behind her glasses.

'Steve?' she whispered back, mesmerised by the colour of his eyes. Periwinkles, she thought. They're the colour of periwinkles.

'God, you're so beautiful,' he said, and a bolt of joy surged through her, spreading her shy smile wide across her face. He helped her up to her feet as if she was a piece of porcelain. Behind them a queue was forming. Carrying her anorak, his free hand under her elbow, he steered her towards the café, holding her so tightly she could feel his heat, thinking giddily that she might never need to wear a coat again.

He'd talked a lot, asking her many trivial questions as they stood in line waiting to be seated. He couldn't shut up. It took a long time for a table to come free, so she happily answered them all, trying to put him at his ease. For once Fliss was with someone who was even more nervous than she was and it felt good to be the calmer one.

Yes, she did like plants and flowers, she told him.

Her favourite were fuchsias. They came in so many colours. And yes, she did come here often as it was just up the road from where her brother worked. What a surprise he knew Christy. Why had they never met before? Ah, so work had taken him away after he went to university, but now he was back. She liked the sound of his voice. She liked the way he smelt. She most definitely liked the way he looked. Her back straightened. Her chin came up. She was feeling really special to be standing beside him. She so wanted this man to feel she was someone special, too.

Her shyness returned when they were finally shown to a table. He was going to have a toasted teacake with his coffee. Did she want one, too? Fliss didn't want to tell him she hated dried fruit in anything because it made her think of rabbit droppings. Wouldn't it make her sound childish? She asked for a Danish pastry instead, completely forgetting that it, too, had sultanas in it. When it arrived with their coffees she was faced with the dilemma of picking them out.

'You're not enjoying that, are you?' asked Steve.

'Yes, I am ...' answered Fliss, ramming a large mouthful in and praying that the sultanas in it weren't going to make her physically sick. Just the sight of them made her nauseous.

'I'm really glad you got in touch again,' Steve said, smiling at her so warmly her heart did a backflip. She nearly choked as she swallowed. 'So you were kicking yourself, were you?' he asked, teasingly. God, he was so sexy when he looked at her that way.

She mentally shook her head, trying to concentrate on what he just said. Had he really just asked if she was kicking herself? What on earth could he mean? She frowned and half-smiled at the same time as she forced herself to swallow the half-masticated pastry. She tried to smile properly, but the lump in her cheek made her smile go lopsided.

The strange smile stopped him dead in his tracks. He, too, was feeling extremely animated and very attracted to her, but his courage suddenly deserted him. It made him rush in saying, 'I'm sorry. I didn't behave well that evening,' he stuttered, smiling a nervous smile in apology.

She swallowed hard. 'It was really odd there were two men called Steve there,' she agreed, trying to reassure him that, as far as she was concerned, all was forgotten now he'd contacted her again. 'I couldn't believe it.'

'Which is why you said you were kicking yourself, then was it?' he asked more seriously.

Kicking herself? She didn't remember kicking herself. Certainly, she'd fallen over her own feet, but she'd definitely not kicked herself that night. Why did he keep using that phrase?

'It made me laugh when I got your message. I

showed the girl I work with who'd encouraged me to join that stupid internet site and she said it was cool of you to think of putting it like that. She said your message was short, to the point and classy. I could never be that clever. That's why I gave you my email. You didn't mind, did you? I can't do short messages. I don't think that way. When you emailed me back, I felt as if I was getting to know you so much better. I don't like those little boxes they give you to send messages on the site, do you? I can never think of anything that doesn't sound contrived, or jokey, or made up. Can you?'

She listened, confused. What message was he talking about? And why was he showing the messages she sent him to a girl he worked with? She looked at him again. Handsome in a nicely balanced and not too flashy way, clean, tidy; certainly he was the sort of man she was looking for; definitely sexy, but she didn't like the idea that he needed another woman to vet his internet dating. She didn't like the thought that there was another woman involved at all.

He was obviously waiting for her answer. She took a sip of coffee, trying to force the lump of Danish pastry further down her gullet and made him wait longer. 'I don't really like internet dating. You never know what idiots you are going to meet,' she said.

She was feeling jealous and it came out in a snide

way. She watched his face fall. A gloom descended over his features far too quickly for her liking. If he reacted like that to a simple slip of the tongue and he needed help from another woman to choose his dates and she remained as much of a klutz as she knew herself to be, what hope was there ever going to be of a relationship between them? The horrifying thought that she might never see him again gave her a courage she didn't know she possessed. One of them had to sort this out, and quick! At this point it looked like it had to be her.

'I'm sorry, Steve. I have absolutely no idea what you are talking about. What's all this about me kicking myself?' she asked.

'It's what you messaged me,' he said, now seriously unsure of himself. 'Surely you can't have already forgotten those special four words.'

'What special four words?' asked Fliss.

Gobsmacked, Steve fumbled around in his pocket, found his mobile, logged on the internet dating website and retrieved the message. He turned the screen around to show her. The message read: **Kicking myself. Try again?**

'I didn't send that message!' frowned Fliss, then, with a bolt of inspiration, she instantly knew exactly who had. She was going to kill her mother when she next saw her!

Furious, she let out a heavy sigh of extreme frustration, but before either could say anything more her mobile rang in her pocket. She took it out, and answered without looking at the display. 'Fliss?' Vera hissed loudly down the other end of the line.

'Mum!'

'Are you with still with him?'

'Why?'

'It's twelve-thirty and you told me to ring you at twelve-thirty to get you out of there if you didn't like him. But you haven't rung. He's a bit of all right, then, is he?' Vera gibbered.

Fliss grimaced, blushing to the roots of her scalp, knowing Steve could hear every word.

He leant back and let out such an explosive snort of laughter, the people on the tables all around looked their way to see what had made such a loud noise. 'You didn't send that message, did you?' he guessed accurately. 'Your mother did!'

Fliss nodded slowly, smiling apologetically back at him and pointing at her mobile. 'Mum,' she said tersely, 'would you like to speak to Steve?' and handed the phone over to him. He took it from her, smiling broadly. Time for the real culprit to feel embarrassed!

'Hello Mrs ...' he looked at Fliss for help. For a moment he couldn't remember her surname.

'Father,' mouthed Fliss.

'... Mrs Father,' went on Steve. 'Thank you so very much for kicking yourself and for making it possible for Felicity and me to meet again this morning. It's been absolutely delightful so far, and I hope it's going to continue for the rest of the day, and perhaps even longer …'

Fliss knew her mother would be squirming. Steve held the mobile out so that they could both hear her splutter, 'You're very welcome. Glad to be of help,' and as he ended the call, they burst into shrieks of laughter. 'I think I might have your mother's seal of approval to date you.'

'That'd be so nice,' agreed Fliss, happiness floating her high on the air.

Chapter Twenty-Three
Start As You Mean To Go On

After enjoying a lazy lunch, Fliss and Steve strolled around the shops hand in hand. Towards the end of the afternoon they bumped into Ian and Etta and Steve suggested they all pop into Claremont's. It turned out the two men were old friends. Steve had gone to the same uni as Ian and they had started their first year on the same floor of their halls of residence. 'I hadn't heard you were back in town,' said Ian, obviously pleased to see him again. 'We must play squash again, eh?'

'My firm expanded and needed larger premises. I couldn't believe it when they decided on the new trading estate back here.'

'Are you working for Hudson, Gleaney then?' asked Ian. Steve nodded. 'I did all their conveyancing,' said Ian.

'Do you work in computers then?' asked Fliss, who suddenly realised they hadn't yet got to discussing what each did for a living. After getting over their shared amusement that Fliss's mother had got them together, their conversation had gone in many other directions.

'Cyberspace security,' Steve told her.

'And you can't think of anything to type in all those little boxes!' teased Fliss.

'I can write a multitude of computer languages in binary, but I'm not very good at the English language unless I think really hard about it. I'm too frightened of being misunderstood, so I tend to get a bit pedantic over what I commit to paper, especially when it's really, really important.'

So what he had written to her had been 'really, really, important', had it? All thoughts of him showing her message to his female colleague evaporated. Fliss was liking every single word she heard.

'What do you do?' asked Steve.

'Stockbroking,' said Fliss.

'Good match!' said Steve, and high-fived her. 'I'll know who to go to now to make a great return on all the money I'm going to earn.'

'You must remember the price of stocks can go both up and down,' she said, mockingly earnest, making Steve laugh and cuddle her close.

Through the half-opened conservatory doors, Vera heard her daughter sounding more happy and vibrant than she had heard her for years. She peeked out to see Fliss standing with the arm of a very nice-looking young man around her shoulders talking to a terribly pretty black girl. Wasn't that Etta? The man who had been standing beside her turned around and she realised it was Ian.

'Your first two successes,' said Olivia, peeking over her shoulder. 'Now, are you still going to tell me you won't be a whiz at this job!'

'Stop jumping the gun,' said Vera sternly.

Olivia backed down, still on her best behaviour. She busied herself tidying, but retained the tiniest of smirks on her face as Vera sat reading through more of the documents she'd given her.

They'd just finished looking around the boathouse and although Vera had already said that once it had been fitted out it could make a very suitable base for the Normal Dating Agency, she was well aware that the biggest problem was Olivia, in whose head, she was sure, the deal was already done. So far all Vera had said was that she would only consider going into the company and running it if the fees were set so exorbitantly high time-wasters would be deterred. Olivia had concurred.

Vera had also been adamant that Olivia must have no involvement with either the administration or the introductions after clients committed to the fee. The deepest of Vera's fears about the efficacy of a personal introduction agency, as she now called it, remained Olivia's exuberance. Wonderful as she was at marketing, Olivia's idea of who might feel comfortable with whom, and who might even start a loving and lasting relationship, was at best off piste, and at worst bordering on the insane.

She watched Olivia tidy and wondered if she could truly trust her. Vera was most concerned that her potential new junior partner, would be unable to maintain confidentiality. The only way this venture could work, Vera was certain, was if Olivia's involvement was kept to an absolute minimum or, even better, that she had no involvement in it at all.

Logic told Vera, however, that this was never going to happen. It had been Olivia's idea, after all, and there was not a chance she would be able to keep her nose out; but Vera also knew, based on those one hundred and fifty slips of paper, that to save all their reputations, the agency had to be opened, and tried for a while. Only when, if, it failed to make money and they could quietly close it, as Vera suspected would happen, would they all come out of this without having egg spread all over their faces, or worse, rotten eggs thrown at them.

'As businesses go, this is up there with the worst type that Olivia could possibly be involved in. She could do so much damage. How are we going to keep her under control?' she asked Angelina, who had obviously also been thinking keeping her sister calm and quiet was going to be nigh on impossible.

'She is taking Claremont's parlous financial

position extremely seriously,' Angelina said and that she'd been thinking it could only work if Vera took majority control. She suggested sixty per cent of the shares in the company go to Vera as she was going to be doing most of the work, she would do the bookkeeping and accounts and would hold twenty per cent for herself. For her twenty per cent Olivia would be in charge of attracting business as she had done so far.

Vera still wasn't sure that would work. 'But she must have been quite discreet to get the amount of names she's got this far,' Angelina argued, 'because you and I only got wind of what was going on at the very last minute. That must mean she is able to keep a secret when she tries.'

It hardly reassured Vera, who was now heavily into damage control, but she could see no other way out of the mess than by starting the business, then closing it down without fuss if it was not making enough money. Money is the key to all of this, she argued to herself. She knew it was the only real thing Olivia understood, and Olivia only understood it when she was running out of it.

'I still think we should change the company name to The Normal Personal Introduction Agency,' she said out loud.

'Too late,' replied Olivia. 'The name's been approved by Companies House or whoever gives the approval, and I've shelled out too much already on the flyers or whatever. Can those expenses go against my shares?'

'Ask the bookkeeper,' said Vera, suddenly very tired now the final hurdles had been surmounted. 'I'm going to talk with my daughter and her new man. Find a bottle of the good stuff and crack it open, but you're paying for it. Don't you dare put it on expenses! Claremont's can pay.'

'Are we going to have these arguments over every little penny, all the time?' asked Olivia.

'You bet we are,' said Vera, walking out, 'but not a hint about our plans yet, and certainly not to those four out there, Olivia! I want to tell my family in my own good time so that they will be well-prepared with a stock response when the word finally gets out.'

The rest of the afternoon was spent in merry conversation. Olivia managed to keep silent about the dating agency and even changed the subject back to the new couples if ever there was a chance anything might be revealed about the new venture. Vera started breathing more comfortably. Steve and Ian went next door to the men's section and both bought new shirts. Fliss and Etta, who had never met before, went through the early stages of getting to know each other by trying on new clothes together, each complimenting the other more than they would if they had known each other better.

Relaxing now a plan had settled in her mind, Vera joined in with their cheerful chattering and made herself stay until the four youngsters made arrangements to have dinner at a pub in the next village together. Ian secured them a table for four, then, while he was on the call, remembered his manners. 'Would you ladies like to join us?' he asked Vera, Olivia and Angelina.

'Good God no!' retorted Olivia. 'We're already old maids. Don't make us gooseberries, too!' to which she received a 'Don't forget you do have a brother-in-law, and I happen to be him,' from Pete who came into the shop to find out why his wife hadn't yet closed up.

'Don't worry about us,' he said to the four young people. 'I've already got our supper ready upstairs. You are staying, aren't you, Vera? Only my boring old lasagne, but there's more than enough to go around.'

Vera realised she was ravenously hungry; something she hadn't felt for very many days. 'I'll stay for a bit, but I don't want to be too late.'

'Goodo,' said Pete, pecking her on her forehead. 'How're you doing, my lovely?' he said, hugging her close.

'Better,' said Vera, appreciating leaning in against his strength, and thought that for the first time in ages she did feel more like her old self.

'I won't be joining you, sorry,' said Olivia throwing her long arms around them both. 'I've got a date,' and she swanned off leaving everyone watching her exit.

Chapter Twenty-Four
New Job - Day One

Pete manoeuvred the cupboard safe into place, breathing heavily. Its door hung open ready for him to reach in and power-screw the metal box to the concrete floor of the boathouse. Vera pointed a halogen work lamp so that he could see what he was doing inside the dark space. When he waggled his hand, she handed the electric screwdriver under his arm to him.

'Don't do it, Houdini,' tittered a voice. 'You'll die in that box!'

'Shut up, Olivia!' commanded both Pete and Vera in unison. 'Go up to the shop. Find someone else to bother.'

'Just wanted to see how our new office is coming on,' she said, walking in, but leaving the door overlooking the river open. The sharp breeze off the water caught and blew an open pack of leaflets for the new agency back into the room. 'Sorry,' she said, trying to retrieve them and kicking the sole of Pete's foot accidentally. Straightening automatically, he bumped the back of his head hard.

'Get out, Olivia!' shouted Vera.

'Okay,' said a miffed Olivia. 'I only wanted to see how you were getting on.'

'And shut that door behind you!' Vera shouted without turning around.

To Vera's eyes, the office in the boathouse at Claremont's was actually looking rather wonderful. It had not held any kind of boat for many years and had just been used as a riverside version of a beach hut by the family. There had been some hilarious parties thrown in the large airy space. On one side at the back Pete, who was competent doing DIY, had installed a small kitchen unit with a sink, a microwave and a kettle behind a false wall. On the other he'd helped the plumber put in a shower room, complete with toilet and hand basin.

'Why do we need a shower?' Vera asked.

'It was cheaper to buy a set than the toilet and hand basin separately,' Pete answered and she didn't argue.

In between the two rooms stood an old double-size, freestanding wine refrigerator. Once, when the shop was at its most profitable, it had always been kept fully stocked with champagne and Chablis, but now its contents numbered only a few bottles of very inferior stuff.

'A pint of milk's going to look extremely silly in there,' pointed out Vera.

'I'll find a way to obscure the glass fronts,' replied Pete. 'Can't have your clients asking to use the loo, seeing loads of booze and getting the wrong idea.' He found posters to stick on the front of each door. They showed pictures of the hothouse at Kew Gardens with its exotic palms.

'Makes the place seem friendlier instantly,' Vera said, much impressed. 'Shouldn't we create a separate room where the prospective couples can sit and chat without interruption?' But after measuring it, she and Pete decided not to create a room but a separate space towards the front of the boathouse, where, if the weather was pleasant, the doors could be thrown open so that clients could look out over the river as they chatted. If it was chilly or cold, the full-sized doors would be kept firmly closed and an ordinary-sized access door fitted into the middle of one of them would be used instead. Vera rang Christy at the builders' merchants. 'Have we got anything in stock that looks like a logburner, but which is free-standing?'

'Just had a brand new delivery in,' replied Christy. 'Electric, but they look just like the real thing. How many do you need?' Vera didn't know, so Christy offered to bring a couple down in his lunch hour.

'Wow. This is looking impressive,' he said as he

lugged one of them in in its cardboard box. 'You'll only need two. They're highly efficient.' Without preamble, he deftly slit open the seal of the box and lifted one out.

The interior shiplap boards of the boathouse had been decorated a neutral shade of grey. The rough concrete floor was randomly covered with second-hand Persian carpets in reds and blues bought cheaply from an auction site. Vera now had a working area in the far corner alongside one of the large windows which could be hidden behind concertina screens. On her desk stood a swish modern computer screen of which she was very proud as it made her feel as if she had finally been dragged into the twenty-first century. Happily, the telephone company had been able to put in a new line rapidly, and Olivia had sourced two sofas and eight easy chairs which had been upholstered in the wrong grey checked material and which were going cheap. The boathouse was still spacious, and the alterations made it a comfortable meeting place.

'Should we be doing all this before we get all the permissions to run a business from here?' Vera worried. Pete reassured her the boathouse was already approved as part of Claremont's shop, but Vera still breathed a great sigh of relief when the last pieces of paperwork finally came through and they were almost ready to open. All they needed now was a steady stream of clients.

The hard work starts now, she thought the first morning she drove herself into work. Both Christy and Fliss had phoned as she was having breakfast. 'You'll be brilliant,' her daughter told her, 'because it's a brilliant idea.' Fliss described most things lately as brilliant, confirming to Vera that she was fully in the first throes of romantic love.

'Break a leg,' said Christy.

'I sincerely hope I don't,' responded Vera, who had been worrying irrationally overnight that the pathway from the conservatory doors of Claremont's to the boathouse could be very slippery in certain weather conditions. What if one of their clients slipped and hurt themselves? Would they be insured? The new insurance policy was the first thing she sought out when she got up that morning. They were, but she still thought it might be a good idea speaking to Pete about her fears.

'There's been non-slip netting laid over it for years,' Pete comforted her when she rang him the next morning at his office at the College of Further Education where he was an examinations officer. 'But, just to reassure you, I'll check it again when I come home. Have you thought about getting some of those large golfing umbrellas printed up with the agency's logo so they can sit in an umbrella stand in the conservatory at the shop just in case? No one had. Vera put it on the ever-present to-do list she carried everywhere with her nowadays.

'Cheers!' The three owners of the newest business in town toasted themselves by clattering mugs of coffee together at nine o'clock on the Monday morning. 'Here's to The Normal Dating Agency,' said Vera.

'And all who sail happily off into the sunset after using her,' quipped Olivia, to which even Vera, who was now feeling as nervous as a kitten, raised a weak grin.

'Here I go,' she said. 'Wish me luck.'

'Want me to come and help you?' asked Olivia eagerly.

'NO!' shouted Vera and Angelina in unison, then Angelina wagged an accusatory index finger at her sister, adding, 'Don't cock this up, Olivia. You know what we agreed. You know your role. You are not to interfere at all after you've met and introduced people to the agency. You are not to get involved in any more! Remember?'

'I'll be good,' said Olivia, collecting the mugs and tidying some stock. Vera and Angelina exchanged a look that said only too clearly that they doubted she could ever manage it.

Vera had already planned how she was going to handle her first day. She would get back in touch with all the people who had written their names and numbers on slips of paper for Olivia to gauge their level of interest. The first one she rang was Toby Goodman from Breeches and Bridles, the old man who had just lost his wife. His name was worrying her. Surely, Olivia had got it wrong when she wrote down that he was looking for a man.

'Breeches and Bridles Equine Stores. How may I be of assistance to you today?' the cheery and very young female voice answered the number listed on the slip of paper. Vera had expected it to be a private mobile number.

'Sorry, I thought this was the number for Mr Goodman.'

'It is,' said the voice. 'The office phone's been diverted to here. Granddad's unloading a mare from a trailer. There's no one in the office until ten. Do you want me to get Granddad? Granddad!' she shouted at the top of her voice. She sounded no older than twelve.

Deafened, Vera held her own phone away from her ear. She switched it on the speaker. 'Don't bother him if he's dealing with a horse,' she tried, but Toby Goodman's granddaughter had already put the phone down and was hanging out of the doorway shouting even louder for her grandfather. Vera had two choices. Either she ended the call, or she hung on and waited. She chose the latter. What if the young girl dialled back and Vera answered 'The Normal Dating Agency. How may I help you?' like she had planned to answer calls? Surely Toby Goodman wouldn't want his family to know what he was doing? No. She had to be discreet and maintain a certain level of confidentiality. Remaining on the end of the line was the right thing to do.

She waited a full fifteen minutes. She tried whistling and calling down the phone so that they might pick up again, but there was no response. She sat sorting other slips of papers into the empty shoeboxes she'd marked up last night. Each had a label written in Vera's artistic hand in different-coloured felt-tip pen. The one for Women Seeking Men was written in pink. The Men Seeking Women, unsurprisingly, was written in blue. Each letter of Men Seeking Men had been picked out in the rainbow colours of the LGBT community, but for the label on the box for Women Seeking Women Vera had chosen a vivid scarlet red as it stood out more. Vera was more than a bit nervous thinking about interviewing lesbians. What would they be looking for? When she reassured herself that as her own sex drive had been reawakened with dreams of enormous erections, she reckoned that she surely wouldn't be giving out the wrong signals, so all she needed to do was relax and let the conversation take its own course. Everyone was looking for their own kind of love, after all, and it was her job to try to help them find it.

'Toby Goodman here.' The very deep voice made her jump. He was completely out of breath. He wheezed, and coughed so hard that when Vera heard him gag and spit, an involuntary grimace contorted her lips.

'Sorry to disturb you,' started Vera, a bit worried he was going to collapse on her. Conscious of her phone bill, she saw from the display that the call had already lasted sixteen minutes now. 'Are you all right? I could call back.'

'Arrr,' he answered in the local drawl. 'Mare's heavy in foal. Her d'aint wanna be moved. Who is it?'

'I'm from the Normal Dating Agency,' Vera started. 'I think you met my colleague, Olivia, at Daniella's a while ago.'

'Her from Claremont's? Arr. I 'ad a good chat 'uv 'er. Bit of all right, ain't her?'

'Yes. Olivia Claremont.'

'I knew her father. 'E were a bit of a dandy, too, weren't he?'

The conversation was going exactly the way Vera had feared it would. Tactfully, she answered, 'It was the business he was in. He had to be a snappy dresser, but I really liked Bill Claremont.'

'Arr. So did I,' Toby Goodman said with relish. 'Could you find me one like 'im?'

Vera had to turn her head away before her involuntary laugh came out. She cleared her throat as she retrieved the phone and turned off the speaker. 'Sorry. Frog in my throat. You're still interested in joining the agency, then?'

When he said he was, and told her when she casually dropped into the conversation how expensive the fees were that 'that foal that mare is carrying'll sell easily as a yearling. Got a pedigree out of the stud book. Yon'll pay for this bit of flim-flam for me. It'll get me out a bit,' Vera transferred his slip of paper into the wallet file she planned to open for every client and opened the appointments page on her swanky new computer to make an appointment for him to come to see her.

'Don't yer do home visits, then?' he asked.

'No. It's more discreet if you come in to see me. I've got an office in the boathouse on the river. Come in through Claremont's and they'll show you where.'

She smiled when he finally confirmed he would, telling her, 'I need some new kecks and underpants. It'll kill two birds with one stone. I might even meet a nice bloke in the shop. Save you some trouble, eh?' He giggled at the thought of it, then coughed and hacked up phlegm again. 'What's your name then?' he asked eventually.

'Vera. Vera Father,' she told him.

'Not Richard's widow from the merchant's!'

'That's me,' she answered, then completely lost it when he asked, 'Found anyone yerself since you lost 'im? I might change my mind as to what I wan' if I knew you woz a-lookin'.' She spotted her reflection in the screen of the swanky new computer, and saw she was actually wobbling with mirth.

By the time she got the old flirt off the phone, she

was desperate for a pee. She'd never tried so hard to keep her laughter in, and as she chatted more to him, she allowed herself to let a few giggles escape, which only served to make him even more garrulous. He had to be old enough to be her father, but life was certainly not repressing him. If this was the type of client she was going to deal with, then perhaps this new job might be more fun than she had expected.

Chapter Twenty-Five
Well, Would You?

Vera broke her own rule on the very first day of trading for The Normal Dating Agency. She told Fliss about her conversation with Toby Goodman and how much it had amused her. She was careful not to give his name, and Fliss never asked it, but once Fliss knew he was an elderly man who worked with horses, it wouldn't take long for her to work out who he might be.

'Well, would you?' asked Fliss, taking another bite of the crab linguine her mother had thrown together for their supper.

Vera took a while answering. After that first conversation, she had wondered what she would do if a man joined the agency that she fancied. It didn't seem right, but then, if he was Mr Right, would she turn down the opportunity? 'I don't think so,' she answered truthfully, 'but then again, I haven't yet been put in that situation.'

'You'd have to give him his money back. You couldn't have him paying you for an overabundance of services,' teased Fliss.

'Felicity Mary Father, what are you implying?' retorted Vera.

'Nothing, Vera Elizabeth Father!' said Fliss, eyes twinkling.

They chose ice cream from the tubs in the freezer for desert, and took their bowls through to eat in front of the evening news. Vera, as usual, wasn't particularly interested in what was going on in the world. Fliss, on the other hand, was unable to turn away from the breaking news. Vera took her empty bowl from her one hand and the spoon from the other without Fliss ever taking her eyes off the TV screen. 'Coffee?' she asked, and Fliss nodded once without moving.

Waiting for the kettle to boil, Vera tidied the work surfaces and loaded the dishwasher. It had been a good day, and she had thoroughly enjoyed it. She'd even done her first consultation; a pretty girl called Emily who had picked up one of the leaflets from the counter in Claremont's and asked Angelina what it was all about. 'It's just what I've been looking for,' she told Angelina. 'There wouldn't possibly be someone I could talk to about joining today, would there, then I wouldn't chicken out?'

They hadn't yet discussed how they would handle approaches like this yet. They'd expected everything to come through phone calls where they would be able to make appointments, but Angelina had quickly rung Vera's line and asked her. 'I can't see why not this once,' Vera agreed, 'but perhaps this ought to be the only time. If not, you could have them waiting in the shop and that would be counterproductive. We might never get a fee out of them if they met someone in the conservatory. Remember we wanted to keep Claremont's and Normal completely separate. Just tell her you happened to see me come into the office and you are doing it as a favour.'

Emily was a sweet enough girl. She worked in one of the high street banks, but she wanted to get out and do something different. She talked a lot about her career, so much so that Vera had to remind her that this was a personal introduction agency and not one that did recruitment. 'Perhaps you could combine both,' suggested Emily. 'I wouldn't mind doing recruitment. I think I'd be rather good at it.'

'Might be a better idea if you stay in the bank if you are looking to find someone to settle down with. Isn't a bank the best place to get a mortgage?' said Vera, getting her back on track to reveal some personal details and preferences. In the end, Emily wanted pretty much the same as any other twenty-four year old girl who hadn't really done that much in her life yet. When Vera asked what she wanted in a man she replied, 'Someone to look after me.'

'Is there anything that would stop you from being interested in a man?' she'd asked next. 'I'm not that choosy,' answered Emily honestly. 'I just want someone to look after me.'

There are going to have to be a lot of young men on our books who are prepared to work their fingers to the bone for their wife and family, thought Vera after meeting Emily. She added a final note to the bottom of her record on the computer. 'Scared of life. Indecisive. Needs someone to lean on and to reassure her.'

Vera poured hot water over the coffee grounds wondering how many such men she would find in the scraps of paper Olivia had collected. Did young men want girlfriends or wives like that any more? Wasn't it a society where men and women were equal?

'Fliss?' she said, passing over her mug of coffee. The News was just coming to an end. The national presenter was doing the handover to news from their region. 'Would you ever ask Steve to look after you?'

'Hang on, Mum. I want to hear about that police raid in Oxford.' Fliss took a huge slug of her coffee and turned her attention fully on the screen. 'I'd like to think he would look after me,' she said when the News was over. The coverage had been five minutes long, and Vera had had many other thoughts during it, so she was incredibly impressed that Fliss was able to pick up the conversation seamlessly.

'I expect he would expect me to also look out for him, but I wouldn't expect him to financially support me, or to listen to all my woes all the time. We only really met a little while ago. We haven't got to that bit yet.'

'But when you were internet dating, was that the sort of man you were looking for?'

Fliss thought about it long and hard. 'I suppose so,' she admitted eventually. 'What's the point of going into a long-term relationship, if you don't expect to look after one another? That's bizarre. Doesn't always happen, though. And, how do you know it will, until you try it? How did you know Dad was going to look after you?'

Vera thought back over time. She honestly didn't know if she'd ever considered it when they first met. The possibility of sex between them was overwhelming, but they'd been of a previous generation. They'd been unable to keep their hands off one another, so their mutual longing coloured all other considerations. Vera had married Richard when she was only twenty because he was the man she most wanted to make love to her. Many others offered, and she had tried a few, but he turned out to be the one she wanted, and she was fairly certain it had been the same for him. Other things did get discussed after she accepted his proposal of marriage, like how many children they wanted and what kind of home they aspired to, but very little was ever talked about how they would conduct their marriage. It had all been a leap of faith.

'I trusted him,' Vera said, suddenly aware that that was what their marriage had been built on. 'And I'm sure he trusted me.'

Fliss sipped at her coffee intently, watching her mother's face move with her internal thought-machinations. 'It can't be that different nowadays then, can it?' she asked, thinking of her own new situation. Isn't that what we're all actually doing? We're looking for someone who we can trust with our love?'

Vera pulled her daughter in close and hugged her. 'Felicity Mary Father. You are one very wise woman.'

'Vera Elizabeth Father,' came the muffled reply. She pulled away and pecked her on the cheek. 'If you'd only let me breathe, I'd tell you I am that because that's what you brought me up to be. Now let me go home, because I haven't done any housework for ages and I need to change my bed before I get into it.'

Vera smirked. 'Any particular reason?' she quizzed.

'Mother!' Fliss blushed furiously and swept out, head down, to collect her stuff from the kitchen. Vera heard the outside door bang and a car crunch over the gravel before she moved. Too much was going through her mind, and all of it was about love.

The strangest thing was that Olivia suddenly popped into her mind. The night Vera had stayed to have lasagne with Angelina and Pete, hadn't Olivia refused to join them as she had a date? And, come to think of it, hadn't Olivia been very much quieter of late? Could that possibly be because she, too, was seeing someone and was keeping it very, very quiet? She'd have to remember to ask Angelina if she knew anything when she next got the chance. But one thing was for certain. Olivia had calmed down a very great deal, and apart from her excitement early this morning, she had kept to her word and she had stayed away from the agency.

Vera jumped to one final conclusion. Olivia had to be seeing someone, and as she was being so secretive, he had to be someone very special indeed.

Chapter Twenty-Six
People Are Strange

The man stormed through the conservatory at Claremont's, straight through the ladies section of the shops, crashed the door open, then turned back to declare at the top of his voice to anyone who would listen, 'She's a fucking charlatan!'

His language brought the assistants from the men's section running. 'What's happening?' asked one. 'Are you all right?' demanded the other.

Luckily there were no customers on either side of the shop. Angelina came running from the office at the back as Olivia and her assistant lost control of and dropped the display stand they were moving to another part of the shop floor. 'Who was that?' asked Angelina, jumping as Vera ran into the shop.

'Did you all get a good look at him?' she asked breathlessly.

'Dreadful jeans,' said Paul, who managed the menswear section. 'Zeigmast rip-offs, mark my words! You can get them off eBay for a song, but one wash and they go saggy round the rear just where you need them to be figure-hugging.'

'Dreadful shirt, too,' agreed his assistant, Rufus. 'Too much bling. And did you see that chest hair! Oooh! That needed waxing.'

'But did you all get a good look at his face?' asked Vera, deeply perturbed.

'I did,' said Toni, Olivia's assistant. It was the first time Vera had ever heard her speak. She always seemed to be sitting cross-legged on the floor folding piles of clothes. 'Isn't he that geezer that sells used cars in Bordenwick? Mum says he's related to gypsies.'

Vera composed herself. She didn't quite know how to handle this. Her palm covered her mouth. 'Spit it out,' said Angelina.

'I doubt we are ever going to be able to help him,' Vera said, even though she was close to laughing. 'Don't get involved with him, please. If he comes back again, you have to let me deal with him.'

She said it so forcefully even Olivia, who had listened with an open mouth, remained quiet, too. 'Perhaps you'd all like to go back to work,' suggested Angelina, turning Vera around and pushing her in to the back office. 'What happened?' she said in a low voice as they quickly walked away. Vera was as white as the lilies in vases in the shop, but her eyes were also dancing with merriment. 'Are you all right?' asked Angelina.

Vera said nothing until the door closed firmly behind her. Only then did she burst out laughing, more from shock than amusement. 'You'll never guess what he wanted,' she spluttered.

'What?' asked Angelina.

Vera choked, fighting back her giggles. Angelina opened the door and called over to Olivia. 'Could you join us for a minute?' she said through clenched lips and so politely Olivia turned around to see if there was someone standing behind her. She wasn't used to be spoken to civilly by either her sister or her friend. Usually they were telling her to butt out, or shut up or simply declaring, Olivia! Intrigued, she left Toni to finish off the display stand and scurried in.

'Get in here,' Vera said, tugging her into the small room unceremoniously. 'I can't believe what he was after!' she spluttered.

'He's not one of mine,' said Olivia, distancing herself from the dreadful man. 'I've never seen him before.'

Vera's eyes turned to heaven in silent thanks. 'I know he's not, but please, whatever you do, don't ever get tangled up with him,' she said. 'He's seriously weird.'

'Why. What did he want?' demanded Olivia, round-eyed.

'He's just asked me if we have any housebound ladies on our books.'

The sisters frowned at each other. Vera was finding it very hard to contain herself. 'Please, don't make me laugh,' she gasped. 'Otherwise I shall never get this out. This is terribly serious and we mustn't make a fool of him.' Despite her attempt to be serious, she sniggered anew.

'Why's he want housebound ladies?' asked Angelina incredulously. Olivia pulled a face as if to say she had no idea either.

'Not just housebound ladies. They have to be seriously overweight and unable to get out of bed.'

That floored Angelina. 'You what!'

'Oh, it gets better. He wants to find a lady so big, all she can do is lie in bed. He specifically said he wanted one so grossly obese they would have to take out a window to get her out of the house.' She collapsed into the fits of giggles which were the only way to handle her shock.

Clutching herself, she laughed so loudly, she couldn't stop. 'He wants a woman who needs him to be her sex slave,' Vera managed to say, finally containing herself enough to tell them. 'He says he's happy to help with her personal hygiene, and he wants to cook for her, massive great meals which will make her only bigger. Apparently he's got a frying pan that can hold twelve eggs at a time! ... And he's used to frying pounds and pounds of bacon crispy! Once, he got started, I couldn't shut him up and I couldn't get a word in edgeways. And you'll never guess what ...' Vera was laughing so hard now, tears were streaming down her face and snot was hanging from her nose. Disgusted, Angelina handed her a tissue at arm's length.

'Go on.' She hesitated, not sure if she actually wanted to hear what Vera was about to tell her.

'He wants to make love to her and feel as though he's ... well, I'll try to repeat exactly what he said,' she gasped, clutching her aching tummy hard. 'He wants to pump away at an enormous human bed of fat. He wants to be able to sink in between her folds and disappear. He wants her to engulf him!'

By now, Vera was incapable of saying any more. The revelation was so bizarre and Vera's laughter so infectious, Angelina and Olivia couldn't stop themselves from joining in.

'What did you tell him?' asked Olivia.

'That sadly we didn't have anybody like that on our books at the moment!'

It took them a long time to calm down, and when they did all Angelina could think of doing was cracking open a bottle. Alcohol was definitely needed to get over the nasty experience.

'Do you think it's a fetish?' asked Olivia, so seriously she made Angelina explode into fits of giggles again. She apologised by holding up both hands as she composed herself. 'No, really,' said Olivia. 'We shouldn't really be laughing at him, should we?'

'No,' Vera agreed. 'But we can't help him either.

How many housebound women who are unable to get out of bed are we likely to have coming in to register with us?'

'They wouldn't be able to afford our fees. They'd be on disability,' said Angelina deadly seriously. Vera and Olivia snorted and she stared them out, affronted. It was now their turn to turn their hands up in apology. 'I was only thinking aloud,' she said.

Vera forced herself to become sensible. The surprise of what she had just been told had been dealt with, but it threw up another problem. 'No matter what anyone ever tells me in confidence, we must never, ever humiliate them. I didn't handle that one at all well. In fact, I handled it badly, but I don't know how else I could have handled it. He did catch me by surprise when he told me with what he wanted. At first I thought it was a wind-up and then I realised he was deadly serious. He really was telling me the truth, and I'm probably the first person he's ever had the courage to tell.'

'So what are you going to do about him?'

Vera sipped on her drink and stared out of the tiny window. Clouds had gathered since she rushed over to the shop after her client. It was threatening to rain. She'd left the boathouse completely open. She ought to go back and close it up, but she didn't feel she could go back just yet. The place would still hold memories of him and his specific needs.

'There's absolutely nothing I can do for him,' she

said. 'He isn't a client. I didn't even get basic details from him. He's not paid a fee, so in reality we have no responsibility to him, but I must keep his secret. I shouldn't have even told you two, but I don't want to get involved with oddballs and weirdos and he was certainly a weirdo, but neither do you want a repeat of how abusive he was in the shop. That's not good and who knows what else he might do? Perhaps we've made a mistake. Perhaps we should never have opened the office in the boathouse expecting people to walk through the shop.'

'But we did it to get more people into the shop,' Angelina reminded her. 'Were we misguided?'

For once, Olivia proved the most sensible of them all. 'It's no good thinking that way,' she said. 'There can't be that many around like him and we did it because we needed to find another source of income to keep the shop from going under,' she pointed out. 'The Normal Agency would have to charge even higher registration fees if we didn't use the boathouse, which costs us nothing.' The others nodded agreement with her. 'The only thing I think we've done wrong is ask them to walk through the shop, and I still don't think there's that much wrong in that. But wouldn't we get so many more coming to the agency if we could open in the evening or other hours, when the shop is closed?'

'I don't want to work any more hours than we agreed,' Vera said.

'You wouldn't have to,' said Olivia. 'It would still be by appointment and you could pick and choose the times you want to work. But wouldn't it be more sensible if we also had a more discreet way to get in and out of the garden? That way clients would enjoy more privacy. And they could choose to come into the shop only if they made the decision themselves.'

Angelina knew exactly what she was getting at. 'The old gate in the side wall,' she said.

'Do you think Pete or some of your men, Vera, could repair it? If we could get that open, we could offer clients the choice. Either they come in through the shop as usual, but they could also slip in and out that way if they don't want to.'

'What about the space you use for your car?' asked Angelina. The side gate was blocked up in order to give more car-parking space.

'Oh, don't worry about that,' said Olivia casually. 'I'll ask my friend if I can leave my car at his place instead.'

Chapter Twenty-Seven
Paint-Splattered

Benji wiggled his body around the gap even before Olivia could open the gate fully. She grabbed him by the collar, worried he might run out into the road, but the dog was too pleased to see his new best friend to escape. He circled her legs, nuzzling her hand for attention. She knelt down and ruffled the long fur around his neck, rubbing her face into the side of his, bonding with him. She loved his organic smell of damp leaves and the riverside, all the things she had grown up with when she was a little girl living with her mum and dad and Angelina above the shop. He must have been out in the garden alongside the river all day.

When they were children, the sisters had shared a bedroom in the eaves at the top of the Claremont building. Facing the river, its construction was of Georgian broad brick. On the street side a much earlier construction of black-painted timbers filled in with ochre wattle and daub narrowed where the building rose towards the roof. The two rooms directly above the shop which served as sitting room and a kitchen diner were square and spacious, but a bathroom had had to be squeezed in on the curve of the stairs on the street side as there was only enough room in the roof space for one large double bedroom on one side and a much smaller room on the other. Angelina and Olivia had shared that smaller room. Their two single beds fitted in one against the side wall and the other against the back with their pillows touching. At night, lying on their sides, the Claremont girls could both look out of the window at the stars as they listened to the sounds of the river with its smell on the breeze coming in through the tiny window.

No one remembered when Olivia first showed signs of the bipolar personality which was going to trouble her all her life. Perhaps it was as a seven-year-old when she decided it would be great fun to see if she could launch herself from their bedroom window and fly with the birds. She never seemed to see danger. Only teenage Angelina, grabbing the long satin ribbons sewn into the side of the waist of Olivia's nightdress and screaming for help as she rammed her feet under the window sill making herself into a human counterweight, stopped Olivia from going in to free fall. Or perhaps it was the winter's morning when they woke up to snow and she refused to get out of bed saying that she had been covered in an avalanche overnight and they should leave her there to die. She'd stayed in bed for four days, refusing food and drink, until her father angrily tore her away from where she had tied herself to the mattress with a skipping rope. As he pulled her out of bed, details for her funeral written in her childish handwriting fell from where she had lain. These included the whole of the upper school choir singing a medley of Abba songs, a white coffin with gold handles adorned with orange roses and white gypsophila and all the mourners wearing outfits in either yellow, orange or bright blue, but not any other colour.

Angelina, already in love with Pete, could not wait to get away from her demanding little sister. Their mother, instead of seeing anything wrong in her eccentric little girl, fooled herself into believing Olivia simply had a vivid imagination and, no matter how bizarre her behaviour, she would grow out of it. Her father thought she was wilful and selfish, just like his own mother had been. He said only a firm hand would ever control her but, try as he might to discipline his wayward daughter, he always gave in when, eventually, she snapped out of her remote and solitary mental wanderings and smiled her cheeky smile at him once again. He was the first to comfort her when her tears were unstoppable as well as the first to congratulate her when she worked herself into exhaustion to achieve her goals.

He loved her unquestioningly and chose to maintain his belief that she was exceptional, and would achieve exceptional things in her life; so it had broken his heart when he had been called to collect her from university six weeks into her first term, a bemused, anorexic girl lying even to herself about how little she was eating. Olivia had been brought home to the family house on the hill where she was nursed by her mother while attending a psychiatric clinic in the next town. By then Angelina and Pete had married and lived in the flat above the shop. 'Come live with us,' they offered, thinking perhaps she was missing her early childhood home, but she refused. That part of her life was now gone, she rigidly maintained, and forced herself to accept that the riverside home she had clung to for comfort had been handed over to them.

Of all the things that remained important to Olivia, uppermost in her wellbeing was the sound of the river and its smell on the breeze. No way could she ever be too far away from it. The river flowing freely through her home town made her feel alive. She gave up all thoughts of returning to university. Instead, she jumped at the chance to work in the shop at Claremont's so she could regularly be beside it. When Ambrose moved into River House she took to popping in for a chat after she finished work whenever he was home, often staying to share his evening meal with him. It meant she could spend even longer in close proximity to the river. Luckily, Ambrose never turned her away. He seemed as keen as her to strengthen their friendship, so she never questioned why he was being so kind to her.

'What have you been up to today, Benji?' she asked the dog. 'Have you been swimming in the river again?'

'Don't put ideas into his head,' called Ambrose from further down the garden where he was slapping paint on the rickety old fence.

Olivia closed the gate and strode across the lawn to join him. Benji stuck like glue to her side. 'I don't know why you're bothering doing that,' she told Ambrose. 'You need a whole new fence. That one's had it.'

'There's a new one on order but while I'm waiting for it to come, this is therapeutic,' said Ambrose, refilling his paint brush with the runny paint. He pulled another, smaller, brush from his back pocket. 'Here, have a go and see if it does anything for you,' he said, lobbing it at her.

Olivia still wore the outfit she had worn to work in the shop. The white trousers and sweater threaded with gold metallic thread were hardly suitable to paint in. 'On your bike, darling,' she said, chucking the brush back at him and hitting him with it on the back of his head.

'Oi you, that hurt,' he said, rubbing where it connected, then rushed at her, dripping paint brush raised, threatening to daub paint all over her.

She backed off rapidly and fell straight over the dog, landing with a heavy bump on a lawn damp with evening dew. 'Want a hand up?' teased Ambrose, holding the paintbrush out of the way. Olivia eyed the splatters smeared over the free hand he extended and refused. She didn't want any of that paint anywhere near her. Benji eyed his master from a distance, sensed playtime and wanted to join in. He raced around the garden until he found a well-chewed squeaky toy which he rushed back with at top speed for Ambrose to throw.

Leaping towards his master, Benji misjudged his leap. He hit Ambrose full in the back sending him flying forwards towards Olivia who, seeing what was about to happen, brought her arms up to protect her face and rolled sideways. Ambrose landed prone where she had seconds before lain supine, all air knocked out of his lungs in one massive groan. Benji circled, thinking it was all part of the game, and ran up his back. 'Get off me, you brute,' demanded Ambrose. 'Your claws need clipping.' The dog, unperturbed, jumped off over his head, turned round, tongue hanging out, and licked Ambrose's face, breathing smelly hot breath all over him. Ambrose groaned as he pushed him away.

Olivia laughed so hard air caught in her throat

and she had to sit up to stem her choking. Ambrose rolled over on one side to check that she was all right. Eventually she stopped coughing. 'So you think that was funny, do you?' he asked, menacingly pushing himself up slowly.

'It was,' agreed Olivia, and stroked Benji, now lying beside her panting heavily.

She didn't see it coming. Ambrose was as quick as a flash. 'Let's see if you think this is funny, too,' he said as he reached out, grabbed the loaded paintbrush, and launched himself at her. He painted a narrow line all the way from the roots of her hair to the tip of her nose.

'Watch my clothes. Watch my clothes,' she said as he threw the brush to one side, pushed her on her back and very forcefully kissed her.

Neither knew who was the most surprised: Olivia, who had been casually wondering for the past few weeks whether she would like it if ever Ambrose made a move on her, but now when he did, went rigid; or Ambrose, who, when he pulled back found himself extremely shocked that he had elicited absolutely no response from her at all. She had just lain there, mouth compressed, motionless, letting him lay his lips on her.

He pulled away, wondering if he should try again, but then thought better of it. After all, she was the first woman other than his wife that he had kissed romantically for the past twenty five years. Was he so out of practice that he'd become a rotten kisser? Or was this no longer the way you kissed a girl? Perhaps he'd misjudged where they were going. She was, after all, at least fifteen years younger than him, if not more. Perhaps they did it differently nowadays. Or was her flirty teasing nothing more than repartee? Had he really read all the signs so badly wrong?

Deeply embarrassed, he turned away from her and swiftly rose to his feet, sure he'd overstepped the mark. He wasn't in the habit of apologising, though he suspected he really should. His modus operandi when he made a fool of himself was to carry on as if nothing had happened and ignore it. 'So, are you staying for dinner again tonight?' he asked, walking away from her.

Olivia, too, chose to act as if nothing at all had just happened between them. She heaved herself up and brushed down her clothes. 'Can't, I'm afraid. Meeting a friend down the gym. You didn't do anything special, did you? You never said you were going to.'

He had, but no way was he ever going to admit it now. Since Olivia had got into the habit of popping in after work most evenings, and after the first few times when she'd eaten most of his dinner, he'd taken to shopping for two. It was pleasant not having to eat every evening on his own and, as it was Saturday and he was due to spend the evening in alone again, he'd bought two rather succulent pieces of fish from the market planning to serve them with new potatoes and a green salad, hoping she'd be able to share them with him.

'I only came over to see if you might let me park my car in your spare parking space when I'm at work,' she went on. 'We need to open the side garden door so clients can get through that way to the boathouse and if I park against it, no one can squeeze past my car.'

'Course,' he agreed instantly, bending to pick up his paintbrush in order to avoid eye contact. 'Whenever you need to,' and with a peck on the cheek to thank him, she fled still wearing the brush stroke of paint from her forehead to the tip of her nose and grass stains all over her bum, leaving him wondering what on earth had just gone wrong.

It was only later much later that evening, halfway through eating one of the pieces of fish, that he faced reality. He saw how she had entered his life when his defences were down. He'd accepted her friendship because he was sore and hurting from the breakdown of his marriage and he'd read something else into friendship. It must have all been wishful thinking on his part.

Suddenly, those little red-haired babies he'd once imagined having with her evaporated. His food became unpalatable. He scraped what remained into the kitchen sink and instead poured himself four fingers' worth of neat scotch, knocking it straight back in one go. Living alone was a bore.

Chapter Twenty-Eight
Faulty Memory

Vera leant back on the back legs of her chair and stretched her arms above her head to ease her shoulders. It had been a good Saturday so far. She made it a rule not to work on a Sunday or Monday and, tomorrow, she was really looking forward to her first full day off since the business started. There had been a long morning of appointments to end a long week during which she had moved mountains of paperwork. She couldn't wait to do more work on the Vera di Milo.

With a nice warm glow inside her, she mentally patted herself on the back that the last remaining slips of paper Olivia had collected had been dealt with. The Claremont's glossy bag was empty and in its place eighty-four wallet files hung in the new filing cabinet. In the end, over sixty per cent of Olivia's contacts had become clients, and, along with the new people who had responded to the flyers and adverts, the Normal Dating Agency now had a sufficiently large pool from which to operate.

Some people still needed to come in to discuss the type of relationship they were seeking. Appointments filled the office calendar. Vera had expected all of the people she'd seen so far to be looking for marriage, but many said that even if the people they met proved unsuitable long term, they would really like the opportunity to spend time with someone just going out on a pleasant date. One extremely well presented and preserved, middle-aged woman called Sandra, who told Vera she was in the throes of divorcing her third husband, was brutally honest. 'The trouble is, when the band starts playing my feet get itchy and I'm looking for a new dance partner. It's not the sex I'm after. I don't really like it. It messes up my hair. What I want is the flirting and the good nights out when I can get dressed up to the nines. I'd rather a man never saw me without my make-up.' At least she knew what she wanted. Vera had already introduced her to two men, both of whom also liked dancing. They'd told her they needed someone to accompany them to social events but nothing more. Sandra became her go-to standby. She even took to ringing in with reports the next morning to tell Vera how the latest night out had gone. There was never any hint of a physical relationship. Vera suspected that one day that might all change, but for the moment everyone was getting what they wanted, so she couldn't see the harm in introducing them. She just had to make sure all parties knew exactly what the score was.

Romance of the true kind was a much harder thing to predict, so when Vera had interviewed a very pleasant young man of twenty-eight called Simon that morning who was phlegmatic that his wife of four months had left him for a man she met at a conference, she was surprised at his pragmatism. 'It was in my critical path analysis that Rachel would leave me,' he said without much regret. 'She told me all the time I was too set in my ways and I was smothering her, but when you love someone, isn't that what you want to do? I want someone in my life to look after. I earn more than enough money. I can provide them with a nice home. I like spoiling a woman, so my ideal partner would be someone who is happy to let someone take care of them.'

Something about the phrases he used and the calculated way in which he delivered them reminded Vera of someone she'd met some time ago. She typed his details into the file and racked her brains as to who that might be. The girls she'd been talking to in the last few weeks were far too independent. Simon was looking for predictability, extreme loyalty and, Vera suspected, the sort of cloying relationship where couples gave each other silly names and giggled at their own jokes to the exclusion of everyone else. He would only find happiness when he was half of a couple truly content in their own company.

Although she went through every file of women seeking men in her mind, she still couldn't determine the name of the girl she knew was somewhere on their books. It was only later, as she was concentrating hard considering how she would paint her own features on the Vera di Milo, that it came back to her.

Emily! Her very first client, from the very first day! Emily had said many times that all she really wanted was someone to take care of her. Could Simon be that man?

Vera rushed into the hallway to get her laptop but couldn't see the extra-large leather designer bag she called her swag-bag in which she carried it. Her coat and handbag were there, but where was the swag-bag? Snatching her car keys from their hook, she went out and searched her car thoroughly, but it wasn't there either.

She leant back against the bonnet of the car and made herself think back. She remembered locking the safe. She remembered switching off the microwave and the kettle in the kitchen. She'd tidied around the sofas in the clients' meeting room, straightening cushions and switching off the standard lamps. Had she locked the filing cabinet? She couldn't remember. Why couldn't she remember? A cold chill spread down her back.

Dammit; because Annie had rung to confirm she'd booked the table for lunch at the Four Feathers tomorrow, but that it had to be earlier than they hoped and Vera had forgotten to go back and collect the swag-bag. Vera now remembered snatching her jacket from over the back of a chair while they were still chatting. She saw herself bending beneath her desk to retrieve her handbag. Then Wyeth had started screeching and they agreed he must be teething. She knew for certain she'd walked out of the door with only one arm in a sleeve of her jacket, struggling to tug the other one through, but her handbag had slipped off her shoulder and she dropped it. In the confusion of righting herself and closing the boathouse for the weekend, she must have forgotten to pick up her swag-bag.

Closing up the boathouse! Bloody hell, she couldn't even remember if she'd actually locked up. She dashed back into the house and picked up the phone. If Pete or Angelina were in, they could go down and check for her. She caught them on their way out to dinner. 'Be quick or we're going to lose the table. Run down while I bring out the car,' Angelina ordered Pete, apparently not too pleased. 'Vera, we'll ring you back one way or the other.'

In the anxious minutes between putting down the phone and snatching it back up again, Vera shut up her own house, this time securing it firmly. She stood waiting by the front door, phone in one hand, car keys in the other, but still jumped when the phone vibrated and Pete panted, 'The boat house was locked, but you'd left the toilet lights on and your big bag was on the top of your desk. I've got to go, Vera, but if you need to collect it tonight, I managed to get the side gate open today so you can get in through there. Just be careful how you move its old wooden door. Its hinges are rusted and the damned thing's very heavy.'

She didn't really need to go down until Tuesday, but her mind was so firmly stuck on Emily, it wouldn't give her any peace until she had satisfied herself that she was the girl who might suit Simon. She could be there and back in twenty minutes and then she could settle down to supper in front of the telly with the memory niggle satisfied. A quick peek at the records would quickly confirm one way or the other and she could, at the same time, collect her swag-bag, but when she approached the High Street, she hadn't considered how busy the town would be on a Saturday evening. She joined a slow-moving stream of cars circling and looking for a place to park. Why hadn't she walked from farther out? It would have been far quicker.

As she sat waiting, an enormous four-by-four attempted to get in to a space far too small in front of her. Before she could pass, it reversed to let out its passengers, blocking her way. She sat fuming. 'This is you all over, Vera Father,' she spoke out aloud to herself. 'Too impetuous by half. Calm down, woman!'

The driver of the four-by-four edged his vehicle forward again, but then couldn't open the driver's door to get out. 'You'll have to park it on The Meadows,' shouted his irate female friend at him as she knocked on Vera's window. 'Give the prat a mo and you can have his space,' she told her. 'It's only big enough for your little car. Why he has to drive that heap, I don't know!'

They're going to have an interesting night out, thought Vera, but was grateful that she was next in line behind him. As she waited for him to negotiate his way out backwards, she glanced across as further down the High Street the side gate to River House opened and a man led his dog out on a lead. The tan and brown dog was large and bouncy, eager for his walk. He circled the man's legs and the lead tightened around him. The man toppled against the wall, his hand shooting out to restrain the dog by the collar. Even though she couldn't hear it, she knew the man had shouted 'sit' firmly because the dog's haunches dropped instantly and his eyes turned upwards to watch his master. With his head lifted, Vera could see he had huge puffballs of greying eyebrows. 'Benji', she said out loud, and it was as if the dog heard her even from that distance.

He strained to look back over his shoulder. The master undid the clasp, unwrapped the lead from around his legs, straightened and tried to re-attach it, but couldn't. Released, Benji lurched towards

Vera's car. His master had other ideas. He grabbed the dog's collar and tugged him around hard, then, securing the lead started to walk Benji the other way, away from the town towards The Meadows.

Behind her other cars hooted their horns. Vera slammed her car into gear and eased it into the now vacant parking space, slipping out and leaning over her half-opened door to watch the dog and his master walk away. There was something about the greying-haired man that made Vera want to get a closer look at him. She watched master and dog walk further away into the distance. 'There's something about the way that man walks,' she said, waggling her index finger. A man passing by turned back and looked hard at her.

Chapter Twenty-Nine
Melancholy and Chocolate

Pete had been right to warn her. The hinges on the side gate of the garden were rusty. In fact, they were so rusty that when Vera gave the bottom of the wooden door a hard kick to release it, the screws gave way and it fell away from her into the garden nearly toppling her over behind it. 'Bugger,' she said and clambered over it, holding the brick wall to stop herself slipping on its rickety, lichened surface. Close to the river, everything acquired a grimy film of slime. Her hands were mucky. She wiped them on her trousers. She was going to have to find a way to secure the gate before she left, but as the light was starting to fade it was more important she first collect her swag-bag and lock up the boat house again.

Dew was forming on the lawn strewn with small sticks and foliage. Squirrels visited this garden. Collared doves nested in the high branches of the trees. She skidded to a halt as she rounded the back of the boathouse. The main light was on inside, its beams forming a spreading beacon across the flower beds. Surely, Pete would have turned everything off? There were no automatic timers or a security alarm. There was little reason to have them. The only valuable things inside were the swanky new computer and half a dozen bottles of inferior wine in the refrigerator. The takings were safely locked up in the safe and she doubted anyone could get at them.

Even so, someone had left the lights on. Could it be vandals? Vera could hear nothing, but just in case, she opened her car keys, secured the fob in her palm with the teeth of the key jutting out between two fingers. If there was an intruder, and she could get close enough, she would either lash out at him with the key's teeth or try to prod him in the eye with it.

Vera crept round to the front of the boathouse. Her heart sank and her pulse rate soared when she saw the small door hanging open. She felt in her pocket for her mobile, keyed in the passcode and brought up the keypad on which she entered 999. With her thumb poised to press the call button, she edge her way into the boathouse.

She could see no one in the outer office, though all the lights were blazing. On the tips of her toes she edged forward, trying to move as quietly as possible. Nothing had been moved on her desk. The swanky computer was exactly where it always stood, still switched off. The filing cabinet and the desk drawers remained closed. Even her swag-bag sat on the top of the desk, just as Pete had found it.

Bash! A groan! And then a sharp kick delivered in what seemed like anger!

Someone was in the back of the boathouse! Vera started running, but as she bumped into the strut of the door, her thumb pressed down the call button of her mobile.

Just as she came face to face with Olivia, a voice asked 'Emergency Services. Which service do you require?'

Vera came to a halt, gobsmacked.

'Hello, caller. Which service do you require?'

Vera looked at the mobile in confusion. 'Caller? Hello? Do you have an emergency?'

'Why are you trying to break into the wine fridge?' Vera asked Olivia, bemused.

'Hello, caller. Is this an emergency? Which service do you require?'

'Where do you keep the chocolate?' asked Olivia.

'Hello, caller!' shouted the person on the other end of the mobile.

Vera came to her senses and spoke back into the phone. 'Oh, sorry, I'm so sorry. I thought I'd got an intruder and I called you before I checked, but it's only my friend, and I don't need you.'

'Are you sure, caller?' asked the emergency controller calmly.

'Yes. Thank you. I am very sorry. I can handle it from here. Just a misunderstanding. I thought it was an intruder, but it's only my friend. I don't need anyone, thank you.' She ended the call. 'The chocolate's not in there,' Vera told Olivia and pointed at the kitchen cupboard. 'I keep it in there.'

Olivia's eyes followed where Vera was pointing, but if she actually saw anything, Vera could not tell. It was as if she was in a trance. Her movements were extremely slow. Her face showed no emotion. Physically, she stood beside Vera, but her spirit appeared to be somewhere far away.

'Would you like some chocolate?' Vera asked gently and went and got the tin from the cupboard. She took off the lid and proffered it to Olivia, who took out a small bar and looked at it blankly. She looked at it as if she didn't know how to unwrap it, so Vera took it back from her and tore the paper away from the end, and then gave it back to her.

Olivia bit off a tiny bite and chewed it slowly. A smile spread across her face, and then, pushing the rest of the bar whole into her mouth, she reached over towards the tin for more. Vera removed the paper from another and handed it to her. Olivia tried to ram it in her mouth even before the previous mouthful was finished. 'Slow down,' said Vera, pulling her hand away. 'It's not going anywhere.' Drink or drugs? She's on something, she pondered.

Olivia's white trousers were stained with grass

marks. She was unusually dishevelled and, what on earth was that brown stripe down her forehead and her nose? It looked like she'd taken eyebrow pencil and scoured a long straight line vertically instead of horizontally.

'Come through and sit down,' urged Vera anxiously, 'then I'll make us both a nice cup of tea.'

Olivia allowed herself to be led back towards the settee. She sat chewing the rest of the chocolate bar, but now more slowly. Vera felt confident enough to go back into the kitchen and switch on the kettle, although she still made sure she could watch over Olivia by leaning against the strut of the doorway as she waited for it to come to the boil.

'River,' muttered Olivia, staring out of the open door.

'What about it?' asked Vera.

'Love the river,' muttered Olivia. Tucking her long legs up beneath her, she lowered her head and started humming a tune Vera didn't recognise. Behind her, the kettle switched itself off. Vera quickly poured boiling water over tea bags and fetched milk from the wine fridge. A paperclip hung out of one of the locks. Had Olivia been trying to force the lock, even though she didn't need to? The wine fridge was never locked. Vera checked her across the room. Olivia still lay in the same position. The tune she hummed was still the same.

'Drink this,' Vera commanded, offering Olivia the

mug of hot tea. When Olivia ignored it, Vera put it on the low table between them and pushed it towards her. Olivia shivered as if someone had walked over her grave. Her eyes sparked, and then just as quickly closed. She stopped humming and went still.

Vera sat watching her, quietly sipping her tea. She'd never seen Olivia like this before, but she had seen other people suffer mental illness. There had been a friend of her grandmother's who would walk into the house unbidden, take the seat by the open fire and rock gently until whatever was afflicting her mind passed. She'd then get up again, walk out and nothing would ever be said. When Vera asked why she did it, her grandmother simply said, 'She's in the grip', but never explained what 'in the grip' actually meant. Vera asked Rosie, but all Rosie was prepared to say was that the woman 'was crying on the inside but the tears won't come out'.

In Vera's opinion, this was precisely what Olivia was doing now. Normally so vibrant and full of fun, it was horrible to see her suffering the exact opposite. Vera watched over her and waited, churning over what to do for the best. She was pretty certain that Olivia was suffering an episode, but she didn't think she was ill enough to call an ambulance, though she might need a doctor. On a Saturday night, how on earth was Vera going to get anyone to come out to see her? She certainly didn't want to tackle A&E,

particularly if Olivia had simply forgotten to take her medications. She was unusually quiet, but she was breathing and moving regularly. There appeared to be no other sign of any kind of pain. Although Angelina and Pete were out somewhere special, she assumed they would be back some time this evening. They would know what to do. She decided to watch over Olivia until she could get in touch with them.

Vera found her mobile and composed a text message to Angelina: **No rush. Finish your meal but Olivia acting odd. We're in the Boat House. PS Pete, Sorry I knocked the side gate over.**

Had she said too much? Probably. Would they feel they had to rush back? Again, most probably. Would they hope that she and Olivia were talking? Again, probably. They were all friends. Would they guess what was happening? She simply did not know how often Olivia had these episodes and what brought them on. Vera had never seen them before, and, in truth, she wasn't certain what form they normally took. It was just that since Angelina had told her Olivia was bi-polar, and to Vera's eyes this looked like it could very well be one of the depression episodes, she'd looked at Olivia through different eyes. This was not a new thing. Angelina would know what to do. Vera would stay with Olivia until they got home.

Which is why Vera decided to send the text and

why Angelina and Pete decided they would forgo the desert course of their meal and make their way home early.

'Has she eaten?' Angelina whispered as she crept into the boathouse.

'Chocolate,' Vera told her, 'but she hasn't moved at all for the last hour.'

Angelina inspected the line on her sister's forehead and nose. 'What's this?' she asked, but neither Vera nor Pete knew. Angelina spat on a tissue and rubbed at it, then stroked Olivia's red curls back away from her face. They were damp and stuck to her forehead. 'Did she say what she'd been doing?' asked Angelina, checking out the brightly coloured trainers she incongruously wore with her white trousers and frowning.

'She only asked for chocolate, then said she loved the river. She's been motionless since I texted you.'

'Same as usual?' asked Pete, closing the door behind him.

Olivia heard the click of the door and screamed 'No!' It shook Vera terribly, but Angelina and Pete seemed unperturbed.

'Leave it open,' Angelina said. 'She has to be able to hear the river flowing.' She removed Olivia's trainers. Vera hadn't noticed it before, but Olivia's calves were tensed and the soles of her feet terribly sore. 'Looks like she's been overdoing the exercise again,' said Angelina. 'That's why she needed chocolate. At least she's taken some calories on board, but it doesn't look as if you could get her to drink.' She pointed to the mug of cold tea.

Vera shook her head. She was starting to feel like an intruder. This was such a personal thing for the family to have to deal with. 'I didn't know whether to call a doctor or not. Or whether she had any specific medication she needed to take,' she said, full of apology for ruining their night out.

'It's too late for that,' Angelina said. 'She's probably gone through her manic phase, and now she has the melancholy. It'll pass, but while she's like this she needs to be by the river. If she can hear it, it soothes her. She doesn't have too many of these patches any more. The latest meds seem to have worked.'

'Did something trigger it?' asked Vera.

'We never actually know!' replied Angelina. 'And she can never remember after the event.' She ran a hand through her hair. 'Vera, would you mind not mentioning this to anyone? As soon as we can, we'll get her indoors and into bed, but she hates anyone else to know.'

Vera understood completely. This was one thing that need never be gossiped about.

'I moved that gate, by the way,' said Pete. He came up and put his arms around Vera. She leant in against his warmth, suddenly needing all his strength. She was exhausted. 'I'll find something else to go in there tomorrow. Can you get yourself home?'

Chapter Thirty
Success Number One

Emily stood up to leave and, like a gentleman, Simon stepped back and held out his arm like a peacock protecting his peahen so that she could walk before him. 'We've arranged to meet again tomorrow,' Simon said. 'Do we have to keep you informed when we meet?'

Vera shook her head, smiling. 'I'll give you both a ring in a couple of weeks. Or you can ring me before if either of you want me to do anything more for you. You have my number.'

Emily appeared to be in raptures. She was googly-eyed and giddy like a child presented with a sweet treat she never expected. Simon had grown in stature. He looked so satisfied with himself Vera nearly giggled. 'Thank you very much. Do we owe you any more?' he asked.

Vera assured him their fee more than adequately covered this introduction. She said no more about what she would charge if this meeting didn't play out and they came back hoping for other introductions. Then a monthly retainer would come into force, but this wasn't the time to mention failure. She had a strong feeling Simon and Emily would not be remaining on the books for much longer. To her eyes, they looked like a couple made in heaven, but who knew? The rest was up to them. They had to do all the hard work of falling in love, deciding what they wanted, and then living the dream. Vera wasn't going to do it for them. She was only the woman who made the introductions.

She gave them time to find their way out of the garden, then walked out and stood on the landing stage overlooking the river. The sun was hot on her face. The weather had taken a turn for the better and long summer days were being predicted. It had even been so warm this morning she'd chosen to wear a strappy summer dress and bare her arms and legs. A slight breeze off the water swirled the soft material around her thighs. She crossed her arms, leant back, turned her face to the sun and gloried in it.

In the distance she listened to the regular swoosh of sculls skimming through the water. People were in training for the regatta. Earlier that morning she'd watched a four-man boat speed past looking as if they were flying over the water, their oars making a louder splash. She was never sure, but did oars go deeper in the water than sculls and that was what made the difference in the sound? She'd have to ask Christy. He used to row before he got seriously into motorbikes. She wished he'd return to rowing, but he'd laughed at her, telling her he was far too overweight and unfit to consider trying again. To her eye, he didn't have a spare ounce of flesh on him, though he was very broad.

Fliss had told her Steve had taken up rowing. He'd had a few lessons and Fliss watched him whenever she could from a discreet distance so that she wouldn't put him off. 'He's not that good yet,' she confided in her mother, then added loyally, 'but he's very enthusiastic.' Fliss and Steve! Steve and Fliss! Either way it rolled off the tongue so easily now it was hard to remember that their relationship was still only in its infancy, but so far Vera had not been told that there were any differences which would turn into problems which could part them. This relationship was already looking as if it was here to stay and she relished watching her daughter finally grow as a woman. She'd even grown her fringe out and was considering trying contact lenses. On the arm of a man she'd walked out of her dark place of shyness into the sunshine and it suited her.

How long ago was it that Vera had hit her own dark place? She couldn't quite put a number of days or months to it, but one thing she did know, light was starting to slip back in to her life, too. She didn't want to go to that dark place ever again, not now she'd arrived where she was today. She was grateful she had a good life. Her children were happy. Her grandchildren were growing up fast. Sunday lunch had been a delight, even if Annie and Christy had got seriously stressed about the mess the children left. That was the beauty of having grandchildren, she decided. It wasn't that you could give them back to their parents again once you were feeling tired or when they were fractious. It was the ease with which you dealt with them because you'd seen it all before and knew you would see it all again. Life went on in pretty much the same way for most families.

So, on this lovely summer day, standing in the warmth of the sunshine, proud that she had introduced another young couple to each other, Vera thanked God for all her blessings. The only thing that was missing was her beloved Richard. That pain would never go away, but even she would admit it was finally easing to a more acceptable level. Did she want another man in her life? She was certainly fed up with flying solo, but she didn't actually need a man. Life was running smoothly enough. She was happy enough, too. She could get most things done, and if she couldn't do things herself, there were enough people she could ask to help. Could she ask for more? Not when she had her health, enough money and people who loved her and who she loved, she decided.

Health! Health was so important. Her mind

wandered back to Olivia and the current trials she was facing. She knew Angelina and Pete had taken her back into their home, but all Vera had been told was that it was because being near the river soothed Olivia. Its steady and constant flow was balm to her soul.

As she stood on the landing stage, she felt like weeping for Olivia, not heart-wrenching tears, but the gentle damask rose dew of the angels, because surely to help her through this, Olivia needed the help of angels. Vera prayed and hoped it would do good.

She was still deep in thought, when without warning an enormous spray of cold river water brought her swiftly out of her meditation. She jumped back drenched, but not fast enough before another great spray had hit her.

'Benji! Stop that! Oh God, sorry!' a man shouted as an enormous and very wet dog swam up to the landing stage, beating the water madly with his shaggy tail. He was trying to heave himself out of the water to greet her.

'Stay! Stay!' She knelt down, urging Benji to stop struggling. 'You're going to hurt yourself. Stay in the water,' she said, but speaking to him only encouraged the dog more. He was frantic to get out to see her.

'Bad boy, Benji!' Further out, the man dipped his head and changed from breaststroke to crawl to catch up with his dog. He was a fast and extremely strong swimmer. He powered in towards the landing stage.

By now Vera was so wet, getting wetter really didn't matter. She leant over the edge, and caught Benji by the collar. Doing the doggy-paddle, the dog licked every bit of make-up off her face, still splashing her with copious amounts of water from his wagging tail.

'I'm so sorry,' said the man raising his face out of the water so close to hers she pulled back. 'Look at you. You're wet through to the skin!'

For a moment, Vera panicked that the water had made the thin material of her dress transparent, but peeking down, although it clung to her in revealing folds that contoured her body, she was relatively decent.

'He's very pleased to see you,' said the man, treading water. 'Does my dog know you?'

'We have met,' admitted Vera. 'A little while ago. I think he likes me.'

They both laughed. Benji, open-mouthed and panting, looked as if he was laughing, too. His tail beat the water with a regular thump, spraying them both. 'I'm Ambrose,' said the man. 'And I know you're Vera.'

So, Benji belonged to Ambrose, which meant Ambrose would have been the man she saw bringing the dog out from the house the other night.

Vera half-smiled. Ambrose. So he was real, not a figment of Olivia's imagination. And here he was in the flesh. Perhaps there was a little too much flesh on show, but it was such nice flesh, just like the smile on the nice face was a nice smile and the twinkling eyes – well, they just flashed with amusement and it made her excited to see that amusement.

'I don't know whether to invite you out, or for me to jump right in,' Vera heard herself saying. Oh no! Could that have come out any more cheesily!

His eyes flashed even more brightly. Ambrose swept his wet fringe back over his head. There was a little bald tonsure at the back. Silver flecked the dark hair around the temples. He was long and lean with muscles in all the right places. He trod water more slowly than Benji doggy-paddled. Benji was getting tired and his head kept dipping back into the water so that each time he came up, he had to shake himself to be able to see through his mane of wet fur.

'He can only get out on the bank that runs down from my garden,' Ambrose said. 'He can't manage this landing stage unless we lift him. Do you think we could manage it between us?'

Vera looked at the size of the dog and baulked. 'Won't he drown you?' she asked.

'Not with you there on hand in case he does. You can swim, can't you?'

Vera could swim. She was a strong swimmer, but she didn't really fancy having to leap in, rescue

Ambrose and manage a hyperactive dog all at the same time, but neither did she want to miss the opportunity of talking more to this handsome man. 'You push and I'll pull,' she decided eventually. 'It won't hurt him, will it?'

It didn't, though once encouraged, Benji fought frantically to get himself out. Ambrose gathered his back legs and shoved him high enough so that the dog could get his front paws on the landing stage. Vera grabbed Benji under his elbows and waited for the next big shove from Ambrose. Benji seemed to understand what was being asked of him. As Ambrose pushed and Vera pulled he scrambled until he got his back legs on the wood of the landing stage and clawed his way up, but not before he had used Ambrose's head as a stepping stone. Ambrose went back under the water and came up coughing and spluttering.

'Are you all right?' asked Vera anxiously. Ambrose held up an arm for Vera to help him, and with a massive heave hauled himself out of the river, bringing enough water with him that Vera was now completely sodden through. Benji pelted off to roll his wet fur on the lawn, wriggling backwards and forwards on his back. Beside her, Ambrose shook his hair equally vigorously, gave her another faceful of water, then swept it back from his forehead again without apparently noticing.

He wiped his wet hand on his wet swimming

trunks, and offered it for her to shake. 'Lovely to finally meet you properly,' he said when she accepted it. 'I didn't get a chance to say much to you at Olivia's dinner party. You were rather the worse for wear.'

Chapter Thirty-One
Fancy A Glass Of Wine?

It was so pleasant sitting on the edge of the landing stage, feet dangling in the water, all inhibitions forgotten by both being as wet as the other. 'I'm going to dry out quicker than you,' Ambrose laughed. 'Skin's waterproof and warmed from the inside.'

'I blame Benji!' said Vera.

'So do I. Frequently!' said Ambrose. 'He's always getting me into deep trouble.'

It flashed through Vera's mind that he could manage that all by himself. She checked out the very expensive waterproofed watch and the heavy gold signet ring on his little finger. 'It's been such a good day,' she said and, when he asked, simply told him that something she had been working on looked as if it was going finally in the right direction. She was sure he must know all about The Normal Dating Agency, but she didn't want him to think she might be touting for business.

'Looks like we're heading for a lovely long patch

of summer weather,' Ambrose said, also wanting to keep things upbeat. The last thing he wanted was for her to get embarrassed and scurry away. He checked her over and found her exceptionally pretty with her damp curls and not a scrap of make-up on her face. The figure wasn't bad either inside that wet dress, even better than when he'd helped get her upstairs to bed at Olivia's dinner party and they'd tried to get her undressed. He blushed now at the thought of the hash they made of it and wondered how much of that evening she remembered. Either she was a damned good actress choosing to make no mention of it, or she really didn't recall it at all, sincerely hoping it was the latter because none of them came out of that story with much glory.

He'd taken so much care that evening that she wouldn't find out exactly who he was. He desperately needed a night off from the depression of the breakdown of his marriage. When they were introduced in a group, he hoped the name his close family called him would be enough to put her off the scent. He never used Ambrose in business, where he was known only by his first two initials. Most people thought his name was Ajay, which he also answered to, so he definitely did not want her to know that he had another persona as AJ Hidrio, CEO and major shareholder of Montaise Holdings, because then she would have known that it was his company that had bought Number Forty.

Negotiations between his property-holding company and her solicitor over its purchase had been at stalemate. She was holding out for the asking price. His company wanted to knock the cost down substantially. Although a good purchase, it could have been easily replaced with other, more lucrative deals. Then, when his wife, Amanda, had dropped her bombshell, thinking it would be good to get out of London and that he might take on one of the apartments in the block for himself while he decided what he was going to do after his marriage failed, he'd taken the train down to see Number Forty; but then he'd seen River House and decided to buy that instead on a whim.

On the train back up to London he'd thought about the two purchases being in such close proximity. At first his inclination had been to pull out of the Number Forty deal completely. The margin of profitability was very slim, but then it occurred to him that if he was going to live in the town, he wouldn't want it getting around that he'd been a time-waster with a local widow. Perhaps she needed every penny she could get with her husband dying so young. Then there was the added complication that the daughter who had inherited River House was represented by a solicitor called Rosser, and Ambrose remembered that was the man who was also representing Vera Father. It was all a bit too close for comfort to be a success.

So, there was no decision to be made. If he wanted River House, then he would also have to buy Number Forty, even though the profit on it would be less than he liked. He needed to find a new home quickly and he had loved River House from the minute he first saw it. He could see himself living there very happily, well removed from the acrimony of his divorce. This town would be a nice place to settle. He could see himself as part of the local community; but to do that successfully he could hardly offend one of the stalwarts of the area by being hard-nosed over money. It was expedient that he back down gracefully and pay the full asking price for Number Forty. After all, it was only money.

When Vera walked into Olivia's dinner party, and he heard her name, he knew he'd made the right decision. The Vera who walked in was charming, and highly attractive. They'd never yet met in person. So far she had only met with one of the company's younger directors so there was no chance she would recognise him, but he still didn't want her to guess who he was. Not tonight. It would only spoil what looked like turning into a fun evening, and after the torrid time he'd just been through, he certainly needed some fun in his life. He'd tried to keep out of her way, but as the evening wore on, they'd all got so drunk and he found he couldn't take his eyes off her. He'd let his guard down and then there had been that stupid incident where he'd let his attraction for her take over.

At first, it had just been a matter of turning his back whenever Vera was near. Then he'd made sure he sat on her blind side at the table. Debbie was a dull girl to share dinner with, but she provided good cover until the teasing between Andrew, Erich and Vera became so hilarious, Ambrose couldn't help but want to be part of the fun. When Vera had gone beneath the table, for some reason he'd moved to the opposite side of the table. He'd already kicked off his own shoes. Andrew and Erich were obviously together as a couple and Vera was looking so damned attractive.

When her stockinged foot touched his a tsunami of desire had engulfed him.

Suddenly the evening had turned for the better. His feet felt like dancing! Had she done it deliberately? Only one way to find out, his sex drive told him. A little footsie under the table, and when she'd giggled in that sexy way she had that sounded like a big cat purring, the chase was on. It was his foot that had shot up the inside of her leg and when she'd come up from playing with it, accusing Erich and then waggling his toes, he'd been captivated.

As he sat beside her on the landing stage staring out of the water, his stomach twisted like a tumble dryer on high speed remembering it all again. How he wished those toes she waggled had been his! He'd waited for a chance to come in for the kill, but then there had been that deep snort and guffaw and the table cloth had gone flying when she'd gone back under the table again. And then she'd knocked herself out.

Thoughts of helping Olivia, Erich and Andrew carry her upstairs when she was lolling and totally blitzed came vividly back to mind. It had been such a struggle trying to keep her upright between them, carrying her with her arms over their shoulders. Her feet had dragged and her legs kept twisting. They were all so very drunk. Ambrose walked behind, ostensibly to catch her if she fell backwards, but actually admiring her bum, until Andrew and Erich staggered and fell to their knees on the stairs, dropping her. Ambrose caught her and swept her into his arms, carrying her the rest of the way. 'Where?' he'd asked Olivia and she'd pointed to a spare bedroom. He could take it from here, he'd said.

But by the time he dropped her on the bed, he was shattered. He bent over, trying to catch his breath, his hands clutching his own thighs. Olivia was already attempting to undress her. Andrew and Erich were arguing that they should just leave her there in her clothes, but Olivia had been adamant. 'She bought those clothes from us at Claremont's,' she said. 'That satin skirt is new season and she paid full whack for it. And she'll catch her nails in that lace if we don't get her top off. Vera takes care of her clothes. She'll be so upset if we don't undress her.'

No one seemed to be taking any notice that Vera

had knocked herself out. Ambrose remembered watching and wishing the others would just go away and leave him alone with her as Andrew and Erich rolled her on her back and sat her up, so Olivia could drag off the lacy top. Then the movement had been reversed to get off the skirt. They'd given up at bra, pants and tights, but not before Ambrose had had a good look and admiring what he was going to have to leave alone in bed that night.

A shiver went down his spine as his carnal memories had an instant effect on him. Twenty-three years married and that night drink had made him as young and reckless as a student! Suddenly, he was conscious all he wore were very damp swimming trunks concealing not very much at all. He didn't want to make the same mistake today. He most certainly did not wish to get carried away and act without decorum. He crossed his legs.

'Are you cold?' asked Vera, bringing him back from his memories.

'Benji and I had better get back in that water and swim home,' he said, avoiding her eyes.

'Or I could fetch the towels I keep in the boat house. Fancy a glass of wine to warm you up?' she asked casually, and his stomach did another cartwheel.

When he told her that would be very nice, she squelched back to the boathouse. Ambrose watched her as she walked away, admiring her greatly.

Inside the boat house, the spare handtowels were kept in a cupboard in the toilet. Vera's dress was starting to dry out, but her underwear was sopping. Quickly, she stripped everything off and dried herself as best she could on the hand towel. She dragged a hairbrush through her curls before trying to put on her pants. They were so wet, she couldn't force herself to. Protecting some of her modesty by holding the towel across her front, she tiptoed through to the kitchen and put her pants in the microwave. Her bra was underwired, so that that couldn't go in, too, but at least she could dry out her knickers. She put them on high for two minutes and threw her bra into a carrier bag to go home, deciding she could go braless.

She chose the best of a cheap selection from the wine fridge, found two wine glasses and set them on the table. She stood naked as she used the tiny towel to wring out as much moisture as she could from her dress, then put the dress back on. It was slightly better and didn't reveal too much. The warmth of the day and the heat from her body would soon start drying it out. When she put her dry pants back on they were deliciously warm from the microwave blasting.

With the other towel draped over her arm like a waiter's, she carried the bottle of wine and glasses out to where Benji and master remained sitting side by side on the landing stage gazing out over the river, the dog nestled under his master's arm. Vera's stomach did a little lurch. She wished she was the one under that arm instead of the dog.

Neither moved until she laid down the wine and glasses and handed Ambrose the towel. Benji dropped down between them and rested his chin on his paws as if he was going to drift off to sleep. He smelt of the riverbank. Blades of grass were tangled in with his matted fur. 'It's going to be a nightmare getting his brush through that,' said Ambrose, drying himself quickly with the towel then putting it around his shoulders.

'Are you sure you aren't getting cold?' asked Vera.

'No,' he lied. 'Come and sit this side to get away from the smell of Benji.' She poured their wine and did as she was bidden, shivering a little as she lowered herself down.

'You're cold,' he said, offering her the towel. It already smelled of him, a toxic mix of the river, his bodily warmth and something else. Vera couldn't quite put her finger on it. Plastic? Chemical, yes, but plastic, no. She sniffed again. Rubber. Oh lor! The smell wasn't from Ambrose. It was coming from her. Dammit! She'd shrivelled the elastic in her knickers in the microwave! No wonder they'd felt so warm!

She started laughing at herself. 'What is it?' he asked, frowning.

'Nothing,' she replied hearing her own high pitch

of a giggle and was over-delighted when he turned and gave her his lazy smile, never taking his eyes off her.

She'd better be very, very careful when she next stood up, or her pants were going to fall down, and how would that look? A wiggly worm of warmth shot straight through the centre of Vera's core at the sumptuous thought.

Ambrose sensed it. Without preamble, he leaned in very, very slowly towards her. Eye contact was only broken as his lips first brushed hers, so when her own parted slightly encouraging him to kiss her more, his heart soared and he kissed her passionately.

Chapter Thirty-Two
Out Of The Window

Since daybreak, from her chair by the window, Olivia had been watching the coots on the other side of the riverbank. A pair were active going in and out of the reeds to their nest. They had very young chicks to feed and hadn't yet brought the chicks out. Appointing herself their sentry, Olivia felt an overpowering urge to keep watch so that nothing bad would happen to the chicks while the parents were out on the water getting more food.

When she was little, she had argued with Angelina over the coots. Angelina was adamant that the chicks should be called babies. You can't call them babies,' said Olivia. 'Only mummies have babies.'

'Ducklings, then,' Angelina teased.

'They're not ducks. They're coots.'

'Why not? Mares have foals. Cows have calves. Sheep have lambs. Coots could have babies called little … cootlings,' concluded Angelina, very proud of herself for thinking of it.

'No, they couldn't,' Olivia had protested, red in the face with fury. 'That's a made-up word,' and had been devastated when, when she next looked over, one of the infant coots had disappeared, presumably taken by a predator. She felt it was all her fault that she had refused to allow it to be called a cootling and had been arguing over the name while it was killed. Today, in her current state of mind, it was more than ever important to her that she never took her eyes off the young family of water birds living on the opposite bank so that nothing terrible could happen again. She sat in the cotton pyjamas Angelina had brought up from the shop, haggard and unwashed. For days now she had eaten or drunk little apart from water from the carafe Angelina refilled each time she came in to check on her.

'If you aren't going to eat, then at least drink for me. I shall only get more worried,' Angelina ordered, judiciously leaving bars of chocolate alongside the carafe. Every day, one of them disappeared, so at least Olivia was getting some sustenance, though it was hardly enough. 'She is taking her pills, though,' she told Pete when he asked. 'But if this episode goes on much longer, I'm going to have to call in the doctor. What if they think she needs to go into hospital again?'

'We'll cross that bridge when we get to it,' said

Pete. 'Are you sure you can run the shop and look after her at the same time?'

'It's not as if she's in the shop most of the time anyway, is she?' said Angelina without rancour. 'She's always out somewhere.' Olivia was too fragile mentally to push into anything. She had to be handled with kid gloves. When she was in the mood to work, her workload was prodigious, but when she wanted to play, she would walk out and leave Angelina to handle everything. She had to be allowed to go her own way. Angelina had learned to be patient to protect her and, of late, she was relieved this way of handling her had paid off. Olivia had had a long run of being well. This was the first spell for a very long time.

This episode, though, was a bad one. It had already lasted many days, days in which Olivia had barely moved out of the bed, let alone out of the room. She visited the bathroom, but only to use the lavatory and to clean her teeth. She then dragged herself back upstairs to the bedroom and immediately got back into bed. If she wasn't asleep, she would lie looking at the ceiling, so, that morning, when Angelina found her sitting on the chair, her hopes had been raised. Even sitting, although barely moving from the chair, was an improvement. Angelina had brought up cereal and tea as well as chocolate for breakfast, but only the chocolate had been eaten.

Olivia had sat watching the other side of the riverbank most of the day. It was only when she heard 'Benji! Stop that!' that her eyes looked away from the coots. Ambrose! She heaved herself out of the chair grasping the windowsill for support. She sensed something about Ambrose was important but, mixed in with the other muddle of irrational thoughts fogging her brain, she couldn't remember exactly what. At first she thought his shout had come from the garden of River House, so she cagily leant to look out of the window to call to him, but when she saw the back view of Vera on the landing stage she immediately pulled back inside. She had an equally strong feeling that she must avoid Vera at all costs, but again, she didn't know why. Her mind whirled faster in the maelstrom she was suffering. She tucked herself behind the curtain, shielding her face, clinging to it for support, peeking out. Whenever her brain was like this, the only thing she could do to ease it was to keep completely still. Eventually, the tornado would stop turning and everything would flutter down back into place.

It was like this, clinging on so she wasn't swept away, peeking out on the world, that Olivia watched Vera and Ambrose get Benji out of the water. She watched Vera go to the boathouse and leave Ambrose dangling his feet in the water. She saw Vera come back bringing wine and glasses and sit down beside him. She watched their first touch of lips which turned into a passionate clinch, and by the time they helped each other up, clinging together, kissing as they walked over to the boathouse leaving Benji to sleep on the grass, something had started to still in Olivia.

The tornado was subsiding. The dust in her mind started settling.

Olivia let go of the curtains, drew them, and crawled into her bed and, for the first time in many days, she fell into a restful and deep sleep.

Chapter Thirty-Three
Before And After

Vera did try to tell Ambrose people could see in through the windows, but his kisses drowned out her protests. In their haste, they even left the boathouse door open, so anyone who wandered out of the conservatory doors of Claremont's into the garden, or any of the people in the boats on the river might just have been able to see in, but he didn't care.

'Benji will bark and warn us,' he said, dragging her dress over her head and nuzzling her breast. Her pants promptly fell down round her knees, unsupported by their melted elastic. 'Why, Mrs Father!' he teased and knelt down to nestle a kiss on her bush as she stepped out of one leg and then raised the other to waggle the pants from around her ankle.

He finished the job for her, slipping the pants over her foot and throwing them away with a flourish. His other arm remained firmly around her waist supporting her ankle in the air. 'Stay!' he commanded huskily, and for a moment she thought he was talking to the dog, though Benji was nowhere to be seen. Excitement surged. She did as she was bidden and froze with one leg suspended in mid-air. When he gently transferred his hand around the back of her knee, and kissed tender little kisses up her thigh, urging her leg over his shoulder, she braced herself for what was to come. His tongue rapidly brought her to a height of pleasure faster than she thought possible. The leg carrying her weight buckled as she climaxed, but as she toppled, he caught and balanced her over one shoulder, then gently twisted and laid her down.

'You are so very, very beautiful,' he muttered as he parted her legs and regarded her. Suddenly she felt shy, aching to cover her nakedness as this was far too intimate, but his eyes willed her not to move a muscle as he slipped off his swimming trunks and knelt in between her knees. Instinctively, her legs wound up and around him, and he rocked back on his haunches, holding them together tightly behind his back.

He was so aroused she wondered if she would ever be able to accommodate him. This was even more impressive than in her dreams. She snaked up and put her arms around his neck, too shy suddenly to look at his manhood for too long. Bringing his mouth over hers, she hung on as if she was never going to let him go. His tongue explored her mouth. Hers responded even more urgently as she fell back, letting him push himself fully inside her.

Slowly they rocked together, neither wanting this to be over too quickly. They pulled back and smiled agreement that they would take their time. As they rocked, they sneaked kisses on to each other's bodies. She nipped his neck and he sucked her nipple in retaliation. Gently, his body slid full length over hers as he nuzzled her neck, still inside her. She rolled him over, closing her muscles to tightly grip him inside as they moved. They rested, stroked each other, stared into each other's eyes, and when his rhythm resumed, she kept pace with him, her nipples bouncing against his upheld palms, until they reached a point where he rolled her back on to her back, and within a couple more rapid movements they were satisfied.

Afterwards, Vera lay in Ambrose's arms, her head on his chest, half-wondering why she didn't feel guilty. She'd always imagined she would and that she would feel disloyal to Richard, but there was none of that now. All she felt was completely sated. Every nerve in her body told her it was the most wonderful feeling.

She'd never discussed it with anyone, not even Olivia when they'd had their heart-to-heart, but since she lost Richard, she'd felt increasingly angry that he had left her alone just when their sex life was still active and terribly pleasant. It was like a penance that she was to be denied that shared intimacy for the remainder of her life. She missed making love with Richard so badly that sometimes it overwhelmed her and she became irrational. Rosie, her mother, had told her to find another man to have sex with, but Vera had never been disloyal to Richard and finding another man just for sex seemed tragic. She didn't want to be one of those women who trawled the pubs, clubs and internet looking for any man. It seemed just too seedy and far too unromantic.

She'd dreamed that, if she was lucky enough to meet someone, a full relationship would develop through mutual attraction, just as it had this afternoon with Ambrose.

She pulled herself upright and looked at him. He was snoozing, half between sleep and totally aware of her closeness. Not wanting her to leave the bubble of togetherness they had created together, he stroked the back of her hair and encouraged her to put her head back down on his chest. 'Lovely, absolutely lovely,' he mumbled and her heart soared with elation.

They lay entwined until Benji crept in and flopped down at their feet with a massive sigh. Ambrose was asleep now. Vera had dozed a little, but woke when she heard the dog padding in. 'Ambrose?' she said, gently nudging him.

'Wha'?' he said, shaking his head to wake up fully.

'Have you fed Benji today?'

He was awake instantly. 'Bugger. I'd forgotten all about him.' The dog clambered to his feet and came round to lick his master's face. Parted, Vera suddenly felt terribly self-conscious and felt around for her dress, one arm firmly across her breasts.

'I think I've already seen them in all their magnificence today,' teased Ambrose, easing her arm away so he could suck one of her nipples.

Benji tried to lick one, too. She shot away. Ambrose let out a deep guffaw. 'I don't know who loves you the most. Me, or my dog!'

Woah! Too much, too soon. Most definitely! Vera slipped her dress over her head and tried to get up. She was as stiff as a bone from making love on a hard concrete floor. Ambrose, however, followed her up without any bother. He was incredibly fit for a man of his age, and then it hit her. What age would he be exactly? Absolutely naked, nothing was hidden. His skin could have been a little less saggy, particularly on his long thin hands and extremely large feet. No wonder he's such a good swimmer with feet like those, she marvelled.

His posture suggested a man who sat at a desk for long hours. His shoulders were slightly rounded and his back not as straight as it could be. Then there was the grey hair at the temples and bald tonsure on the top of his head. She would have to wait to see whether he wore spectacles, but that had nothing to do with age, she reasoned.

Vera guessed that he might be younger than her, and that made her even shyer. Her hair was fully grey. She'd had two children and her flabby belly displayed that. Her boobs hung lower than they used to. Nowadays her skin was a nightmare, terribly dry and needed constant moisturiser.

What on earth had he even seen in her? It must have been a spur of the moment thing, and that bothered her. This was going to make things awkward. She started to feel terribly uneasy. 'I must be getting home,' she said, checking the time on her mobile.

'I was hoping you might join me for dinner,' he said, slipping his swimming trunks back on.

'That would be lovely, but how are you going to get home?' she added anxiously. 'You're not wearing many clothes.'

'I'll have to walk around,' he said calmly.

'Through the High Street on a Saturday night! And what about Benji?'

'He'll walk beside me.'

'It's Saturday evening. Town will be heaving and you're planning to walk out into the High Street like that, with no shoes on! It'll be all over the county in ten minutes. And what if anyone's seen us? What are my children going to think?'

Ambrose took her hand, guessing it might only enhance his reputation, making him seem suave and devil-may-care, but for Vera, it would be a disaster. She was a pillar of the community. She ran a dating agency now. She'd been a property developer before. Her family ran businesses in town. Both of her children worked here.

'If I swam home, could you walk Benji round to the house?' he asked. 'I don't want to ask him to go back into that water again today.'

Relief surged through Vera that he understood her predicament. 'Would he walk for me off the lead through a crowd of people?'

'You haven't got any string here, or anything you could use as a lead?'

Vera looked around, mentally assessing what was in the boathouse. The Normal Dating Agency had no use for string. She shook her head. 'What about the towels? Could we tie those together?' She held up the small pieces of cloth. Even tied together they would be so short Benji would choke if he pulled, which he was likely to do. He was a big dog and Vera doubted she would be able to hold him if he wanted to chase anything. 'What am I going to look like anyway?' she said holding out her arms in her still damp dress. Her pants wouldn't stay up and her bra was in a carrier bag waiting to go home. After their passion, even her curls had gone haywire.

Ambrose bit his lip, trying to stop himself from

laughing. The way she looked would definitely cause massive speculation if anyone who knew her saw her. She'd have to say she'd fallen in the river, and then they'd have something even better to gossip about. 'Where's your car?' he asked eventually.

'In Olivia's space, just outside the garden gate,' she answered brightening as a solution came to her mind.

'Where is she anyway?' he asked, suddenly aware he hadn't seen her since the dispassionate kiss.

Vera blanched. Should she tell the truth? No. It was nobody's business other than Olivia's and what would Ambrose think if he knew she was holed up in the bedroom overlooking the boathouse at the top of Claremont's?

'Having a break visiting friends,' she lied hastily, bending to pick up all her bags so he couldn't see her face. 'What if I put Benji in my car and drive him round to you? You could swim home then and we wouldn't be seen together.'

'The gates are locked to the High Street. I always keep them locked on busy days. You'd have to wait for me to swim round, and then there be the same risk someone would see you. How did Benji know you so well anyway?'

The dog perked up hearing his name. His chocolate-brown eyes beneath his puffball eyebrows stared first at Ambrose, then Vera, waiting for clues as to what they wanted him to do. Vera reached out and stroked him. He nuzzled her hand for more. 'He's been to my house, haven't you, Benji? Angelina brought him that day she was looking after him for you.'

They looked at each other, each thinking exactly the same thing at the same time and smiled. 'What if you take Benji straight home with you now in the car, I pick up his food for him and fish and chips for us, and we all have dinner at your house?'

'Perfect,' said Vera, high-fiving the palm he held out. Even the dog thought it was a brilliant idea. He jumped up, resting his front paws on Ambrose's shoulders, and woofed.

'Just one little thing,' said Ambrose as he walked out and told Benji to go with Vera. 'Benji knows where you live, but I don't.'

Chapter Thirty-Four
Rosie's Unexpected Visit

The front door was open and there were suitcases inside the front door when Vera drove up her drive. What? Vera peered at them as she eased her car into its space. She recognised those damned cases! They were her mother's. What was Rosie doing here now?

Benji bounced in before her, his tail wagging as he sniffed around to see if any other dogs had invaded what he already saw as his territory. Rosie came out from the kitchen, wine glass in hand filled to the brim, at the sound of someone coming through the door. Benji backed away. His back legs went down, his hackles went up and he barked like fury.

Rosie screeched like a scalded parrot and dropped her glass of wine. It shattered between the wooden flooring and the beige runner. Benji crouched, quivering, his nose down on his paws with his tail between his legs.

'Don't worry, boy,' said Vera, dropping down

beside him and holding him close. 'But stay where you are. Don't get any of that glass in your pads.' The dog licked her hand and never took his eyes off Rosie. He hated her instantly.

'Please don't tell me you've only gone and got yourself a dog!' Rosie said, standing her ground. Benji growled. Vera stroked him. He quietened, but the growl continued in the back of his throat.

'Can you get that glass out of the way?' Vera said. 'There's a pan and brush in the utility.'

'Not before I've poured myself another glass of wine,' said Rosie, turning away and leaving the mess on the hall floor. 'I need something to calm my nerves after coming face to face with that brute.'

'You'd better pour Benji one, too, then. He's had an even worse shock than you.' Vera shouted after her, exasperated. 'Come on, Benji. Let's take you through the sitting room and put you out in the garden. You can stay out there until your master arrives with your food.'

The dog was only too pleased to get away from the scary woman who threw glasses at him. He stuck to Vera's side as she led him by his collar. Out in the garden, he found a spot he fancied on the lawn and lay facing the house, standing guard, waiting for the next contretemps, ready to leap into action if Vera needed him to protect her.

'Lovely to see you too, darling,' said Rosie sarcastically when Vera pushed past her to collect the dustpan and brush. She took a deep slug of her wine, then poured the remainder of the bottle in on top. Two glassfuls from one bottle, Vera thought mutinously. And I bet it's one of my best wines!

'What exactly are you doing here, Mother?'

'Well, that's a nice way to speak to me. I had to ask the taxi to drop me here because I've brought your house keys instead of my own. I can't get into my own house!'

Vera cleared up every piece of the broken glass before she spoke again. She found old towels and mopped up the spilled wine. Rosie always drank red wine, so there was a nasty stain. Vera fetched the cellar and sprinkled salt copiously into her carpet. It was particularly bad around the tassels. That's going to be a bugger to clean, fumed Vera, straightening up stiffly. On hard floors twice in one day, she thought. My poor old knees can't take it.

'Why are you looking such a goddamnawful mess?' asked Rosie, watching everything she was doing. 'Are you wearing a bra?'

'No, Mother, and I'm not wearing any knickers either!'

That was enough to stun Rosie into silence. Vera left her to think about it. She stormed upstairs to throw herself in the shower and put on fresh clothes before Ambrose arrived. Oh lor! Ambrose! She had to get rid of her mother before he turned up, so instead of getting into the shower, she tied a satin wrap around her, and skidded back downstairs, heading for the study where the keys to her mother's house were locked in the safe. With a bit of luck she could pack her off in a taxi before he turned up.

She hadn't shut the front door. As she came back down, he was standing there looking spectacular, freshly showered and dressed, and carrying a bag full of delicious-smelling fish and chips. Her stomach growled with hunger. 'Are we eating these first, or going straight for round two?' he asked, wide-eyed at confronting her dressed only in a wrap.

'Yummy,' came a voice from the kitchen. 'Good girl! You've already ordered take-away. I'm starving.' Rosie came out and stopped dead when she saw Ambrose. Again, she had an overfull glass of red wine in her hand. 'Bloody hell, are you the delivery man or a stripagram?'

'Watch the wine,' shouted Ambrose and Vera at exactly the same time. Rosie jumped, some wine spilled out over her hand and the glass slipped out of her hand. It broke in exactly the same place as before.

'I give up,' moaned Vera, sitting down with a bump on the stairs and putting her head in her hands. Outside, Benji started barking again furiously. 'Mother, meet Ambrose. Ambrose, Rosie,' she introduced them through her fingers.

'Shut up, Benji!' shouted Ambrose calmly, quickly striding over the broken glass, hand outstretched to shake Rosie's. She took it and simpered. Vera could have smashed her mother in the face. Ambrose took instant control. 'Why don't you put these in the oven to keep warm, Rosie? Go upstairs and take your time, darling. You must be getting cold,' he said to Vera, parting her hands and kissing her fulsomely on the lips for the benefit of her mother, 'and I'll take care of the mess if someone will only tell me where the dustpan and brush is.' He turned around, picked a dog bowl filled with dried food up off the doorstep and shut the door. 'But first I'd better feed my poor dog. It's long overdue for his supper.'

When Vera came back down dressed and with hair still damp from the shower, she found everything under control. The mess in the hall had been cleaned up, though the stain on the carpet was even larger. The table had been laid. A fresh bottle of wine had been opened and three smaller glasses had been poured. Benji had been fed in the garden and, now that his master was here and in control of the scary lady, he was happy to sleep by the conservatory door, although whenever Rosie moved one eye crept open just to check what she was doing.

'Sorry, I've been so long. Did you manage to keep the fish and chips warm?'

'They'll be slightly soggy, but I'm so hungry after all the exertions of today, I could eat anything. What about you?' asked Ambrose, eyes twinkling in her direction as he opened the oven door and brought them out. They looked edible. All three of them took a chip, blew and then munched on them.

'Dish them up, Ambrose. I'm not going to let these get cold,' declared Rosie. 'I'm ravenous!'

Ambrose grinned as he skilfully stretched the two portions between the three of them. He'd even warmed the plates. Rosie patted his bum as he bent over to get them out of the lower oven. Vera felt the knots in her neck tighten, but Ambrose just ignored Rosie's forwardness.

'So, how did you meet this gorgeous man?' she asked as she tucked into her portion, eyeing Ambrose appreciatively. Vera choked and reached for a glass of water.

'At one of Olivia's dinner parties,' said Ambrose non-committally as he patted her back. 'Vera's toes touched mine under the table and the rest is history.'

Rosie snorted with laughter. Thank God her daughter was finally getting some fun!

Chapter Thirty-Five
You Can't Keep Good Gossip Quiet

They'd packed Rosie off to her own home in a taxi with a pint of milk, a loaf of bread and her oversized luggage. She would have stayed chatting the night long, but when Vera went silent and Ambrose sat beside her on the settee stroking the back of her neck, Rosie actually took the hint and left them.

'Am I staying the night?' he asked as they stood together in the doorway and waved her off. 'Otherwise I shall have to call another cab for me and Benji. I've had too much to drink.'

'Do you think Benji will settle?'

'He will, if you ask him nicely,' said Ambrose, eliciting a quizzical grin from Vera. He kissed her passionately before they even closed the door. 'I did take a chance and brought his bed. It's in the car. May I bring it in?' he asked when they finally parted.

Vera felt enervated. Every nerve in her body tingled with excitement. This was going so fast, but she didn't care. It was bizarre how she'd only been thinking how much more content with her life she felt when she was standing on the landing stage, and that she didn't need a man. Then within what seemed like minutes one had swum into her life.

And he even had a dog! Of course she wanted them to stay. She didn't want this to end. 'Would you like to stay here tonight?' Vera asked Benji as if he was a child. The dog reciprocated by stroking himself around her legs, wanting fuss. 'But it'll be in the conservatory,' she added, smelling her hand from where she had stroked him. 'You still stink of the river. Tomorrow it'll be the hosepipe for you, young man.'

In her king-sized bed, their lovemaking was different, but infinitely more satisfying. It went on well into the early hours of the morning. Ambrose was affectionate and sweet, this time not so commanding, asking her permission to try out anything new. It had been a long time since the early days of their marriage when she and Richard had been so delicate, finding what each preferred. I wonder if it never changes, no matter what age you are, Vera thought as she drifted off to sleep with her back tucked close against his side, her neck supported by his outstretched arm. First the passion, then the polite exploration, then the long years of taking each other for granted, almost forgetting to give a little of yourself when children demanded so much, and then the final stage when lovemaking became a comfort, a reassurance that as the body aged, the attraction remained the same. She never decided. Sleep overtook her before she came to a conclusion.

When she was woken by Benji moving about in the conservatory the next morning, Ambrose was still asleep on his back. He snored, but it was rhythmic and regular and she quite liked it. It was like having an animal in her bed. It was nearly ten o'clock. The dog probably needed to go out. Naked, she slipped out of bed and found her wrap. She padded downstairs in bare feet and opened the door for Benji. He romped straight into the garden, sniffed around, urinated on the lawn, then after sniffing a lot more went through the archway, emptied his bowels and proceeded to kick the ground with his back paws all over the poo. Most of it shot up and hit the half-finished Vera di Milo.

'The boobs aren't big enough,' said Ambrose, coming up behind her and wrapping himself around her back. 'But your face on that is as lovely as any goddess.'

'Flatterer,' protested Vera. 'She's no goddess.'

'I can tell that,' said Ambrose seriously. 'She's cross-eyed.'

Vera turned round and punched him hard on his

naked upper arm. He wore only underpants. 'Bully!' he groaned, rubbing his arm more than it could have ever hurt. 'Come back to bed and try that again.'

'And what are you going to do about it?' asked Vera, showing him a bunch of fives.

'I'm sure I can think of something,' said Ambrose, lurching in for a slobbery kiss.

Vera pulled out of it, grinning broadly as she wiped the slobber off her face with the back of her hand, thinking, how did he get so practised? He'd got this flirtation thing down to a fine art. Richard wouldn't have been like this if I'd been the one who died. He'd have been shy and fumbly and would have apologised all the time. Ambrose was almost too slick.

Her heart stopped. She panicked and worried whether she was just another notch on his bedpost?

'Tea?' asked Ambrose, interrupting her thoughts.

Benji had finished checking out the garden and now lay on his side watching the birds. 'Will he be all right out there?' Vera asked.

'Sure he will. He prefers to be out in the garden at River House, too. He's relishing the space. We don't have enough room for him in London.'

And there it was! The 'we'. Vera didn't even know whether he was married, divorced, or what, but the 'we' confirmed there was a relationship and he'd even said 'we don't' as if it was still on. With a sinking heart, she realised she knew absolutely nothing about Ambrose and, consumed with desire, she hadn't even thought to ask. Everything between them so far had been primal. Even Rosie had fallen for his charisma. One guffaw when she told him her last man had been called Benjamin and he'd also been a dog, and she and Ambrose had become firm friends.

Well, Vera wasn't going to be drawn in so easily. She was better than that! 'Are you married, Ambrose?' she asked very quietly, dreading the answer.

Her worry showed on her face. 'Very recently separated,' he answered truthfully.

'How recently?' she asked, heart sinking. All she could hear was that he was married.

'Very,' he said eventually, eyes hardening, face setting into seriousness.

She moved away from him, not quite knowing what to say next. Please God, don't let this be happening, her whole being screamed. I've let a man in under the radar. He has a wife and he's going to break my heart; and I simply couldn't bear to go through that pain again.

Ambrose moved a step closer. She stepped back away from him, not wanting him to touch her, knowing that if he did she would melt in to his arms instead of pressing for answers she most definitely did not want to hear. It stopped him dead. The phone rang right behind her and, without thinking, she reached down and picked it up.

'Hi, Mum,' she heard Fliss say brightly on the other end of the line.

'Hello, darling,' she answered in the quietest of voices.

'Oh God, Mum. Sorry! He's there with you, isn't he? Granny said he'd brought his dog, so she thought he would be going home. But he hasn't, has he, Mum?'

Vera turned her back on Ambrose. He strode out of the room to go back upstairs to dress. In the garden, Benji was rolling, scratching imaginary fleas off his back.

'Yes,' answered Vera eventually, her emotions suddenly terribly flat.

'Now I don't know what I ought to do,' Fliss babbled. 'I was ringing to say we'd invited Granny over for afternoon tea so she can meet Steve, and I rang Christy, too. He's bringing the family over to see her. And I was sure you'd come, too, but do I invite Ambrose as well? Would he want to come? We can't have the dog. There's not enough room in my little house, not with Mickey crawling now and Wyeth trying to join in. Would it be safe to have a dog around them at this age? I never know ...'

Vera heard nothing more. All she could think was that the gossip was already out. Her own bloody mother had made absolutely sure of that.

Chapter Thirty-Six

Family

Vera had to give Ambrose his due. He came back downstairs fully dressed, still with overnight stubble, but with his hair combed perfectly. He excused himself with great formality, not even blaming his hasty retreat on Benji. 'With Rosie coming home unexpectedly, I'm sure you all want to be together as a family. I was going to ask you if you'd like to take a long walk with Benji and me later, but I can see you really need to be with your loved ones today.'

Loved ones! At least he didn't have the temerity to include himself with that group.

He retrieved Benji's bowl and bed instead, finding his car keys in his pocket as he called Benji in. The dog went straight to Vera for fuss. 'He really likes you,' Ambrose said and part of her ached for him to add, 'but I like you more,' but he didn't.

Nor did he ask for her number, or suggest when

they should meet again. 'I shall probably be up in London most of the week,' he said casually.

'What's happening to Benji?'

'I've hired dog-walkers to come in twice a day. That will do him. He'll stay out in his kennel otherwise.'

So, he was coming home every evening! Her heart lifted a little that he wasn't staying in London with his wife. It briefly crossed her mind that she was being silly and that she might offer to go round to check on the dog. Angelina and Pete had looked after the dog before, but if Ambrose was going through a separation, she couldn't bear to be involved. She was still too fragile emotionally to get involved in someone else's problems and she certainly didn't want to have hope for something she might never be able to have. What if this was nothing more than revenge sex? She couldn't risk it. It would be too demeaning, and if that was so, then she must also say goodbye to Benji. It wasn't right to use the dog as an excuse to get closer to Ambrose. They pecked one another goodbye on both cheeks, leaning over Benji's bed, and then Ambrose was gone without another word, looking steely serious.

Better to let him go now before he does me even more damage, she thought when, totally deflated, she closed the door and leant her back against it for support. She never moved as she heard his car tyres turning on the gravel, then the acceleration as the sports coupé sped away.

'So, when are you seeing him again?' asked Annie, cornering Vera in Fliss's small kitchen that afternoon.

Vera shrugged, unable to bring herself to say out loud that she never expected to see him again. She'd already convinced herself she'd made it obvious to him that she couldn't handle his still being married. Irritated that Rosie had told her children about Ambrose before she'd had a chance to speak to them, she was sure Rosie would have embellished the juicy story. She couldn't be more angry with her mother if she tried.

'Rosie turning up's made a bit of a cock of things, hasn't it?' asked Annie astutely, closing the door a little more. 'If you don't mind me saying, I can't believe your mother's appetite for men. She bounces back more often than a ping-pong ball. I heard her just telling Fliss she's now seeing someone called Henrique.'

'Henrique! Henrique from next door?'

It was Annie's turn to shrug. 'Apparently he had a younger wife, but she's just bled him dry and run off with a Romanian waiter, so Rosie's stepped in to cheer him up.'

'She hated Henrique a month ago!'

They both sniggered. It broke Vera's bad mood. Vera pulled her daughter-in-law in close, sighing deeply as she clasped her tightly. 'God! You've got it bad,' said Annie, again extremely astutely. Vera couldn't speak. She had. One day, one night with Ambrose and she was this much of a wreck. She was right, walking away. She simply could not handle it.

The kettle boiled and they made a fresh pot of tea. In the next room, Wyeth screamed for attention. 'He's ready for a feed. Do you think Rosie will pick him up?' Annie asked cheekily, knowing that once Rosie had done the obligatory coos, told everyone how very special her latest great-grandson was going to be, had her photograph taken with him and then given him back to Annie, she would take no notice of him for the rest of the afternoon.

When they came through with the fresh mugs of tea, Christy stood up to let his mother sit down in his place, then sat on the arm of the chair, his own arm resting around Vera's shoulders. Fliss's room held too few chairs for everyone. Some people had to sit on the floor, and when anyone moved, there had to be a major rearrangement of legs. Mickey was having the time of his life crawling from one willing adult to another. Steve was particularly good with him, pulling faces, making farm animal noises and making him chuckle.

'He's fitting in okay, isn't he?' remarked Christy, indicating Steve. Vera nodded. 'Wonder when he'll be moving in?'

Vera looked around in surprise. 'Has Fliss said anything to you?'

'Doesn't have to,' said Christy with a slight turn of his head towards his sister who was opening a bottle of wine. Rosie already held up a glass, waiting for it to be filled. 'Look at her. Have you ever seen her this relaxed?' Vera squeezed his knee in agreement. Fliss was glowing. They watched as she poured the tiniest amount of red wine into Rosie's glass. Rosie stuck her nose in and smelt it, then held the glass out to be filled. Fliss poured in a soupçon more and got a hoot of derision from her grandmother.

'You drink far too much, Granny,' they heard Fliss tease, then she relented and filled up Rosie's glass. Everyone else refused wine. 'Looks like you're drinking this all by yourself then,' said Fliss, leaving the bottle behind Rosie on a windowsill well out of the children's reach.

'What about you, Mum?' asked Christy. 'Is it going well?'

Vera chose to ignore the obvious. 'It is, darling. The Normal Dating Agency looks as if it's just had its first success. Nice young couple. It'll be interesting to see how that works out.'

'Did you ever find anyone for Toby Goodman?' Christy asked casually.

'How did you know about Toby Goodman?' Vera shot around, surprised.

'Don't worry. Nobody's been talking. He told me himself when he came into the merchant's to get fencing.' Vera relaxed beside him. 'You do know

Rodney from Stores is on the lookout. You ought to introduce them.'

Vera twisted round and stared her son full in the face in disbelief. 'Oh yeah,' he said in answer to her unspoken question. 'All the lads know. He's a deacon at the church, still lives with his mother, serves on the parish council, but Rodney's out there. Just keeps shtum about everything. He had a special friend, but he died recently. Perhaps you could get them together.'

Vera had been dreading dealing with Toby. If she managed to find someone, she didn't want it getting around town that she had been instrumental in the introduction. She grasped the opportunity. 'Could you suggest Rodney serves Toby next time he's in, and if it's a goer, I'll forego Toby's fee. I don't think there's much hope of me finding anyone for Toby. I've only had a couple of men register.'

'Well, gays wouldn't, would they?'

Vera looked him blankly.

'Think about it, Mum! You are called The Normal Dating Agency,' Christy said and finished off his tea.

Of course! It was obvious why only straight people were registering. The trouble was in the name. What homosexual man was ever going to expect success with a personal introduction agency called The Normal Dating Agency! No wonder few of the names on the slips Olivia had collected at the Maid Marion had chosen to register. It had been one after the other refusing, and Vera had wrongly concluded it was because of her, that she was an older woman, not because they thought they wouldn't meet anyone. How wrong had she been?

'But it is normal,' she protested. 'Normal for everyone, no matter what normal means to them. We deal with anybody.'

'Just saying, Mum.' Christy shrugged. 'But most folks are really stuck in the mud in this town, even if they make out they're open-minded and bang on about diversity. They may say it to your face, but everyone knows that's not what'll be gossiped about behind your back. We all know about the Maid Marion, but no one admits to going in there, do they? And, if you were a bit nervous about coming out, would you use the local dating agency? Get real, Mum!'

Vera bit her lip. He was right. Gossip was rife in this town and a lot of it was downright nasty, but, before they could discuss it more, all conversation ceased when Mickey clambered over Steve and a tiny foot hit him in his testacles. Steve groaned and quickly lifted Mickey out of the way. For a moment he couldn't get a word out. Fliss shot to his side, clambering past Annie, now sitting on the floor breastfeeding Wyeth.

'Crikey, Mickey! Don't damage the wedding tackle,' Steve moaned in a high pitched voice.

'Told you,' said Christy and started humming the

wedding march. Vera slapped him hard on his knee.

'So? Come on, Mum. You avoided it very neatly, but I haven't forgotten. What's this about a new man?' he demanded.

'Christy!' protested Vera, rather more loudly than she would have wished. All eyes turned as one towards her.

'The extremely glamorous Ambrose! If you don't want him, Vera, I'll have a go,' swooned Rosie dramatically. Annie snorted at her tactlessness.

Vera saw red. If ever she was going to say anything, now was the time. She handed Christy her mug, and got to her feet. 'Listen to this once, my family. And that especially includes you, Mother, because I haven't yet dealt properly with you. Yes. Ambrose and I spent the night together last night. Yes, we did have sex, but that's absolutely all I am telling you! It's my business and I don't want to hear another word about it from any of you.'

All eyes stayed firmly on her, even Wyeth's, who stopped sucking on Annie's milk and stared serenely up at his grandmother. No one dared utter a word.

Vera stared back at them, defying anyone to interrupt as she went on. 'None of you are to make any more of this than there is. He hasn't asked me out. I haven't yet decided if I would go out with him anyway, but he is the first man I've been with since your father died and I would very much like it if you would all show me some respect and let me handle this in my own way. This isn't yet anything to do with any of you!' She promptly sat back down with a thump and a bright crimson face.

'Oh,' she said as an afterthought, and stood back up. 'Mother, if I hear one word that you have gossiped about me, or spoken to anyone in the street, or telephoned any of your friends, and particularly Aunty Eileen, I will personally grab you by the hair, take you down to the airport and send you back to Majorca. And I will never let you come home again! You will be banished permanently.'

'What's all this got to do with me?' pleaded Rosie. 'If he was such a disappointment in bed, then just replace him. It's no use telling us your problems. Just get on with it and find another man.'

Chapter Thirty-Seven
The Fallout

Olivia woke gagging from a very dry mouth. She peered at the bedside clock. It showed three-thirty, but was that in the night or the afternoon? She lay with eyes closed and allowed herself to come up to full consciousness slowly. Her mind was no longer so confused. She was feeling less distant. There was birdsong outside. She could hear the swoosh of the traffic on the bypass. Beside her, the clock was ticking.

Easing herself upright, she ran her fingers through her tightly knotted curls, and then rubbed her face vigorously. When her eyes fully opened, she could see slits of daylight coming in around the edges of the curtain. Overnight, she'd had the most wonderful sleep unpunctuated by troublesome dreams. She yawned and stretched, threw the bedclothes back and dropped her feet to the floor.

'I thought I heard you moving,' said Angelina

coming in with a fresh carafe of water. 'Want these opened?' she said, indicating the curtains.

Olivia nodded and drained a glass of water. Another followed, then a third. 'Take it easy,' advised Angelina,' or you'll drown.'

'Is Vera in?' Olivia asked.

'Vera? No. Why should she be? It's Sunday afternoon.' Angelina opened the window fully to let fresh air in. Neither the room nor Olivia smelled very fresh.

'I thought I heard her talking to somebody,' said Olivia heading for the bathroom.

Angelina stripped the bed and hung the duvet half out of the window to air. She tidied chocolate wrappers into the waste bin, and put the used carafe and glass on top of them. When she passed the bathroom clutching the bundle of bed linen and the waste bin high so she could see where she was treading, she could hear the shower running.

'Over?' asked Pete, looking up from where he was sitting reading the newspaper in the sunlight streaming into the kitchen.

'Hopefully,' said Angelina, shoving the bed linen into the washing machine. 'I'll take her clean clothes up in a minute and see if she wants anything to eat.'

By the time Olivia came down into the kitchen she had recovered much of her buoyancy. She strode across the room and hugged Pete tightly, holding on to him as if it had been a very long time since she last saw him. She swung open the fridge door, peered in, ate several slices of ham straight from the packet, then took out the cheese box and cut herself a huge hunk of cheese. 'Have you got any chutney?' she asked, throwing open cupboard doors.

Angelina took bread from the bin and sliced a chunk for her. 'Butter that,' she said. 'There is chutney somewhere, but as only you ever eat it, it's probably at the back of the cupboard.'

Pete pulled out a kitchen chair, took Olivia by the elbow and urged her to sit down. She did as she was bidden, munching on the bread, elbows on the table, until her chewing got slower, and eventually she discarded the remainder that she couldn't eat. Her colour drained away. Beads of sweat came on her forehead. She belched, then rammed her hand over her mouth. Pete sat back on the legs of his chair as she swung past him heading for the bathroom where she promptly brought back up everything she had just eaten.

'I thought all that was in the past,' Pete said dispassionately to Angelina.

'Give her time,' replied Angelina. 'Looks like she's staying with us for a while longer,' she said and hugged her patient husband in mutual sympathy.

Vera rang on Tuesday to say that she would be working from home for a couple of days. 'The phone's already diverted. There are no appointments scheduled and if anyone rings I have the laptop with me here. My mother turned up Saturday night and we've got some family business to sort out.'

'How is she?' asked Angelina politely.

'Oh, you know ...' said Vera, trailing off.

'Do what you have to, Vera. We're all right here. Take as much time as you need.'

What Vera actually wanted was to go to bed and never get up again. Remorse, guilt, regret, she didn't know exactly what words to use to describe the black cloud which had descended. If this was depression, it had flown in on Concorde and landed square at her doorstep. 'How's Olivia?' she asked.

'Better. Up and about. Getting there.'

'Has she said what brought it on?' asked Vera, who was worried Olivia had been doing too much work for both Claremont's and then burning the candle at both ends visiting the clubs and pubs advertising The Normal Dating Agency. Most of the clients had come through Olivia's effort.

'She never knows. It just comes on.'

'You'd have thought something triggered it,' said Vera, who knew very little about mental illness apart from what she'd read in the papers. 'Give her my love, will you?'

Vera appreciated her own problems were nothing like as serious as Olivia's. If she was feeling low, it was because she had made a fool of herself with Ambrose, and that, combined with Rosie turning up, had tipped the balance. She'd been feeling so much happier. She was enjoying the work. It was a new challenge. She liked meeting new people. There was plenty of money in the bank from selling Number Forty. She even starting to get over Richard, and then along came Ambrose.

She'd heard nothing from him. There had been no phone call, no knock on the door. When she drove past River House, the gates were firmly locked. Although he'd said he was working in London all week, it was as if he had never even been there.

Stop being so stupid, Vera berated herself. You met a handsome man. You had fantastic sex. A lot of women would be satisfied with that.

But it's not enough for me, her inner devil taunted her, and she groaned with sheer frustration.

Benji's poo was still visible under the archway. She needed to clear that away, so she found two carrier bags, put one over one hand, scooped up the mess and firmly secured everything in the other. The Vera di Milo was still dirt-spattered where he'd scratched soil up and thrown it into the air. Vera fetched the dust brush and eased it away from the mural. It was dry and most of it came away easily. If she was working from home, perhaps it was time to do something positive.

She worked solidly painting the mural for a couple of hours, had a quick snack, then drove down to Robin Redbreast's to buy plants called Vera to go around the archway. She bumped into Fliss on her way out. 'What are you doing here, darling?' she asked.

'I'm just on my way back from a half-day seminar. What are you up to? Aren't you working?'

Vera put down the heavy bags of plants. The plastic handles of the bags were cutting into her fingers. She stretched them out, showing Fliss how deep the marks were. Fliss took her mother's hands and rubbed the circulation back into them. 'Mum?' she started, still holding on to Vera's hands.

Vera waited. 'Have you heard from Ambrose?' Fliss asked, then bit her bottom lip.

Vera shook her head. Around her the noise of the busy High Street suddenly ceased. A cloud seemed to have crossed in front of the sun, even though the sky was cloudless. People scurrying by seemed to be frozen in time. It was obvious she was about to be told something terrible. Although Vera had warned her family in no uncertain terms that she wanted no interference in her personal life as far as Ambrose was concerned, she could see Fliss knew something and it was troubling her, but obviously didn't want to be the one to tell her mother what she knew.

'Spit out whatever you have to say, Fliss,' Vera said, so quietly it almost made Fliss's heart skip a beat. Her hand instinctively went over her heart. 'Felicity?' urged Vera.

Fliss looked from left to right. There were so many people pushing by them, this was definitely not the right place to break difficult news. 'Not here,' she said, picking up Vera's bags and elbowing her towards Oysters. Inside the pub was half-empty. Fliss dropped the bags on a vacant seat in the corridor and scurried her mother towards the Ladies' loo.

Vera could hardly breathe. What awful news did Fliss have to share?

Fliss checked they were alone. 'I know you said we shouldn't say anything, but this is too important.'

Vera waited. She could hardly breathe. 'Fliss, for God's sake tell me.'

'Did you know that Olivia has been seeing an awful lot of Ambrose? In fact, she's been seeing him practically every evening after work. Mum, I think Ambrose is the boyfriend Olivia's been keeping secret.'

Vera, panicking, had to get out of the confined space of the Ladies. She grabbed the door and lurched out with Fliss closely behind her. In the corridor, she stopped to collect the carrier bags filled with plants, then thought better of it. 'I need a stiff drink,' she groaned and dropped them back down.

From the far corner of the bar, Rosie called over. 'Wonderful idea, darlings! Make mine a large one.'

Chapter Thirty-Eight
Come Back With Me To Majorca

Vera ignored her. Fliss went to the bar and ordered three red wines. 'I don't want that,' Vera said, pacing. 'Give me a whisky. Neat!'

Charlie Powys, the only other person in the bar, sat quietly behind his broadsheet. He peeked around the edge of the newspaper never expecting to witness Vera Father ordering neat whisky this early in the day. She was too upright a member of the community. She never put a foot wrong. His ears pricked up. He sat back and listened, using his newspaper as cover.

'What's he done?' Rosie guessed immediately, eyes sparkling in anticipation.

'Wouldn't you like to know,' said Vera, downing the first glass of red wine poured in one go, and scrabbling to find her purse. Fliss's eyes twisted back and forth from her mother to her grandmother nervously. This was not going to end well.

Louise, the barmaid, already held a smaller glass under the optic. 'Single or double?' she asked.

Vera slapped a twenty-pound note down on the counter. 'Double,' she confirmed and when she was served it, knocked that back, too, in one go. 'Same again,' she said pulling out another twenty-pound note.

'Put that away,' said Louise, covering her hand, 'and I'll make you a strong coffee. I don't want to be clearing up your sick today.'

'Louise,' pleaded Vera.

'Sit down with Rosie, Vera! Either of you girls want coffee, too?'

Rosie and Fliss shook their heads. 'Aren't you supposed to be at work at this time of day?' Rosie asked her granddaughter.

Fliss took off her business jacket, loosened the top button of her white shirt, and checked her watch. 'They can wait,' she said. 'This is more important.'

Across the room, Charlie Powys propped his newspaper against his beer glass and turned up the volume on his hearing aid. It emitted a high-pitched buzz which nearly deafened him. He turned it back down again. Fliss eyeballed him, warning Vera not to say anything, but Vera was too wound up to notice. Fliss placed her hand over her mother's forearm and swivelled her eyes in warning towards the opened newspaper.

'What?' demanded Vera.

Rosie was highly amused. She sensed a juicy bit of gossip in the making, particularly when Fliss waggled wide eyes in Charlie's direction and Vera got the message, but instead of keeping quiet, she stormed over and hovered over Charlie until he lowered the paper and looked up to her. 'You might as well turn that hearing aid of yours back up, Charlie' shouted Vera. 'You too, Louise! Then you'll both conveniently overhear what I'm going to tell my mother and, as fast as you like, you can tell the rest of the town,' she said. 'Ready? Are you listening closely? Then I shall say this only once.'

Challenged, Charlie was a coward. He tried to slope out of the door. Louise, affronted at being called a gossip, turned away with lips pursed and raised the volume on the background music, but there was nothing anyone could do to stop Vera shouting at the top of her voice, 'I've just had sex with Olivia Claremont's boyfriend!' and with that, she stormed out.

'You couldn't have handled that any better,' said Rosie, scurrying after her to the car park. 'That told them.'

Vera couldn't find her car keys in her handbag. She rounded on her mother. 'What are you still doing here?' she demanded. 'Haven't you got some good gossip to spread now?'

Her mother ignored the jibe and snatched the bag out of her hand. 'No way are you driving,' she said, finding the keys in the front pocket and opening the door. 'You've had too much to drink. Are you coming, Fliss?' she shouted to her granddaughter, who had followed them out of the bar, then run back to retrieve the carrier bags filled with plants.

'You can't drive, Granny. You've had too much to drink, too,' she said, dropping the heavy bags to the floor.

'What are you talking about?' demanded Rosie. 'I'll be fine. I'd only had the one.'

'To top yourself up!' shouted Fliss back. 'Granny, you're a lush. You're permanently drunk.'

Rosie's retaliation was only stopped by Vera bringing back up the red wine and whisky all over their feet. 'Oh lovely, Mother!' said Fliss stepping back from the mess. 'I'll drive. I never touched my wine.'

Fliss drove them to Vera's house in silence. In the back, Vera hung her head out of the open window in case she was sick again while Rosie sat in the front and glowered at Fliss. By the time they reached Vera's house, Rosie had forgotten all about Vera's own very public declaration and had now convinced herself she was the aggrieved party. She moaned as much to Vera, but Vera was so overwrought, she was having none of her mother's self-centredness any more.

'Fliss is absolutely right! You do drink too much, Mother,' she fumed. 'And you embarrass me all the time with your come-to-bed eyes, your succession of men and your constant need to be the centre of attention. Why did you ever have to come back this time?'

'Don't blame me if I walked into your love nest and spoiled your bit of fun,' snapped Rosie spitefully.

Fliss blanched at her nastiness. Was this really the grandmother she loved?

It was, however, exactly what was needed to make Vera stand up for herself. Frustrated; she clenched her fists and shook them in the air. Her voice wobbled when she spat back at Rosie, 'It wasn't just a love nest, Mother! It was the first time I'd been able to allow myself to get close to another person since Richard. I never asked for it. It came out of the blue, but I've needed it, so badly, for such a very long time, and now you're reducing it to just a bit of fun! It wasn't just a bit of fun to me, Mother. It was my way of moving on.'

'And you went and did it with Olivia Claremont's boyfriend,' sneered Rosie.

Vera leant back against the wall and closed her eyes. 'What am I going to do now?' she asked herself, distraught.

Rosie would never understand how badly Vera was suffering. It simply wasn't in her personal make-up. 'There's no use us falling out over men,' she said. 'Olivia will forget all about this tomorrow.

Leave her to be the one angry at this Ambrose. You! You've just got to move on. Come back with me to Majorca, and then you'll see some real fun.'

Chapter Thirty-Nine
Tails Between Legs

Christy called in on Vera on his way back from the airport. 'Did she say anything?' asked Vera guiltily.

'Not a word,' lied Christy, who had argued with his grandmother all the way down on the long drive but didn't think it expedient to tell his mother that Rosie remained intransigent in her view that Vera was being overdramatic and, just like buses, there would be another man along in a minute. However, he did suspect Rosie knew how wrong she had been in the way she handled Vera, and that she probably had her tail between her legs, but she refused to show it. She had simply packed her bags and she fled. 'Straight back into normal Granny mode,' he said, accurately assessing his grandmother's motives. 'Says she's missing Henrique terribly, so she has to get back.'

'She hated him a month ago!'

Christy put his arms around Vera and gave her a

tender hug. He noticed how fragile she felt. She'd always been like a sturdy pit pony ready for work, never fat, with a nice figure, always much stronger than she looked. Now it felt to him as if she could break from the slightest blow. His father's death had taken so much out of her, but she'd been so good at hiding her true feelings. She'd tried to protect him and Fliss from the worst of the shock, but now he could tell from how much her body had changed she'd lost a lot of her inner resources.

When she made coffee for them both, he took a good look at her from behind. Her clothes were much looser. She seemed to have lost height. How had none of them noticed? Guilty, Christy came up behind her to give her another big hug.

'What's this for?' asked Vera, not pulling away.

'Because you've been having a torrid time, and you just need it,' Christy said and wasn't surprised when Vera starting weeping. He held her tight as the tears flowed. Two damp spots from the tears from her eyes and the dribble from her mouth soaked through his shirt on to his chest. He held her until he felt her gulps started slowing.

'I'm sorry, darling, but Granny gets me so wound up,' Vera said, pulling away and wiping her face with kitchen roll. 'But perhaps I shouldn't have been so hard on her.'

After the argument he'd just had with her in the car, Christy was hardly going to agree. He was now convinced Rosie could take on an invading army and absolutely nothing would change her mind. 'Don't worry about Granny,' he said tactfully. 'She's super-tough. She's a survivor.'

'I'm not,' sighed Vera and flopped down on a chair. Christy collected their coffee and then came to join her at the kitchen table.

'Drink that,' he ordered. Obedient as ever, she took a sip from her mug. 'And don't be so hard on yourself. You are still grieving for Dad.'

Vera's eyes filled with tears again. 'I miss him so much,' she whispered. 'But I can't have him back.'

When Christy finally left her, he decided not to go to work at Father and Sons, but instead made his way home to see Annie and the boys. It was lunchtime and he knew they would be home. He felt so emotionally drained, he needed the comfort of his own family. Annie shot to the door as she heard his key in the lock carrying Wyeth over her shoulder. He was grizzly and the muslin under him showed he had been sick after his feed.

Without a word, Christy took him from her and smelled his nappy. It was full. 'That's the third time this morning,' moaned a weary Annie.

'Where's Mickey?'

'Gone down for a nap, thank God.'

As soon as Christy changed Wyeth's nappy, he settled. Very soon, he was asleep and his father could lay him down. Almost on cue, Annie came out of the kitchen with a plate of sandwiches and, putting them down, kissed Christy. 'Was it that bad?' she asked.

'Granny was her usual nightmare, so I chucked her out outside the terminal and just drove off,' sighed Christy. 'But it's Mum I'm worried about. I called round and she's been crying again.'

Annie munched on her sandwich and let her husband talk. 'I'd have thought she'd be coming out of it by now,' he went on, 'but, Annie, I put my arms around her and I couldn't believe how much weight she's lost.'

'Eat your sandwich,' Annie said, pushing it towards him and, while their sons slept, they finally managed a full conversation without interruptions. Annie reminded Christy that he was also still mourning the loss of his father. Christy said he thought he was doing all right, but things like this brought it right back up again. Annie praised him for how well he had done taking over the lion's share of running the business. He told her no words could ever describe how much he appreciated her support. She told him she didn't need words from this man who she loved more than her own life. She knew how much he'd been hurting and hadn't been able to show it. He'd had to be strong for everyone, and she was so proud of him.

Christy couldn't finish his sandwich. He pushed it aside and, without realising, Annie picked it up and took a huge bite, pushing bits in with her finger. Christy chuckled. 'That's why you can't lose the baby weight. You're still eating for two.'

'More like four,' she mumbled with her mouth overly full, putting the rest back down on the plate guiltily, but happy that her husband could still laugh at her. He appeared to be better now he'd confided so much.

Later, when she took the dishes back to the kitchen and he followed her purely because he didn't want to be out of her comforting presence, she threw him the tea towel for him to dry the dishes she hand-washed. 'You know you said your mother was still grieving?' she started.

Christy nodded.

'Well, I'm not sure this is the same sort of grieving,' she went on. 'This isn't about your dad this time. I reckon this blow-up with Rosie is about Rosie and the way she treats Vera. Vera's put up with a load of crap from that woman over the years. I thought Rosie was being a right cow sometimes, not just to Vera, but to you and Fliss, too. Does she pick up our babies? She only touches them when they are given to her so she can be in the photographs. She expects everyone to listen to stories about herself, but so many she should never tell in front of her grandchildren, let alone her great-grandchildren. Don't get me wrong, I like Rosie. She's very generous, but it's always on her terms.

She's had this roasting from Vera coming for a very long time.'

Christy stared out of the window at the garden strewn with the toys of small children. The lawn needed cutting. There was hardly a bloom left in the flower bed; Mickey had picked them all off. 'But where does that leave Mum?' he asked.

Annie was adamant. 'In a much better place? This has come for a reason, sweetheart. It's been a long time coming, but finally Vera has done exactly the right thing for herself and nobody else. She's put herself centre stage in her own life, and it's about time. Vera doesn't need sexual fun and it was cheap of Rosie to make out this was what it was all about. Vera needs to know she has a right to be happy again after losing your dad. Standing up to Rosie is a sign she's no longer putting up with all her crap simply because she's too sad to fight. I think your mum might be coming out of the worst of her bereavement. She'll get over this quicker than you think.'

Christy pondered. His beautiful wife could well be right, but then he thought of something else.

'But what about her sleeping with Olivia's boyfriend?'

Annie smirked. 'Does it really matter? If he's as attractive as Rosie says then I might even consider having a go myself, even if he is an older man. He sounds like he's a bit of all right!'

Christy looked at her wide-eyed. He saw the sexy merriment in her eyes, rolled up the tea towel and whacked her straight on her backside, and then lurched at her to prove that he, too, was a bit of all right himself.

Chapter Forty
The Confrontation

Vera could put it off no longer. She felt so guilty, she had to apologise to Olivia. She couldn't live with herself if she didn't. Their friendship was longstanding. They were in business together. Olivia was seriously unwell and she certainly didn't want to put any more pressure on her at all. Vera had now been at home for three days, hardly eating and drinking, and she was in torment.

Annie called round with the boys and tried to reassure her she had done nothing wrong, that Ambrose was a free man and old enough to make his own choices. If Olivia was so upset, why hadn't she been in touch with Vera? Vera cuddled Wyeth, drawing comfort from the baby's warmth and smell, and changed the subject, expressing her delight that the boys were growing so fast. How could she tell Annie that Olivia was cooped up at the Claremonts' fighting her own demons? Angelina and Pete had managed to hide Olivia's illness from her for this long, so they must have done so from everyone else as well. It wasn't her story to tell, and she certainly wasn't going to be the one to disclose it. She was no gossip.

Fliss and Steve brought round a take-away. 'We've got something to tell you,' they said, avoiding all talk about Rosie. 'We're moving in together.'

'Where?' asked Vera, delighted.

'My house to start off with, before we start to look for something bigger,' confirmed Fliss, glowing with happiness. Steve gave Vera a huge portion of the Chinese food they had brought with them, but she hardly made a dent in the pile on her plate. When she went to the bathroom, Steve and Fliss exchanged worried questions. 'What about suggesting she takes a holiday?' Steve asked.

'She usually goes to Granny in Majorca. That's out of the question now, isn't it? I bet she never goes again,' said Fliss, very worried about her mother after having a long talk with Christy who had told her everything he knew.

'Perhaps we could take her for a short break somewhere,' suggested Steve, not really believing what he'd just said.

Fliss snorted in amused derision. 'Do you really want my mother to come away with us? We're hardly getting out of bed when we're together. It'd be like going on holiday on her own!' In answer to which, he leant across and kissed her so passionately that Vera returning from the bathroom turned around and walked back out of the kitchen again.

No one dared mention Ambrose. Vera had already made it perfectly clear that she wanted no interference, but Christy was angry enough to tell his sister he was going around to River House to challenge him. 'Don't you dare!' warned Fliss. 'We've never met the man. All it would do is make matters worse. If Mum chooses to put this in the past and ignore it ever happened, then it'll be the best for all of us. At least she knows now she can still manage sex,' she added as an afterthought, making Christy screw up his face in horror at the thought that his mother even still wanted sex. 'Get real,' Fliss told him.

On the fourth day of her self-imposed exile, Vera got out of bed and waited until the hands on her watch showed nine in the morning. She didn't want to ring Angelina any earlier at her flat. She dialled Claremont's shop number expecting Angelina to answer the business phone, so was taken aback when she heard Olivia's cheery voice on the other end of the line. 'Good Morning. It's a beautiful day and you are speaking to Olivia at Claremont's. How may I be of assistance?'

'Olivia?'

'Vera! Where the hell of you been? I haven't seen you for ages. Are you all right? We heard you'd had a right go at Rosie outside Oysters and then she shot straight back off to Majorca. Come on, I need all the goss.'

Vera leant back, stunned into silence at hearing Olivia's voice and her sounding so chirpy.

'Vera?' she heard Olivia say on the other end of the line.

'Vera! Are you still there?' Vera heard Olivia call over to Angelina, 'Vera's not talking ...' and Angelina's footsteps clacking on the wooden floor as she ran over to the phone, snatching it away from her sister.

'Vera! What's the matter?'

'Angelina? Don't worry. I am all right. It was just such a shock ...' But before she could say more, Angelina had interrupted.

'Oh thank God, Vera. I thought you were having a stroke, or something.'

Vera sagged. 'No. I am all right, honestly. It just stopped me in my tracks hearing Olivia. How long has she been back?'

'Sunday,' Angelina said lightly and Vera instantly knew she meant from the illness. 'You are coming in later, like you said?' Angelina prompted, giving Vera the signal that she needed to see her.

Oh God! There was no getting away from it now. She was going to have to face Olivia and she was going to have to do it today.

Walking in through the front door of Claremont's

was one of the hardest things Vera had ever done. She'd already planned what she wanted to say. She was going to tell Olivia and Angelina that she was pulling out of the Normal Dating Agency. She would leave her money in, but she wouldn't work there any more, so when Olivia rushed up and threw her arms around her, checking her out and declaring, 'Vera! You look awful. You didn't get that dress from us. It doesn't fit you,' as if absolutely nothing had happened between them, she found it very hard to know what to do next. Resigning was the only honourable thing to do.

'My heart's not in it any more,' she told them simply after she broke the news.

They had all walked down to the boathouse to talk without being overheard and now sat on the settees in the meeting area. Before, when Vera went ahead to unlock the doors, Angelina slowed Olivia down and asked, 'This is all right, going back in there, isn't it? Vera knows you've been unwell. She was the one who found you in the boathouse.'

'You never said!'

'You weren't well enough to tell. Do you realise how bad it's been this time?'

Olivia hadn't even considered it. She remembered nothing of how the episode started. Like a pendulum, her mood had once again swung from deepest gloom straight through to elation and she had long learned that there was no point in asking what had happened when she was in the deepest throes of the melancholy. She never truly remembered it exactly as it actually happened anyway. She could have flown to the moon and she would have remembered it as a distant dream. Her only fear was that she might hurt someone else when she was in this state. 'It could happen,' her psychiatrist had told her and her family, 'but the most common way it's presenting in your case is that you shut down completely. It's highly unlikely that will change now. You're more likely to make rash decisions when you are elated. Have you found yourself talking out of turn?' she asked tactfully and everyone, including Olivia, laughed.

'I do it all the time,' she confirmed, 'but usually I remember most of it.'

Angelina, stroked her back in encouragement, unsurprised that Olivia was the most upset about Vera's news. 'You can't leave,' Olivia said. 'You're brilliant at all of this. Look at how many people have come to see you. What about that couple who were an instant hit? We've only just got going. There's going to be loads more matches, mark my words. Tell her Angelina. She can't go, can she?'

'I simply can't stay either,' said Vera quietly.

'Why not?' asked Olivia, looking from one to the other.

Vera fiddled with the material of her dress, trying to find another way to persuade Olivia that her mind was made up. It was impossible to think they could ever again make this business work now she'd broken the trust between one of her best friends and herself, and all over a man who was still married to someone else. She needed to confess she'd been a bad friend to Olivia's face before the gossips told her, but how could she say she was sorry she'd slept with Ambrose? She could apologise to Olivia for being a bad friend, but she could never say sorry for making love to Ambrose. It had been the catharsis she needed and it had been wonderful. It meant way too much to her, far more than Rosie's idea of just a bit of fun.

And it was with that thought, as she sat, head down, with her mind churning and two of her best friends waiting for her next words, she finally stared square in the face a truth she was hiding even from herself.

Vera would never be able to apologise to Olivia and truly mean it because she had already fallen in love with Ambrose, and she simply couldn't bear the thought of him preferring another woman over herself.

Chapter Forty-One

Silly Vera

A surge of heat overpowered her. Vera couldn't breathe. She had to get out of the boathouse. She needed to cool down. She ran out on to the landing stage, where she crouched holding her chest, gulping in great gulps of fresh air.

Olivia started to follow, but Angelina held her back. 'What did you tell Vera about you and Ambrose that night she found you in the boathouse?' she asked. She wasn't expecting an answer, but there could be an outside chance that Olivia might just know what had caused her rapid decline and was refusing to tell anyone about it. The gossip going around town that Vera had slept with Ambrose seemed suspiciously close to Olivia's illness, and Angelina suddenly didn't believe that Vera only wanted to give up running the agency because, in her own words, 'her heart was no longer in it'.

There was more to this than met the eye, and

Angelina had a good idea what it was.

'Ambrose? Nothing. I don't remember. I don't even remember Vera being there.' Olivia bent and slapped her palms on the side of her head, trying to force her brain to function. 'Angelina, I can't even remember being in the boathouse,' she cried in dismay. 'When was I in the boathouse?'

This was causing more harm than good. Angelina pulled her close and hugged her. 'It's nothing, darling. Don't get yourself worked up, please. Not again.'

Olivia struggled out of her grasp and doubled down over her knees, her arms clasped around herself, rocking as if she was in physical pain. 'I'm so fed up with this, Angelina,' she said. 'There's always something I can't remember and it's always important, and everyone else knows about what I've been doing, but I never know myself. I hate being this much of a burden. I cause so much trouble and I get so much wrong.'

Angelina stroked her back, waiting, knowing that after the remorse, Olivia would bounce back again. It was a regular pattern, but Olivia obviously wasn't fully out of the episode yet, although it was close. Angelina prayed it was just a matter of time before the rocking would still, Olivia would unwind and, like a butterfly coming out of its chrysalis, her sunny side would return again.

With each stroke of her back, Olivia did calm. Her

breathing regulated. She slowly unwound, and threw her head against the back of the settee stretching her body out. She yawned deeply. She wiggled her face back into a comfortable place. Angelina handed her water and she drank deeply, stopping with the plastic bottle mid-air as she suddenly thought of something else. 'What was that you said about Ambrose?' she asked.

Angelina could see the change. She tried again. 'I asked what you told Vera about you and Ambrose.'

'Me and Ambrose?' Olivia was confused. 'Why would Vera want to know about me and Ambrose?'

Angelina went still. How was she going to handle this one? Should she tell Olivia the gossip that was going around town? She finally decided it was better coming from her rather than anyone else, and braced herself for the fallout.

'Vera announced to everyone in Oysters that she and Ambrose slept together,' she said as calmly as she could. 'It's the talk of the town.'

Angelina certainly did not expect the reaction she got. It was as if an electric shock shot from her toes to the top of her head through Olivia. The cogs in her befuddled brain fell into place. The lights came on and suddenly she could see very, very clearly. She rushed out of the boathouse so fast, she left Angelina open-mouthed.

'Vera!' she shouted, jumping onto the landing stage, making it shake. She was laughing maniacally.

Vera, still crouching with her back to Olivia, spun round on her heels as Olivia tried to tug her to her feet, dreading that Olivia was furious at her.

'Silly Vera,' laughed Olivia, trying to hug her.

Vera pulled away, missed the edge and promptly fell backwards into the river. The tidal wave of cold water she displaced drenched Olivia, who screeched at full volume as it hit her warm skin.

Chapter Forty-Two
All Sorted

Olivia found it so hilarious, she couldn't help Vera out. She laughed so hard, it left her coughing and spluttering. Angelina was forced to dive in and save Vera herself.

When Olivia held out her hand to drag them both out, she got even wetter. Vera's dress was ruined from complete immersion. Angelina's pale cream trouser suit clung to her and was covered in river slime. 'What's happened?' shouted Paul, the manager from the men's section, as he came running to find out who had screamed, closely followed by the other two staff.

'Don't touch us,' screamed Angelina, 'or I'll be replacing even more clothes from the stock!' She looked over towards the back of the shop and couldn't believe how many customers were streaming out onto the lawn to see what was going on.

'There's a coachload of tourists just walked in,' explained Paul, 'but none of them are likely to be buying now.'

Angelina, braced herself, brushed her soaking bob back from her face, straightened her back and strode up the lawn towards the customers, scurrying her staff before her. 'Welcome to Claremont's,' she said, taking command. 'There's nothing to worry about, thank you very much. Everyone is all right,' and then hissed to Paul, 'Get this lot back into the shop and make sure nothing's missing.' Paul ran off at top speed to do as she asked.

Angelina took the first shower, quickly dressed and left Olivia and Vera sitting wrapped in bath towels, drinking hot tea. 'I'll go and find you something to wear from the shop,' she told Vera.

'So you slept with Ambrose, then?' asked Olivia as soon as Angelina was out of earshot.

Vera dropped her eyes guiltily. 'I'm sorry,' she whispered.

Olivia pursed her lips and observed her. She sat for a very long time, just looking at Vera, her face stiff and unsmiling. 'I saw you, you know. I watched you.'

'What?' asked Vera, horrified.

'Well, I watched the start before you went into the boathouse. I was up in my old bedroom,' she said, tipping her head to indicate upstairs in Claremont's. 'I watched you out of the window.'

Vera blanched. This was awful. She felt rotten to the core for having made love to Olivia's boyfriend. 'I'm truly sorry,' she whispered, even more quietly.

'There's just one thing I want to know,' said Olivia.

Vera raised her eyes and was more than slightly surprised to see Olivia's sparkling like diamonds. She was really enjoying this! Or, was she going into another episode? Vera got even more nervous. Should she call Angelina?

'Was he any good in bed?

Vera very nearly fell off her chair. She half-nodded, having no idea what to say.

'Oh, thank God for that,' went on Olivia, desperate to tell her story now. 'When he kissed me, I felt absolutely nothing. It was such a shock. I'd waited for ever. He'd been such a gentleman, I never thought he was going to get going. I've never met anyone so damned slow. All he seemed to want to do was talk. And then, out of the blue, when he knocked me down and kissed me, I didn't like it. Oh, Vera. I got in such a muddle I had to go up to my room,' she said, indicating the bedroom above them again.

'Was that where you were all the time you were away?' Vera asked incredulously, just as Angelina reappeared carrying a selection of dresses and underwear from the shop from which she could choose.

Olivia acknowledged her presence. 'Angelina and Pete look after me whenever I'm ill,' she said, reaching out and squeezing her sister's hand in a gesture of thanks.

'Did I just hear right as I was coming up the stairs,' asked Angelina, laying the clothes down over the back of a chair. 'Did you say you didn't like being kissed by Ambrose?'

Olivia grimaced violently as if even thinking of the kiss brought back horrid memories. She undid, readjusted and then retied the towel under her arms and shook her bright red curls back from her head. 'It was like kissing a dead fish,' she said archly, and for good measure shivered at the memory.

'So who are you sleeping with, because sure as hell you've been sleeping with someone?' demanded Angelina. 'I was sure it was him because you were spending so much time at River House.'

'Wouldn't you like to know?' teased Olivia.

'Actually, I would this time, Olivia, because you've just put us through hell,' exploded Angelina, suddenly worn out by her sister's antics. 'You've got to stop both the gossiping and the secrecy. You like to know everything about everyone else, but you're sure as goddammit never going to tell us anything about what's actually going on with you. That's not your illness talking, Olivia. That's your true personality. You are a damned gossip. But, when you never let us in on anything, it means that each time you have one of your turns, we think we might have done something wrong. Was it Ambrose that caused it this time?'

Olivia refused to answer. She stood up, ambled off and the next thing they heard was her singing in the shower.

Vera felt trapped, but she couldn't leave Angelina to deal with this alone. Angelina flopped on a chair beside her, pushed back her hair from her forehead, and let out a deep groan. 'I don't know how you cope with it,' said Vera eventually.

'Neither do we,' confided Angelina. 'We're at the end of our tether with her. Why do you think we've never had children?'

Vera's heart went out to her friend. She was so patient; so uncomplaining. She ran a business that gave her worries, and still she gave fully of herself to Olivia. Vera called that true love, both from Angelina to Olivia, but also from Pete, who was prepared to be the rock on whom they both leant.

'Try some of those on after you've had a shower,' suggested Angelina, calming now and getting back to practicalities. 'Do you mind me asking,' she said, looking slightly abashed, 'how did Olivia watch you get together with Ambrose?'

'We met on the landing stage and we ended up in the boathouse,' Vera admitted, her heart now so uplifted that Ambrose hadn't slept with Olivia, she couldn't help but smile a very satisfied smile.

'It was that good, was it?' teased Angelina, putting her hand over Vera's.

'Good, better, best!' admitted Vera, turning her own hand over and holding her friend's. 'I honestly never thought it would happen again after Richard, but …' she sighed, unable to go on, she felt so excited now the ordeal with Olivia was over.

Angelina gave her hand a big squeeze back. 'At least one of us is getting somewhere,' she said.

'It can't go any farther. He's married and I won't get involved with a married man. But what we've had has certainly helped me. I never thought I could feel like that again. There's a bit of light suddenly shining at the end of my tunnel.'

Angelina leant across and hugged her just as Olivia strode back in, freshly dressed and made-up. They both turned around. 'Shower's all yours' she told Vera, as if everything was normal. 'Oh, if you really have to know, I've been sleeping with Jez for months now, Angelina . We haven't told anybody because it's nothing more than a mutually satisfying arrangement and he doesn't want me called a cougar 'cause he's twenty years younger than me.'

'Jez from the gym?' asked Angelina, taken aback. Olivia nodded and grinned lasciviously. 'What the hell have you been doing to give you such sore feet?' Olivia air-swiped side to side of her sister's face and stuck her tongue out at her.

Vera relaxed, watching the two sisters settling

343

back in to their normal behaviour until Olivia told Vera, 'Oh, and when I was in the bedroom, I rang Ambrose. He's on his way over. He has something to tell you. He'll meet you in the conservatory.'

Chapter Forty-Three
Normal Service Resumed

After being on his own most of the week, Benji refused to let his master go out again without him. Ambrose freshened up, feeling incredibly nervous about what he needed to tell Vera, but when he went to leave the house, he was so preoccupied, the dog shot round him and straight out on the street. 'Stay!' shouted Ambrose, trying to lock the door at the same time as checking where Benji was. Further down the pavement, Benji, stopped and looked back over his shoulder at Ambrose as if to say, 'Come on then. I'm in a hurry,' but when Ambrose started to catch him up, Benji loped off again.

Traffic on the High Street was nose to tail. The pavements were crammed with people. It was the height of the season, Regatta Week, and the town was full of tourists coming to see the rowing. 'Sit!' screamed Ambrose, terrified Benji was going to be hit by a car as the dog weaved his way around pedestrians' legs, frequently bounding off the pavement into the road.

Benji ignored him. 'Benji! Sit!' shouted Ambrose even louder. 'Can somebody please stop my dog?' he pleaded. People turned around to look where the shout came from, but no one helped. Benji kept running. Ambrose nearly knocked over a middle-aged woman. 'Watch where you're going,' she complained unpleasantly as he tried to apologise.

By then, Benji had disappeared. He was nowhere to be seen. Ambrose's tension spiked. He ran past the open door to Claremont's, then skidded to a halt and ran back again as, out of the corner of his eye, he spotted a wagging tail disappearing towards the conservatory through the shop filled with customers.

'Lost someone?' asked Vera when Ambrose finally got there, too. The dog had leapt up on her shoulders and she was laughing as she leant back to avoid his over-enthusiastic licks.

'Bad dog!' said Ambrose, letting loose his frustration. The dog turned his head around, his mouth open, tongue hanging to one side. Ambrose could have sworn Benji was laughing at him.

'You look like you need a drink, Ambrose,' said Angelina, proffering an Angosec. 'But do you mind if you drink these in the garden. I really don't want Benji's hairs all over the stock.' She handed another glass to Vera and pointedly opened the door for the three of them to go outside.

Ambrose gave her a squeeze in thanks and took a much-needed glug from the glass before he followed Vera and Benji. He was feeling exceedingly nervous. He didn't know how Vera would take his news. Was he being far too presumptive too soon?

'Shall we go down by the water?' she suggested, equally nervous as she had absolutely no idea what Ambrose wanted to say to her. After the mess of her own family life he had just witnessed, she was convinced it was going to be bad news. No sane man would want to hang around with all that going on. She'd already convinced herself he was going to tell her there was no point in continuing seeing one another. She suspected he was going to say he was going back to London to make it up with his wife and he would soon be selling River House.

'Would you rather go to the boathouse?' asked Ambrose indicating her dress. 'That's so beautiful. Won't it spoil if we sit on the wet planks?'

Her stomach lurched and her heart soared as he admired her.

Angelina had made a good choice. Vera did feel beautiful in her new dress. It was simple, tight in the bodice and full in the skirt, and its swirl of soft pastel colours suited her well. So what if Benji had messed up her make-up!

'Perhaps that would be more private,' she said. Although nothing could make up for the stupid glow she currently felt inside simply because he was there beside her, she braced herself for the disappointment she expected to come. In one fell swoop he had made her feel alive again, but if now was the time to let him go, the last thing she wanted to do was break down in public.

She ached for him to kiss her, but there was no hint of any familiarity from him. He was stiff and formal, every inch the businessman, no longer the passionate lover. He stood to one side as he held the door ajar for her to enter the boathouse in front of him. Vera straightened her back, and stood proud as she passed so close she could feel his warmth, telling herself nothing, ever again, could possibly be as bad as losing Richard. This is only a simple matter of pride, she thought. I can handle this.

'You've made a really good job of setting up this business,' Ambrose said, staring around when he took the seat on the settee she offered. She deliberately chose to sit opposite him. Benji flopped by her feet. She was glad of his support. She needed it. This was torture.

She reached down and petted Benji, who turned his chocolate-brown eyes up and stared at her adoringly. 'I won't be here much longer,' she told Ambrose, equally business-like. 'I'm pulling out. I expect Olivia and Angelina will close it down after I've gone.'

Ambrose was truly shocked. 'Why would you want to do that? Olivia says you're absolutely brilliant at hooking people up.'

Vera had had time to do a lot of thinking in the past few days. 'She's exaggerating as usual,' she said, wondering how much more Olivia had told him. 'But, if you don't mind, it's not as simple as hooking people up. I introduce people to see if they might like one another. I respect their confidences and provide them with a safe place to take their time. Internet dating hooks people up. We give the personal touch,' she said, suddenly wanting to have a dig at Olivia. 'It's a business where you need to tell, and be told, the truth.'

Ambrose heard the inflexion in her voice. He could see she was angry, and knew it had to be at him because he was angry at himself, too. He'd berated himself for being such a fool, walking out that Sunday morning and forgetting to ask to see her again. He should have phoned but, just like now, he hadn't been thinking straight when he'd shot back up to London. He'd been unusually impetuous because he was rattled, driven by what he had to do, knowing how urgently he needed to sort out the other part of his life.

'But we've hit a problem and I can't see a way around it.' He zoned back in and realised Vera was still talking about the agency. 'We've really only got white people like me and my family on the books. There are no coloured people registering. There are only a couple of gays and not one disabled person. We can hardly call ourselves The Normal Dating

Agency. More rightly we should be called the Abnormal Dating Agency,' she said, and smiled nervously at her own joke.

He laughed involuntarily. His face lit up. When she half-smiled back, it took his breath away. His eyes sparked at the sight of her beauty, but when anxiety gnawed at his stomach again, his face fell.

Momentarily Vera was mesmerised by the crinkles around the corners of his eyes which deepened when he laughed. Her stomach lurched. She loved each and every one of his crinkles. She wanted to be able to see his lovely, crinkly, smile many more times again, but as she was so certain that wasn't going to happen and that she was going to have to accept it, she stopped talking, her mouth slightly open.

Ambrose wanted so much to dash across and kiss that mouth, but he forced himself to hold back. It was now or never. He had things that needed to be said, and after they had been said he worried she would never want to kiss him again. He had to explain everything so she could forgive him. She needed to hear the truth and she needed to hear it from him and no one else. He was well aware how much Vera hated gossip because, whenever she gossiped, Olivia always ended her story with something like, 'but my friend Vera thinks I shouldn't have said it. She doesn't like people talking'.

He sighed unhappily. 'Do you know who I really am?' he asked.

Vera frowned. 'No,' she ventured.

'I bought Number Forty from you. I'm A J Hidrio from Montaise Holdings,' he said, sternly business-like.

'Okay ...' she said. 'So?'

That stunned Ambrose. 'I thought ...' he started, but she interrupted him.

'Nice to meet you A J Hidrio. Thank you for buying Number Forty.'

'It was a mistake,' he said, distracted. 'I was planning to knock you down even further. Number Forty wasn't worth anywhere near what you were asking,' he added.

For a moment, Vera wondered if he was asking her to buy Number Forty back. She panicked. She couldn't buy it back! She needed that money.

'Sorry?' Vera asked and stopped stroking Benji. Benji nuzzled her hand to remind her he was there. This wasn't making sense. 'I don't understand,' she said. 'Why would you pay more than you thought it was worth? That's crazy!'

'It's mainly the reason you and I got involved,' Ambrose said.

'But I never met you until long after the sale had gone through,' said Vera. 'So what's the problem?'

He couldn't find an explanation. Still angry at his own impetuosity that day, Ambrose shrugged in such an arrogant way and pulled such an odd face that Vera could only take it that he meant he regretted what he had paid her. Her hackles rose. Did he think she had cheated him in some way?

'Spit it out, Ambrose,' she snapped. 'Did you only have sex with me to get back at me because you paid me too much money for a block of flats!'

'Oh no. Please no. It's not that.' Ambrose saw Vera's pretty face harden, and it cut him to the quick.

'Well, it damned well sounds like it,' said Vera, her voice rising along with her shame that she'd been duped. All her fears that she was nothing but another notch in his bedpost came flooding to the front of her mind and were confirmed. 'So why did you conceal who you really were from me then?' she demanded.

'Olivia told me ...' he began and her fuse was lit.

'Bloody, interfering, gossiping Olivia again!' she said, slamming her hand down so hard on the table between them that it bounced.

Benji yelped and pulled away, frightened by her anger. He wriggled and tried to hide behind her legs, quivering violently. When there was no room, he put his head on her knee and licked her hand to make her look at him. 'It's all right, Benji,' she said, preoccupied by her fury.

Ambrose was so nervous he could feel sweat pooling down his back and under his arms. 'I'm no good at this,' he said.

'If you're going to tell me that what we did was all one big mistake and you never want to see me again, let me do it for you, Ambrose! I'm past caring. You're a married man. You never told me. I suppose you're going back to your wife now, and you'll both have a good laugh at me, the little widow who needed sex so badly!' she ranted, working herself into a real tizzy.

'Get out of my life now, Ambrose, bloody, Hidrio. Please! Have a good laugh at my expense, then go! I've made the biggest fool of myself over you, and it will only be a relief when you put me out of my misery and disappear. I can go back to my old life. I was safe there. No one gossiped about me. No one wanted anything of me. I could live in my own world. You've just made me a fool of me,' Vera raged.

Benji skulked away and found a safe place in the corner. Ambrose watched him go, so angry at himself he didn't trust himself to speak. Instead he got up, walked out through the door and ended up on the landing stage, staring out, fighting back red-hot fury. He'd handled all of this so very badly.

'What the hell are you doing out here? Why was Vera shouting?' demanded Olivia, emerging from behind the tree where she had been skulking with champagne and glasses in her hand, ready to be the first one to congratulate them. 'You haven't told her, have you?' she guessed accurately. Ambrose nearly shot out of his skin. He stared at Olivia blankly.

'God, you are so repressed, Ambrose Hidrio. Get back in there and tell her exactly how you feel about her. Tell her how much you love her.'

Ambrose didn't move.

Olivia groaned in frustration and headed towards the boathouse. She stuck her head in through the door and commanded, 'Get out here, Vera Father before I come in and get you out myself.'

'Bugger off, Olivia,' retorted Vera.

'Humour me,' Olivia urged. 'You can't leave everything like this.'

Ambrose went to walk away, but Olivia grabbed him firmly by the forearm and made him wait on the landing stage until Vera came out, still very shamefaced that she had exploded with rage.

'Stand there,' Olivia ordered, pointing to a place facing Ambrose. When Vera hung back, she grabbed her hand and pulled her over. Ambrose tried to walk away again, but Olivia held him firmly. 'Oh no, you don't!' Olivia said and made him turn back to face Vera. They both looked at each other sheepishly, but did as they were told. Olivia waited until she was confident enough to let Vera's wrist go.

'Right!' Olivia said bossily. 'Let's try it this way. You are the clients and I am the person making the introductions. Vera this is Ambrose. Ambrose this is Vera. I think you are both very well suited, but let me tell you a little bit more about one another, because I'm the gossip who talks to everyone and knows everything, so I know everything there is to know about both of you.'

Vera and Ambrose looked at her askance.

'Potted history,' went on Olivia. 'Vera, Ambrose paid the full asking price for Number Forty because he came down here to look at it and fell in love with River House. His wife, of … what was it, Ambrose?'

'Twenty-three years,' answered Ambrose.

'Twenty-three years … had just chucked him out because he wouldn't go with her to Italy to find herself and he had no idea what finding herself actually meant anyway, but if he'd known me then, I could have told him that men never do, so he wasn't being stupid, and he should have just let her go on her own. He didn't want to go, cos he realised he no longer loved her and she no longer loved him. Well, she can't have done, because she kicked him out because he bought Benji, or something like that, so he needed somewhere else to live. Is that about right, Ambrose?'

Ambrose nodded. 'Good!' said Olivia. 'So, your turn, Vera, He knew you lived in the town and he suspected it would be hard for him to be accepted here if he bought River House and then it got around that he had shafted a recently widowed local woman by paying less than her asking price for Number Forty.'

Vera turned sharply to look at Olivia. That was a different way of looking at things!

Olivia was starting to enjoy herself. 'He was right! The gossips would have had a field day, and just like you, Ambrose doesn't like gossips. And then he found out that the solicitor selling River House was our friendly local solicitor, Martin Rosser, who was also acting for you. The chance of anything leaking out of that leaky old office was too great, so he knew for sure it was best he paid full price for Number Forty to you so it didn't happen. See now?'

Vera looked at Ambrose. 'Is that right?' she asked, not quite sure she was getting everything Olivia said. Ambrose nodded, and reached out a hand to her. She took it without thinking.

Olivia smiled to herself. 'We can rush through the next bit. While Ambrose was moving down here to the town, I started the Normal Dating Agency, you started making people happy, but you still weren't happy yourself. And then Ambrose kissed me and I didn't like it and had my meltdown and ... now I'm not actually certain about this part because it was when I was in a bit of a world of my own, so I'm only going on what Fliss and Annie told me ... but, am I right that Rosie turned up just after you and Ambrose got it together, you lost your cool at Rosie for being a gossiping old cow and ... are you two keeping up?'

Vera and Ambrose had moved closer together and were now holding each other's hands. They were both smiling at Olivia and nodding.

'Now this is the important bit.' Olivia held out both hands and spread them in the air like a conductor taking applause from his audience. 'Tra-la!' she sang.

'Ambrose. Vera is no longer uptight about being a widow since she had sex with you. She's made a fool of herself telling the whole world about it, but survived. I reckon that means it was pretty important to her, but what she doesn't know, because she doesn't listen to gossip, is that her street cred has shot through the ceiling, so she's got no reason any longer to be scared of the gossips anyway.' Olivia prodded Vera hard on her upper arm, making her squeal. 'And that includes me, Vera Father!'

Vera sniggered. Ambrose moved in closer and put his arm around her. Both were now fully enjoying Olivia's performance.

'But even more important, I suspect she could no longer give a shit,' Olivia kissed her finger tips and raised her hands to the skies, sending up a prayer of thanks, ' because she's finally stood up to that stupid old soak of a mother of hers and sent her packing. Vera has found herself Ambrose! See, that's what finding yourself is all about! I told you, you'd get it one day.'

Ambrose burst out laughing and leaned over to kiss Olivia on the cheek.

Vera pulled him close. 'Not yet,' she said. 'There's more isn't there, Olivia? There has to be more.'

'Oh, you can bet your life there is!' said Olivia, completely and utterly proud of herself. 'This is the very best bit. Vera, Ambrose has just got a quickie divorce from his wife, so he's no longer married ...'

Vera leant back in delight, searching his face for confirmation. The crinkles were back! In fact they were even wider and deeper than she had ever seen them. Ambrose nodded so vigorously, he couldn't stop. Vera dragged him into a long and passionate kiss.

'... but I have a feeling that won't be the case for very long,' said Olivia walking away.

'How did I do as a personal introduction counsellor for the Normal Dating Agency?' she asked Angelina coming the other way with more glasses and champagne and a dog chew for Benji.

'Benji,' Angelina called and the dog came running to see her.

Angelina looked across to where Ambrose and Vera were chattering away, reassuring one another that all the revelations were true. 'Bit rushed and ham-fisted,' said Angelina, pulling a face. 'I think you're better working in the shop.'

'But, I've just done the introduction for marriage number one for the Normal Dating Agency!' said Olivia, punching the air in self-congratulation.

'Abnormal!' shouted Vera and Ambrose from the landing stage, and then kissed through their laughter as Benji shot for safety across the lawn with his dog chew in his mouth, running away from the pop of the champagne cork that Angelina released from the bottle.

The End

If you would like to know more about what Vera, Olivia and Angelina get up to next, read

THE NEW NORMAL

by

Jan Caston

The Normal Dating Agency is going from strength to strength. Vera's fast becoming highly respected as a matchmaker. Gossip is getting around town, and for once, it's all good. The business is booming and even more lonely people are signing up to find a long term partner.

Even Olivia is calm and has stopped worrying about Claremont's. The extra income from the dating agency she started in their boat house has helped the dress shop avoid bankruptcy and now that Angelina has found a new, and more reasonably priced, supplier, the customers are flocking back into the shop.

Christy and Annie are thoroughly enjoying bringing up their two little boys. Fliss and Steve are looking for a new house together and an engagement is imminent. What could possibly go wrong?

With the differences starting to show between them, Vera slams on the brakes on her new relationship with Ambrose. It's all going too quickly. She's frightened and she's thinking about calling the whole thing off...

... but first, there's the most horrific accident...

THE NEW NORMAL

Will be available mid-2018.

For regular updates on its progress follow
www.jancaston.com

but for its opening chapters, please read on...

Chapter One
Life Changes

Her scream started split-seconds before she applied the brakes. Judging correctly that she was never going to be able to stop in time, a warning at the top of her voice and evasive action was all that remained to save both of them. Coming down the hill, crouching to get maximum speed from his skateboard, the youth heard her, but it was too late. Helmetless, without knee or elbow guards, oblivious to any danger, he careered on the wrong side of the road directly into her pathway, completely unable, or even willing, to alter his trajectory on the two foot long board mounted on nothing more than four sixty-millimetre wheels.

She had no option. They were on course to collide. She gunned her motorcycle, swung the front wheel round and aimed for the hedge, years of experience kicking in to tell her that if she could hit it at the right angle, the hedge might save her. She shifted her weight over the back wheel, crouched over the fuel tank, lifted the handlebars and tried to do a wheelie.

She partially succeeded. The hawthorn hedge was newly planted and still sparse. She got enough lift from the front wheel to mount the bank and ram forward through it, never expecting the back wheel to get such purchase that she took off and crashed over into the field on the other side. The bike landed on its front tyre throwing her over the handlebars. It cartwheeled and landed on top of her, crushing her pelvis and leg with the extra force its momentum created.

The youth didn't stop. He carried on down the lane and disappeared into the distance. A plumber travelling close behind in his van witnessed it all. Forced to slam on his brakes in an emergency stop to avoid the skateboarder going over the bonnet of his van too, the plumber told the Police afterwards that the kid was laughing his head off as if he didn't have a care in the world as he sped away, stopping all other traffic coming in either direction on the hill.

As the plumber clambered through the hedge to get to the motorcyclist, the elderly woman who had been travelling behind his van called the emergency services. 'The bloke on the motorbike didn't stand a chance,' she babbled in shock as the Emergency Controller tried to calm her down and get details of where the accident had happened. She couldn't remember the name of the road.

'Let me talk to them,' said the portly man who, in turn, had had to slam on his brakes to avoid going into the back of her car. He put a comforting arm around her shoulder. 'You sit back in your car, my love.' He shouted to the builders from the lorry behind his car, taking control. 'Check on that fella that's gone over the 'edge, mates!' The two men in high-vis jackets had already jumped out of their cab and ran carrying a green first aid box towards the hole in the hedge as the portly man gave concise details of where the accident had happened to the emergency controller. He walked into the middle of the road, hand held high, stopping the traffic coming in the opposite direction.

'What's happened?' asked a woman in a four by four.

'Accident, missus,' he told her. 'Put your 'azzard lights on, will you? We need to keep this road clear for the emergency services to get through.' They could hear the sounds of sirens now and see lights flashing in the distance.

'Stay on the line for instructions and tell them not to take the biker's helmet off,' advised the emergency controller on the other end of the line as the man clambered through the now broken down hole in the hedge.

'Too late mate. It's already off, and it's not a man. It's a woman,' he said, spotting the long black hair highlighted with red fanning out around the head of the contorted body. The plumber stopped the back wheel spinning as he and the builders anxiously discussed how to lift the motorcycle off the lower part of her body without causing more damage. Groaning in agony, the biker had already pushed off her own helmet. Blood was pouring from both a nasty gash above her eye and her broken nose.

'Is she breathing?' asked the Emergency Controller.

'Yeah,' answered the man. 'Can't you hear 'er moaning? But she's trapped under the bike and 'er leg's all in the wrong place. Can you ask 'em to get here quick? This is bad'

'Try to keep her absolutely still. Don't let anyone move her unless she stops breathing. Leave the bike exactly where it is until the ambulance comes. Don't move anything.'

The portly man stared around looking worried, then let out a strangled, 'They're here,' as he saw the ambulance come to a halt in the road. A paramedic jumped out and was pushing his way through the hedge even before the brakes were on. 'Thank God, you got here so quick,' said the portly man and, without thinking, switched off his mobile phone.

The paramedic raced towards the woman, kit bag on his back, his partner following shortly afterwards, carrying a clutch of equipment. Together, they held the woman still. The paramedic instructed the plumber and builders when to lift the heavy motorcycle. It took the three of them to lift it away. 'Hello. Can you hear me?' he asked the newly released woman, checking her vital signs.

The woman groaned in agony.

'Can you tell me your name?'

'Annie,' she managed to whisper. 'Annie Father,' and then passed out completely.

The paramedic pulled off one of her leather gloves to put the oximeter on her finger. He pushed up her jacket-sleeve exposing a sleeve of tattoos.

'My God,' gasped the middle aged man. 'It's Christy Father's missus. From Father and Sons,' he told them. 'I've got Vera's number in my phone. She's that girl's mother-in-law. Should I ring her?'

Neither of the paramedics answered. They were too busy attending to Annie. The Policeman clambering through the hedge answered the portly man's question. He rushed up behind him, and stopped him from pressing the number he had stored in his mobile.

'Let me do that, Sir,' the Policeman suggested. 'Best if it comes from me,' he said turning the now shaking portly man away. His female partner, rushed passed them and checked the motorcycle was switched off and secure at the same time as telling the plumber and the builders she'd need them to give statements. 'We'll need you too, Sir,' said the Policeman to the portly man. 'So, please stay here for the moment.'

The Policeman rang the number the portly man

gave him from his own mobile phone. 'Is this Mrs Vera Father?'

Shock had finally hit the portly man who now stood frozen to the spot and white faced as he listened in. He heard Vera confirm it was. 'This is the West Counties Police. Can you give me a number on which I can contact your son?'

They both heard the urgency in her voice. 'He's here. Right beside me... Christy!'

By the way her voice faded, it was obvious she'd already handed the phone over to her son.

Chapter Two
By The River

Up until then, they'd been having such a lovely walk and talk. Christy carried Mickey on his shoulders, chattering away to him as they stopped to watch the swans gliding under the bridge.

'Ducks,' said Mickey, pointing every time he spotted another one.

'Swans,' corrected Christy. 'Ducks are green or brown. The white ones are swans.'

'Ducks,' said Mickey again.

Vera couldn't help but smile at her elder grandson. In the pushchair before her, his brother, Wyeth, stared at the sky contentedly, his nineteen month old eyes moving as he surveyed the clouds. 'Can you see an elephant?' asked Vera. Wyeth's deep chestnut eyes turned fully onto hers. They were so full of merriment, his gaze made her smile broadly back at him.

He pointed up at something. As Vera turned to

look up at what he wanted her to share, her mobile rang. 'Hello,' she said distractedly as she stared at the floating clouds.

'Is this Mrs Vera Father?' she half heard.

'Yes,' she confirmed.

'This is the West Counties Police,' the person on the other end of the line said, and her attention shot back fully to the phone call. 'Can you give me a number on which I can contact your son?'

'He's here.' Her hand started shaking inexplicably, and she thrust the mobile towards Christy. 'Right beside me… Christy!'

'It's the Police,' she mouthed; unaware she had instinctively lowered her voice so the boys wouldn't hear.

'Not another break-in at the merchants!' Christy groaned in exasperation, pulling a face and shifting Mickey's leg out of the way so he could put the mobile to his ear. 'Hello,' he said so he could hear. 'Christy Father here.' Vera watched his expression drop from cheerful to deadly serious as he listened.

When Christy blanched and started running back in the direction of the car, Vera knew this was far more serious than a break-in. 'Where are they taking her?' were the only words she managed to catch as he bolted off with Mickey bouncing wildly on his shoulders.

'Daddy!' Mickey screamed and clung to his father's hair trying to hold on.

Vera turned Wyeth's buggy and ran after them. Torn away from his cloud-reverie, Wyeth burst into tears. 'It's alright,' consoled Vera.

'What's happened?' she shouted after Christy. She couldn't keep up with his loping gallop. 'Christy! Stop! Put Mickey down!'

Before her she could see that although Mickey had wrapped his arms around his father's head, and Christy ran with one arm up trying to keep his elder son on his shoulders, the four year old's legs could no longer maintain their hold. Mickey started lurching backwards. 'DADDY!' he screeched at the top of his voice as he scrambled to save himself.

Christy stopped dead. It broke the little boy's grip. Vera watched in horror as, at first, Mickey slipped slowly, arms flailing, but then all his attempts to cling on failed. He dropped with a heavy crunch to the ground. His head bounced. It took the wind out of him. Momentarily he fell silent; then the howls of shock started. 'Oh God! Mickey. I'm sorry,' said Christy gathering him up, trying to stem the flood of shocked tears.

'Did he hit his head?' demanded Vera, feeling for lumps. The child had a mop of long, thick auburn hair. She could feel nothing under it. 'Mickey!' she said sharply. 'Look at Grandma. Show me where it hurts.'

Mickey stopped screeching and turned two watery blue eyes towards her. 'Daddy hurt me!' he said pitifully.

'Daddy didn't do it on purpose,' Vera consoled as Mickey fought to get out of his father's arms and safely into hers. She took him and clutched him closely, rubbing his back and head, still checking for any serious damage. 'What's happened?' she asked Christy over the top of Mickey's head.

'We've got to go. Now!' was all Christy said as he lifted Wyeth out of his pushchair and tried to fold it down before running to the car. He tugged her elbow and urged her to run with him. It was obvious from the lift of his eyebrows and the twist of his head that he couldn't speak in front of his children. His ashen face confirmed this was extremely serious.

That could only mean it had to be something to do with Annie.

Vera ran after him as fast as she could towards the car.

Christy bounced the wheels of the car onto the pavement outside Accident and Emergency. As Vera got out to take his place in the driver's seat, across the roof he managed to tell her without the children, still safely strapped into their car seats in the back, hearing. 'They said it's bad, Mum'.

'Is she alive?'

Christy nodded, but without conviction.

'Go! I'll take the boys home,' Vera commanded. Christy hesitated, appearing suddenly uncertain as to which door he should go towards. Vera pushed him in the direction of the ambulance bay. He started running.

'Your phone!' Vera shouted after him when she spotted it beside the driver's seat.

He skidded on his heel and ran back to collect it. She pecked him on the cheek before letting him go. 'She's a fighter, Christy. Ring me as soon as you know anything,' she said. 'I've got the boys.'

Christy couldn't reply.

'Where's Daddy gone?' asked Mickey as she drove away.

'He won't be long,' she told. 'There's nowhere to park the car here, so you, me and Wyeth are going to take it home, and Daddy will come home later in a taxi. Does that sound okay?'

'Okay,' agreed Mickey. Vera looked in the driver's mirror at his reflection. He was staring out of the window completely oblivious to the developing crisis.

Ambrose arrived with takeaway pizza before Christy rang again. He had rung once so far, and only to say that Annie had arrived in the ambulance, was alive but unconscious, and that he would ring again once he knew more. 'She's in an awful state, Mum,' was all he was willing to say. 'She hasn't woken up. They say she's bleeding badly from somewhere. They've taking her straight into theatre.'

'Any more news yet?' asked Ambrose walking through to the kitchen and dropping boxes of pizza onto the table. Wyeth dragged himself up to his feet, then toddled towards him. 'Wow. You're getting fast, young man,' said Ambrose scooping him up for a cuddle.

'Me! Me,' demanded Mickey holding up both arms.

Ambrose shifted Wyeth onto one hip, then wound his free arm around Mickey's waist to lift him high. Mickey clung to his neck and smacked a slobbery kiss somewhere near his ear. 'Thank you!' said Ambrose and pulled a funny face at Wyeth who chortled from the bottom of his stomach in response. It made Ambrose throw his head back with a laugh of sheer delight. 'He's going to have such a deep voice,' he told Vera.

Vera leaned in for her own kiss. As Ambrose's lips found hers, from either side her grandsons landed pecks on either of her cheeks.

'See, all your men love you,' teased Ambrose, but the smile she returned him was so taught with tension; he quickly put down the boys and pulled her into a hug.

'Nothing at all?' he whispered in her ear. She shook her head slightly and leant her face into his shoulder, the warmth of his body the support she'd been craving.

'Let's get this pizza eaten then,' he suggested. 'Are you boys hungry?' he asked, being practical.

Vera was too nervous to help. She let him take over.

To be continued in The New Normal by Jan Caston

Acknowledgments

The idea for Normal Dating came after an hilarious, but far less naughty dinner party than the one related here, thrown by my good friend, Julia Hunt, where the conversation turned to the disasters of internet dating. Around the table every person had some story to tell, many of them far too unbelievable to be ever recounted in this book.

Normal Dating was written exceedingly quickly. It seemed to want to tell its own story and I wondered afterwards where the characters sprung from; but in truth, thinking about it more deeply, they came from the life I've lived and the many parties I've attended or thrown - the amazing 'dos' we've enjoyed over the years here at home in Jersey, balmy summer sizzles and winter warmers with Mum and Dad, and John and Barbie Price at Owl Hill (and no, Barbara, I did not go and put on fresh make-up before I met the hunky firemen who came to tackle your blazing hay field. I was in line filling buckets from your pond with everyone else - just to put the record straight!).

The book was line and copy edited by Hilary Johnson Authors' Advisory Service. Thanks Hilary and team for working out all those tricky little details with me, although at times, Hilary, the way you kept trying to tempt me to have another dog took a lot of resisting!

The beautiful book cover was hand-drawn by Susan Lintell at Susan Lintell Fine Art. Susan bought and renovated a new house whilst she was working on the cover and we had many more conversations about that project than ever we had about the book cover.

Marketing is handled by Leonie Hervé of Leonie@Harmonie. Many of our lively conversations have been about the sorry state of dating for today's generation, always jollied along with good food and a glass or two. We've found it's good to talk!

My writing buddies, Gwyn GB, Sue du Feu and Elizabeth (Monty) Lawrence have always been there with recommendations, sterling encouragements and witticisms. Debs Carr (aka Georgina Troy) gave me invaluable advice. Cheers girls! The drinks are on me next time.

But primarily, my thanks go to all the people I've met over the years who have inspired me to keep writing. I'm so glad you did.

ABOUT THE AUTHOR
JAN CASTON

It's rather nice having three very different strands to my life. In one I'm a contented step-mum and step-grandma; in another I'm a film and TV writer/producer, but today, here in this book, you will be meeting my third strand – writing contemporary romance.

Why do I love contemporary romance so much? Probably, it's because I am just like the women about whom I write. Theirs is the life I've lived; one happily filled with laughter and drama in equal measure. Luckily, so far, I've always come up the other side, though often not quite smelling of roses. I've been lucky enough to enjoy the warmth of fantastic parents, family and friends, and most importantly, the love of a wonderful man who suited me in every way.

But it wasn't easy to find him. He was elusive for a very long time!

I'm sentimental in that I believe there is love out there for everybody, but I'm also sufficiently cynical to know it never arrives in quite the way expected! I also believe that when it arrives, it usually comes with a laugh attached.

There's been a lot of adventure and mishap in my life – some horribly scary, some hilarious and irreverential, some so uplifting I wanted to share it with the world. From flying Concorde to being broke and slumming it, I have been privileged to do so many things.

To me - that's what life is all about. Living it!

Of course some of my full and rich life crosses over into my books, but don't worry any of my wonderful family and friends. You've been present at all the important junctures of my personal adventure. You've constantly inspired me, but I'd never divulge any of the secrets we share with the wider world.

Apart from my little charity book *Living With Cancer - The Year When Even The Dog Got Cancer*, all my other work is entirely fiction.

So, whenever you pick up one of my books, make yourself comfy and settle down to enjoy another of the stories inspired by my crazy life.